I0831681

SHERLOCK HOLMES AND THE GIANT SUMATRAN RAT

Book #1 in the Confidential Files of Dr. John H. Watson

C.J. LUTTON

JOANNA CAMPBELL SLAN

spot on publishing

CONTENTS

AUTHOR'S NOTES

Whenever possible, I have adhered to the British manner of spelling. Also, I have used the word "Chinaman," which is sadly a pejorative, but is in keeping with the times. I do this after wrestling with myself. In the end, I hope that including such an offensive term will stand in stark contrast to the noble character it references, and therefore, remind the reader that prejudice is a peculiar form of ignorance. —JCS

OTHER BOOKS BY JOANNA CAMPBELL WITH CJ LUTTON

Sherlock Holmes and the Giant Rat of Sumatra

Sherlock Holmes and the Father of Lies

Sherlock Holmes and the Nefarious Seafarers

Sherlock Holmes and the Time Machine

For more information and purchase links, go to:

http://www.booklaunch.io/joannaslan/thesherlockholmesstories

OUR GIFT TO YOU

Dr. John H. Watson has written a background report on the famous Diogenes Club. If you are interested in all aspects of Sherlock Holmes' world, this is a must-read! To claim your copy, go here —

https://BookHip.com/TNQTC.

Joanna Campbell Slan

Spot On Publishing

9307 SE Olympus Street

Hobe Sound, FL 33455 / USA

http://www.SpotOnPublishing.org

http://www.JoannaSlan.com

http://www.theSherlockStories.com

Publisher's Note: This is a work of fiction. Names, characters, places, and incidents are a product of the author's imagination. Locales and public names are sometimes used for atmospheric purposes. Any resemblance to actual people, living or dead, or to businesses, companies, events, institutions, or locales is completely coincidental.

Cover by Dar Albert, Wicked Smart Designs

http://www.WickedSmartDesigns.com

Revised 09/02/2020

FROM THE CONFIDENTIAL FILES OF DR. JOHN H. WATSON

One never knows.

At least, I certainly did not. When I first released details of my life with Sherlock Holmes, I had no idea that my efforts would turn my flatmate into a celebrity. Nor did I know my work would change my profession from that of doctor to author. In the event, my books also opened up my life, and that of my subject, to public scrutiny, and to public discourse. I should have realised as much. When one steps into the harsh glow of the footlights on the public stage, one is stripped naked as a babe. 'Though I understood this to be the case for performers, the idea held no truck with me regarding my occupation as a mere scribbler of words. How could I have prepared myself for the multitude of opinions strangers felt compelled to foist upon me? And when they came at me, as fast and furious as the bullets that whizzed by when I was in Afghanistan, my corporeal response was to seek shelter as I had on the battlefield.

Alas, there was nowhere I could hide! Given the teeming masses of London, given our location in the heart of the city, and given our proclivity to be out and about, with the addition of nicely drawn inkplates in various newspapers that revealed our visages to the masses, Holmes and I were easily recognisable, if we did not take the trouble to obscure our features. Day to day, such disguises were not only impractical but also time-consuming and irritating.

So there was no help for it but to hold one's head high and sally forth. Each morning, I steeled myself for the onslaught of slings and arrows cast my way. As I stepped from 221B out onto the street, I reminded myself that I had reaped the rich rewards of celebrity—in fact, they jingled in my pocket. The curse of such celebrity must also be borne in good humour. For the most part, I managed my popularity with all those elements attributed to a gentleman. I signed autographs, I shook endless hands, and I listened to long-winded prattle that covered every element of the Holmes adventures in tedious detail without adding a single smidgeon of new thinking. I did this, secure in the belief that I owed these members of the public my attention in exchange for their hard-earned cash.

Yes, it could be almost comical when a fellow countryman ventured a fulsome and lively opinion on the characters or the action in my books. As if I could control people and their behavior! Some readers seemed to think I am a puppet master, and all I need to do is pull strings. Rather than remind them otherwise, I do my utmost to smile and nod politely. Once such encouragement fades, I am ofttimes late for my appointments or errands, and this indubitably makes me cross, as I am a punctual man by habit. How could I have prepared myself for the multitude of opinions strangers felt compelled to foist upon me?

Concurrently, as the number of my readers has increased, so has the clamour for me to share every detail I can about Holmes and his cases. There seems to be one common complaint: readers want to know about the Giant Rat of Sumatra. They hark back to the offhand comment made by Holmes about the "world is not ready for such a tale." Of all I have written, no phrase has aroused more curiosity nor engendered more comment than that passing reference. Holmes and I discussed the matter at great length. We both knew that the details of the case, when revealed, could impact the security of our nation and indeed the entire continent.

I was hesitant to commit this particular story to paper, much less hold it up to public scrutiny for many reasons. First and foremost, Holmes and I once again found ourselves delving into events that cannot be explained by science or the rational mind. To wit, we were forced to accept an occurrence that can only be classified as unnatural. Or more accurately, supernatural. This rankles me, as all my training as a doctor goes against admission that such phenomena does exist. And yet...in this unusual and poignant case, I am forced to believe it does!

Furthermore, Holmes had cautioned me that exposing such dark events to the public would surely result in the ridicule of my efforts. He worried that those of my readers with a scientific bent might actually think I was daft. Of course, there was another voice to consider, that of Mycroft Holmes. Sherlock Holmes and I both knew that his older brother would object to any transparency regarding the situation in the strongest of tones.

And yet, a decade has passed and I have determined Mycroft's worries can no longer blanket this adventure in secrecy. This story cries out to be told! The world needs to hear, take note, and appreciate the courage at the heart of this yarn. Particularly given that three of the main actors were so young! More importantly, there are elements of this episode well worth considering carefully. I believe it is both a cautionary tale and an inspirational one.

Therefore, I have decided to write all of the details down in a coherent narrative without any further delay.

At the time that everything happened, the whirl and excitement of the case made clarity a scarce commodity. We were like prize ponies in the hands of an inexperienced rider. Our heads were jerked this way and that, willy-nilly, as the force that dominated us struggled to decide where we should go. At the end of our journey from darkness to light, we were sore and wet and bone weary, so I think I can be excused if my thinking is rather muddled.

At the very least, I pray that my readers will judge this case and remember that Holmes and I were as astonished by the incidents as anyone. Since that time, we have seen much that was presumed invisible and done much considered impossible.

But back then, we were much more innocent and trusting...

꧁ I ꧂

The most unimaginable adventures oft begin with a mundane act. Certainly there was nothing afoot to signal that this day, above all others, would launch the most fantastical adventure of my friendship with Sherlock Holmes.

Holmes and I had finished our breakfast and the maid had removed the tray. A light spring breeze riffled the curtains at the two big windows, causing the fabric to rise and fall. Despite the fact that London streets are always subject to horse droppings, this particular day brought us a present, the fragrant scents of spring flowers, specifically the spiciness of geraniums and the sweetness of petunias. The clement temperature eased the ache in my wound that I had received whilst I was serving our Queen and attached to the Fusiliers as a doctor. All in all, this was the sort of morning that made me happy to be alive.

My flatmate Sherlock Holmes had appropriated his favorite of our two armchairs in order to work his way systematically through the stack of daily newspapers he is fond of reading. With his little black devil, his small dirty pipe, in his mouth, he puffed a steady stream of tobacco while I laboured over creating an index for my journals, a task I'd procrastinated on for months.

A messenger knocked on our door. He was a young lad and the note he'd clutched in his hand was grubby and creased. Nonetheless, I gave him a handful of coins and watched his thin face light up with the anticipation of food, no doubt.

The note read as thus:

Dear Dr. Watson,

I trust this missive finds you well and in good spirits. As you might remember, after my recovery from wounds received in Afghanistan, I went directly back to my family home in Wiltshire. However, my life did not work out there as I had hoped. I have recently accepted a position at the Bethlehem Hospital. That is precisely why I am writing. We have an unusual case here, one that I believe you might find intriguing. The man in question has seen action in a military theatre abroad.

Please let me know if you are available today. I hate to impose, but this man's condition is serious and in decline.

Yours sincerely,
Thomas Henry Knopf

P.S. I should also like to renew our friendship.

The signature brought a flood of memories, as Thomas Henry and I had served as surgeons in Afghanistan.

The Bethlehem Hospital. *My, my.* The Bethlehem Hospital, known colloquially as Bedlam, was a blot on our nation's copybook. What had started as a charitable institution with the best of intentions, had become a cesspool so foul that admittance there was little better than a death sentence. Decades ago, public shame brought the place's horrifying conditions to the light of public scrutiny, and the outcry that followed served as incentive to make long-needed improvements. Even so, I wouldn't send my worst enemy to Bethlehem.

The very idea that Thomas Henry had wound up there was intriguing. As I recalled, Thomas Henry was a scion of a very wealthy family, a man wholly unused to the deprivations and hardships of the battlefield. Of all my colleagues, he whinged on and on the longest, decrying the state of the world and bemoaning the deplorable lack of leadership that caused our nightmare in the sandy wasteland named Afghanistan. As I recalled, Thomas Henry expected to return home from HR Majesty's service and once safely returned to the bosom of his familial surroundings, he planned to go back to his small practice in the village that his father owned, a satisfactory reward for Thomas Henry having done his duty to Queen and Crown.

But now, he was working as a doctor in one of the worst possible hospitals in the country. Of course, I would heed his request to visit posthaste. At the least, this visit would satisfy my curiosity; at best, I might be able to offer assistance and make the conditions of one person's life better.

Whilst ofttimes I ask Holmes to accompany me, particularly if I think the case in question might prove interesting, today he seemed content to read the various agony columns with total concentration. The upraised newspaper, cut from newsprint to fit the span from a man's left hand to his right, shielded my friend's face. Rather than disturb him, I scratched out a note and put it on the dining room table.

MUCH HAS BEEN WRITTEN ABOUT THE BETHLEHEM HOSPITAL, AND correctly those charged with administering the place turned it into a national disgrace. What had been built with good intentions planted a seed in the imagination of the public that illnesses of the mind rendered humans into spectacles of derision. For the small charge of a shilling, the public could tour Bethlehem Hospital just as they did the London Zoo, and indeed, the comparison is apt because the patients were treated no better than, and often worse than, animals. They were kept in hanging cages furnished solely with straw on the floor. The caregivers were oblivious to that very human need for privacy and condemned those who were already suffering to a sort of entrapment that would drive even the most strong-minded individual to lunacy. Onlookers would taunt these poor confused creatures, tossing them food and calling out rude names. Sadly there was no way for the sufferers to escape! No way to hide from the inhumanity visited upon them.

Those who had access to funds (or relatives willing to come up with money), paid the orderlies for the barest of necessities. Of course, there was no way to make sure the orderlies compensated the sick fairly. Thus the exchanges were always one-sided and weighted towards the free rather than those who were confined. Added to this egregious situation was the capricious manner that caused many to find themselves residents of Bethlehem. If a woman annoyed her husband, if he found her inconvenient, or if he simply tired of her, he could have two doctors sign papers against his wife. This alone was enough to open the gates of Bethlehem and slam them shut for all eternity. Many a wealthy woman found herself stripped of her fortune and her dignity by such scoundrels, but worst of all, these women found themselves shut away in cages, never to see the light of day again! And why? Because two doctors were paid to confirm their hysteria, a singularly feminine ailment.

Whilst supplied with a steady stream of patients, deranged medical practitioners enjoyed a free hand at experimentation. With no governance and no hierarchy to watch over their activities, those charlatans with a bent towards nefarious actions contrived tortures disguised as treatments. One, the spinning chair, was notorious for rattling a patient's brains until inducing violent sickness and prolonged inability to stand upright. But did it bring back sanity? No, it did not. Nor was it based on sound medical research.

As a young man receiving my medical degree, I remember taking a turn of duty in Bethlehem. Needless to say, I came away both shaken and infuriated. It had taken only one night for me to confirm my worst suspicions. Vulnerable people were made to lie upon mouldy, foul-smelling, and damp straw for all the hours of the evening with no respite. A precious few had blankets. All had fleas and lice. If they were lucky, their slops were contained in a bucket that could be emptied the next day. If they were not lucky, they used the same dried grasses that were their bedding. They were offered no opportunity to clean themselves. Nor were they allowed the soothing caress of fresh clothing. Suffice it to say, the stink of these individuals was a cloying fug that caused one to heave repeatedly. Worse yet, to my mind, the stench seeped into the cloth of my own limited wardrobe. No airing could whisk that pungent smell away!

Which reminds me of how poorly these patients were fed. As to their victuals, I can say with great certainty that nothing they were offered came up to the lowest of standards that most would demand and expect. Weevils were common, and for those who had been in this place long enough, such intruders barely warranted a second's hesitation before they were popped into a starving mouth.

So it follows, as day and night do each other, that Bethlehem bred infirmity of the body and of the mind and even more sadly, of the essence of humanity.

And so I entered this stinking, frightening medical failure with trepidation. A matron led me to the third floor, and towards the center of the building, where she ushered me into an antechamber. The room was plain, musty smelling and populated by chairs lining the walls. I presumed this was where those wishing for a consultation waited.

"Dr. Knopf's office," the matron said, pointing towards an open door. From my vantage point, and peeping through the aperture, I could see dark wood bookshelves from floor to ceiling. The tomes on the shelving were untidily arranged, and more than a few were on their sides. Dust motes danced in the sunbeams, and a dank smell rolled towards me on a wave of overheated air. As I neared the doorway, I spotted two fine leather-covered chairs placed side by side. Behind them was a horsehair divan positioned on a carpet. I doubted that the floor covering was expensive, but it did add a note of cheer to its dreary surroundings.

"Halloa?" I called, before I crossed the threshold. "Thomas Henry Percival, it is I, John Watson."

"By all that's holy, Watson, it's you!" Thomas Henry rose from his seat behind his desk to clasp my hand and offer a hearty handshake. I was struck immediately by how sallow his skin was, and the way his tendons stood out from his neck, under a wattle I'd never previously seen. In my memory, he was a vigorous young man, and 'though hardship ages us all, I had never expected to see my colleague looking a decade older than when I'd seen him several years ago. As he shook my hand in greeting, I also noted the slight tremour, oft a sign of a man who badly needs his next drink. In addition, his jacket collar stood out from his neck, suggesting he had lost a great deal of weight and had not bothered to go to a tailor and have his jacket taken in. This puzzled me. In my memory, Thomas Henry had been extremely conscious of his wardrobe. Even excessively so.

"What a fine office you have! A very nice set-up indeed," I said. "Good for you, old man!"

"What are you doing with yourself these days?" my old comrade asked, settling back into the rolling office chair behind his desk. How curious his office looked, given the oppressive setting. His large oak desk was flanked with bookcases. The shelves were jammed with papers, books, and pamphlets. All these reading materials threatened to explode at any second and cover the floor in a deep layer of messy paper. Two leather chairs faced the desk and bookended that horsehair sofa. In the dim lamplight, I could not distinguish what colour the furniture was, if indeed, it had any colour at all!

"To answer your question, I am consulting here and there. Along with my pension, there's more than enough money to make ends meet. I bump along, one might say."

"Have a seat, Watson. We must get caught up." He leaned forward. "You were injured, were you not?"

"Yes, and my wound still pains me. The dysentery proved debilitating as well. I'll never be able to return to active duty. Not that I would care to."

"Too right. Too right by half." He resumed his former seat, settling comfortably in his chair. "I was injured as well. Half of my left foot is missing. Plagues me like the devil. I say, Our Queen asks too much of us. She and our Country took everything from me. Everything I loved and valued."

This astonished me, as I had long ago decided that returning with my life and a minor injury was cause for celebration, given that I had personally attended to scores who died or suffered with such severe wounds that their lives would never be the same. Furthermore, every man must die, so giving one's life for one's country seems to me to be the noblest manner of departure one might desire. At least I knew that if I died on the battlefield, I would have been heralded as a hero, with my name inscribed on a tablet in the Scottish village where I was born. Better that than being hit by an omnibus! Lest I seem overly cavalier, of course I had misgivings, but during my tour of duty I had seen such extraordinary actions of valour that I put those aside and decided, with some firmness of mind, that to die serving these young soldiers was a fitting use of my talents.

Thomas Henry must have discerned that I was puzzled by his remarks because he expanded on them, saying, "I came back to find my childhood sweetheart had married another, my brother had bankrupted the family business, and my mother had squandered the family fortune. The long and short of it, old chum, is that everything I fought for disappeared before I could return to that which I held most dear. No, my life has been ruined. I'm not considered the fine catch I once was. I walk with a limp. When my foot was injured, I was knocked to the ground and struck up the side of the head. The damage I incurred has resulted in terrific headaches."

Sliding open his desk's upper drawer, he reached in and withdrew a fountain pen. It was remarkable in that the body of the writing instrument was made of onyx, obviously an expensive piece. He fiddled with his fountain pen, twirling it over and under his fingers. "So whilst the Queen's eldest son dallied with singers and actresses and all manner of married women, I wasted my vigor and my youth fighting for His hereditary wealth, His title, and His Mother. Yes, Queen Victoria cares naught for our sacrifices, only that She is undisturbed in Her grief whilst Her son frolicks around London, spending Our Nation's funds with the same sort of free hand She spends Our Countrymen's lives!"

I was at a loss for words. Thomas Henry's complaints surprised me and caught me on the back foot. "I didn't know about your hardships. I am sorry to hear about them." And I was. I shifted my weight in my chair. Was this diatribe the purpose for which Thomas Henry had brought me to this hospital? To hear him talk about what he had lost? Whilst I understood his need for a sympathetic ear, I felt the tickle of irritation start to grow.

"If not for the stipend this job pays, I should be destitute," he said. His expression was bitter. Thomas Henry stared down at his fist as he clenched and unclenched the pen whilst it rested on his desktop. "Instead, I am privileged, one might say, to tend to the ills of those less fortunate than I."

Rather than hear him dwell on his miseries, I thought it best to move ahead. "Yes, and is that why you asked me to meet you here? Can I offer you my skills as a physician? Prescribing something for your headaches?"

"No. I am perfectly capable of taking care of myself!" His eyes quickly locked on mine. The oddest procession of emotions was parading across his shovel-shaped face. His lips pursed in a sneer—and then, he caught himself and he relaxed his muscles so to resume a parody of politeness. "No, I wanted to catch up with an old friend, and I have a particular case that I need a second opinion on. As it happens, I was at luncheon at the Diogenes Club, and my companion mentioned you were in town. I believe you've done some scribbling, old chap? He said you're a published author. A sordid book about crime, or so my friend said."

This was shortly after my second book about Sherlock Holmes had been published, and although I would by no means call myself a national treasure, I had received a modicum of approbation. As a result, I was justifiably proud of my endeavour. To hear it dismissed as "scribbling" irked me beyond reason. I had heard this sort of disrespectful talk about writers before, and anyone who shows no respect for the hard, sustained efforts of an author, deserves the sort of fury the writer visits on him. Thus it was my turn for a parade of emotions to march across my visage. I was angry, indignant, offended, and furious.

"Oh, dear!" said Thomas Henry. "I must have offended you. Heavens! Nothing would be further from my aim. Please accept my abject apologies."

I muttered, "Of course. Now, let's get to the matter at hand. I should like to see your patient."

THOMAS HENRY LED ME THROUGH HALLWAYS LINED WITH ROOMS that ranged from clean and orderly with inhabitants who seemed docile enough to spaces that were little more than cells harbouring wild animals. At the end of our sad tour, we happened upon a cell where a man was buckled firmly into a white cloth jacket with arms that crossed over his chest and secured one to the other in such a manner as to totally inhibit movement. The patient sat slumped on a pile of straw with his eyes closed. At first glance, I thought the poor fellow to be dead. Such a thought continued until Thomas Henry pulled a large iron ring of keys from his back trouser pocket and unlocked the door.

"Dr. John Watson, please meet Mr. Wren. He was found wandering the streets of London. Not only has he suffered a severe vitamin deficiency that has caused a discolouration of his skin, but he's also severely dehydrated.

"Attend, please," said Thomas Henry. He squatted and dug into the canvas straitjacket so as to uncover the back of one of Mr. Wren's hands. Next, he gently pinched a piece of Mr. Wren's skin between his fingertips and let it drop. Very, very slowly the skin returned to its accustomed place. The slow "tenting" was, indeed, a common but effective manner of ascertaining whether Mr. Wren's fluid levels were low. And yes, the poor man was extremely dehydrated.

After wordlessly performing this experiment, Thomas Henry got to his feet. He walked over to the iron bars that formed one side of the square that housed Mr. Wren. With a sigh, Thomas Henry leaned against the bars.

As a matter of habit, I stooped closer to see my patient, and then I reached over and took the man's pulse. It was slow but steady. His skin felt like his temperature was normal. Both of his eyes were terribly swollen, suggesting he'd been hit with a fist in the face, over and over. The yellow tinge to his skin was exceedingly worrisome. Gingerly, as I muttered soothing words, I touched his body. At length I discovered he was surprisingly muscular. Or rather he had been muscular and was now wasting away.

I peeled back one of his eyelids to find a cloudy eye. The man flinched.

"Sir?" I ventured. "Please know you are among friends."

Mr. Wren responded by sheltering his face as best he could within the crook of his arms.

"Mr. Wren, please tell me about your injuries," I said, putting a gentle hand on his head. The man's hair was dirty and unwashed and looked to be jet-black in colour.

"No," was all he whispered.

I tried repeatedly to get him to talk to me before giving up.

Getting to my feet, I asked, "What sort of background do you have or can you share with me, Thomas Henry?"

Joining me in staring at the trussed-up man who was lying limply on the hay in front of us, he said, "He was brought in by the police. They found him hiding amongst several wooden barrels being stored behind a pub. When asked his name, he said, 'Wren,' but that was all. We had thought to feed him and fatten him up before sending him back out to the street or even the poorhouse, but last night something rather extraordinary happened. This man, with his evident weakness, surprised an orderly, overpowered the man, and raced out of the hospital. Hard to credit, isn't it? And yet, another orderly saw it happen! Of course, all of this was before we fitted him for a straightjacket.

"When he was found, this creature was covered in all sorts of disgusting matter. There was blood, offal, feces, feathers, and grasses, to name a few bits of the debris washed off of him. He also sustained a boil on the back of his neck. It's rather enormous, and I thought that the contents of such a festering wound might give us a hint as to what is bothering him. Would you assist me in lancing it and extracting the disagreeable matter inside?"

"Of course." During my time in the service, I had seen the most disgusting, and yet fascinating, parade of parasites and infections that could flourish beneath a man's skin. When left to their own devices, these colonies leak poisons into the bloodstream, sickening the entire patient. I had no doubt that a sore such as Thomas Henry had described was wearing down of the health of Mr. Wren.

Thomas Henry had a surgical room prepared at the other end of the hallway. After instructing an orderly to bring Mr. Wren to us, we waited and discussed what sort of procedure would be most efficacious.

An hour later, I was back in a growler on my way to 221B Baker Street. Knowing the insatiable curiosity of my flatmate, I carried with me in my jacket pocket several glassine envelopes. Inside these were materials collected from the body of Mr. Wren. After assuring Thomas Henry that Holmes was trustworthy and had expertise in such matters, my old colleague had agreed to allow me to take these samples to the detective. I wondered what Holmes would find. Surely some portion or another of these samples would provide information about the strange Mr. Wren.

As it happened, Holmes was racing out of the flat as I was alighting from the growler. "Stop!" Holmes shouted. "Wait right there!" He flagged down the vehicle. "Watson, that means you and your driver."

With that, he ran past me and jumped into the backseat of the growler. Despite the athleticism his gymnastics took, he managed to snag the crook of my arm and half-drag me along, too. "Watson, you must come."

With only a little reluctance, I climbed back into the growler and resumed my already warm spot on the bench seat. Once I had composed myself, I asked "What is so all-fired important?"

But Holmes was busy looking at a street address that had been hastily scrawled. With two thuds on the roof of our conveyance, he signaled for the driver to move on. When we stopped at a cross street, Holmes handed the address to the cabman and our journey continued.

"They are trying to bury it. To hide it. Sweep it under the rug," Holmes muttered. "Insane! You cannot have a string of murders so bloody, so brutal and silence all who see the carnage. You cannot keep a tragedy like this from the masses. It will out. Furthermore, the tongues that wag regarding it will manage to pick apart the most sensational aspects and exploit them. Better to let the press in from the earliest days. Tell them the truth, and make them dependent on you! That's how you control this."

"This what?" I asked.

"This spate of brutal attacks. Did you hear? Another young woman has been found in an alley on the East End. She, too, has been partially disemboweled. Lestrade sent this note to me." He waved the crumpled piece of paper.

"And what is this about?"

"Another one, Watson. That brute has slaughtered another one."

❧

CARNAGE IS TO BE EXPECTED ON THE BATTLEFIELD BUT NOT IN THE streets of the city. The sight before us was piteous in the extreme, and without my time as a medical doctor attached to the Fusiliers, I should not have withstood the horror and shock we'd been asked to examine closely. Scotland Yard Inspector G. Lestrade, a weasel-faced man of short stature and a paucity of imagination, had arrived before us. Holmes had been invited as a consulting detective, a man whose keen insights were unparalleled when it came to modern crime investigations. Holmes had asked me to come in my role as a doctor, presumably to offer a professional evaluation of whatever form human misery was taking today.

That question was answered almost as soon as we stepped out of our cab. In a narrow alley between two buildings, a sad clutch of policemen and onlookers had gathered around a form on the cobblestones. As Holmes and I drew closer, the group parted to let us through. My immediate reaction was so visceral that I almost wished they hadn't stepped aside.

The sad creature before us was as close to being decapitated as I had ever seen without a clean blow being struck. The white gristle of her windpipe gleamed against the vermillion of her wet blood. The pink of her flesh had been torn jaggedly along the rich red pulp of her neck. Her blue eyes had frozen open in horror and her pretty mouth formed a perfect "oh!" of surprised horror. Tendrils of her corn silk hair fanned out in a corona around her head, even as the curling strands were semi-submerged in puddles of drying blood. Some kind soul, or a person of offended sensibilities, had tossed a horse's blanket over her so that from the clavicle down she was covered. The rank odours of coppery blood, urine, and feces hung over her like a dirty veil. Smears of blood on her outstretched hands proved that she had not traveled to the other world willingly. Indeed, the crisscrossed rips in the flesh of her forearms suggested she had fought valiantly for her life.

As for her honour, who could tell? Under normal circumstances, a doctor might examine her internal organs to determine whether the poor woman was a maiden or a lady who sold her favors freely.

I say "under normal circumstances" because this was anything but a normal circumstance. Holmes and I had decided to share a flat together comparatively recently, and thus I was still learning about the scope of his work. This presented a struggle as I attempted to understand exactly what a consulting detective did. Now I found myself gazing down at the cooling body of what had once been a woman and wondering what on earth to make of this desecration of a young person.

Using my fingertips, I attempted to drag the horse blanket away from the victim to afford me better viewing. As I had feared, the blood was congealing, mixing with the fibers and stiffening the fabric. After several unsuccessful tries, I gave up on delicate maneuvers and bent closer to the prone form. With one gloved hand outstretched, I grabbed a corner of the dusty wool and dragged the cloth away from the bloody torso so I could examine the body.

A voice shouted, "Stop! Stop right there."

A man in a rather expensively cut bespoke suit appeared out of nowhere, or so it seemed. He railed at the inspector. "Lestrade? Step away! Tell that man to leave her alone!"

Holmes and I gave each other sideways glances, a silent conference that proved he was as curious about the interruption as I was. I let go of the dirty horse blanket.

"Begging your pardon, guv," said Lestrade in an obsequious manner, "what we have here is a nice-looking young lass. Or at least she might have been once, but I don't know exactly how she was killed. Dr. Watson here, he might tell me."

"Watson is a surgeon and a battlefield tested one at that," added Holmes.

"I don't care if Watson was Admiral Nelson himself, he's not to touch those remains," the well-dressed man said. "Neither are you, Lestrade. I am a representative of Her Majesty's government, and as such, I am ordered to make sure you cease and desist all examination." The man was rather out of breath from running to stop us, but his errand was so urgent that he gasped out these words without waiting to regain his wind.

"We have here a crime, and it's on my beat!" Lestrade protested.

"That doesn't matter. Your beat, Lestrade, is yours only by the powers invested in you by Scotland Yard. If we say you have lost your sinecure, then so be it!" The newcomer had moved from breathless and urgent to strident and demanding.

To this day, I am not sure whether or not poor Lestrade understood the insult rendered when his job was labeled a "sinecure." Whatever the policeman understood, he latched onto enough of the diatribe to decide to back away from the dead girl. I, however, was not as ready to be cowed. Holmes and I had traveled a long way to get here, and now that I was to be cheated out of doing my duty, I felt irritable.

"See here," I said, "Lestrade wanted an expert opinion and that is exactly what I intend to provide." But when I moved forward to touch the blanket again, Holmes grabbed me by the upper arm.

"Don't," he said, in a voice entirely unnatural to him. Turning to the newcomer, Holmes added, "Too bad. I should have at least hoped for a chance to open up her stomach and take a look at her last meal. That might have directed us to a local pub, easily enough."

I swallowed bile. The fact that Sherlock could speak so calmly of food brought a fresh wave of nausea to the gathering of policemen. Almost as one, their Adam's apples bobbed in unison while their flesh turned more towards green than healthy pink. One constable noted for his brusque manner turned on his heel and raced away, but not fast enough to spare us the sounds of his retching. My hand flew up to cover my own mouth rather than chuckle out loud. Actually, the policemen had every right to be disgusted. I'd seen men *in extremis* but not young women. Having been taught at an early age to protect the ladies in my orb, I found the dead girl disquieting, to put it mildly.

"See?" Lestrade piped up as he faced the newcomer. "I brought Holmes and his pal because they're good at thinking crimes through. Not as good as me, but they have their uses."

"How many does this make?" asked Holmes. He had no need of elaboration; we all knew what he was asking.

"Five." Lestrade lifted one shoulder in a half-hearted shrug. "At least that's what we're counting as this fiend's work. Some say we should include more. I don't know."

"You've done an admirable job keeping details of these murders out of the press," observed Holmes, ignoring the man interrupting his investigation. "Is that fair, Lestrade? Don't people need to know that a beast roams the streets? That an animal who preys on young women is loose among us? Wouldn't it be fair to warn everyone, but especially young women, to go out and about with caution?"

Lestrade said, "They aren't but prostitutes, so don't worry yourselves much. The East End is full of them. You can't toss a rock and not hit one. Disgusting, I say. I ought to lock up the lot of them."

Holmes turned narrowed eyes on Lestrade. "Yes, but only if you lock up their customers, too. Look at her! She can scarcely weigh eight stone! Do you honestly think she enjoys selling herself to the highest bidder? Does she look like she'd had an easy life? What say you? Can you see the slightest hint that she had something to look forward to, given how gaunt she is and how dirty, except merely surviving one more day? And now some heinous wretch has taken even that away from her. Jack the Ripper, indeed! If he killed her with one quick blow, smiting her senseless, then he'd be an angel of mercy, I'd warrant. But he did not. He played with her as a cat does a mouse. Only a few East End residents live beyond that tender age of thirty, and so this young woman was not allotted much more time here anyway!"

I opened my mouth to chime in, but Holmes had had enough. Casting an angry glare at the well-dressed man who'd interfered, Holmes said, "Come on, Watson. These men don't need our help. They've got this well in hand. This makes the fifth woman identified as being the harvest of one killer. More might be on his list as well, but they've chosen to assign those murders to this fiend. This one is freshly slaughtered, and no real progress has been made, but the great machinery of English crime prevention does not need our help."

Reluctantly, I turned, planning to walk away along with my friend, but as I did, Holmes shook his fist at Lestrade and his supervisor. "You're naught but one slippery rung ahead of her on life's ladder, you fools! Lestrade? You brought me to look at this impoverished wretch to make me feel as hopeless as you do—but we both know that you have all the resources you need. The problem is *not* that you can't catch this madman. It's that you don't care to! You'd rather see women like her die!"

2

The time for our luncheon had passed, and by silent agreement, neither of us felt eager to sample the foodstuffs of those miserable establishments that dotted the East End. Holmes waved down a cab. After we'd taken seats, he rapped sharply on the roof and shouted, "To the Diogenes Club."

Willing my face not to reveal my shock (and delight), I turned to stare out the window. I found it curious that a man who was thrifty with his lodgings could afford membership in one of London's most pricey private establishments, but then again, Holmes was full of surprises. Each day I opened my eyes and wondered, "What next?" I might leave the comfort of my room to find him hunched over his chemicals and deep in the midst of an experiment that could bring the house down around our heads. Or I might find him behind a pile of open books. And then there was the notable time, he was tinkering with the severed hand of a victim, trying to ascertain if traces of gunpowder could be found on the fingers.

It was our great good fortune that our landlady, Mrs. Hudson, was congenial to the extreme. For a reason I can't fathom, she considered Holmes both odd and amusing. Even his small mishaps, such as setting fire to a needlepointed cushion because he'd shoved his lit pipe into a back pocket, evoked only the most muted responses from that dear lady. Confronted with the burned cushion, she could only shake her head and marvel, “You managed to ruin it right proper, Mr. Holmes.”

Just when I thought she might light into him like one cock lands on another in the ring, she smiled and added, “I have never cared for that particular pillow. My aunt did the stitching, but she complained with every tug of her needle, and I cannot set eyes on that piece without remembering how dour she was. Good riddance, I say! Let me toss it out for you.”

The sonorous strikes of Big Ben grew louder and louder as we approached the Diogenes Club. Rather than risk embarrassment later, I lodged a mumbled protest about the prices. Holmes gave me a puzzled look and cocked his head in surprise. “I thought you knew?”

“Knew what?” My blood pressure was rising. That sensation of being caught off guard is unpleasant, to put it mildly, and yet here I was, feeling out of sorts.

“Nothing, old chap. My fault entirely. I neglected to tell you that my brother Mycroft is one of the club’s founders. Since I intend to speak with him about the murder we saw, I feel totally comfortable with putting a good meal on his bill.”

“Should you ask him first?” I was horrified. As wonderful as the food was, I couldn’t justify the extravagance. The fact that Holmes was saddling his brother with such an expense shocked me.

“No need,” Holmes assured me with a laugh. He hopped out of the cab and I clambered out behind him. “By the way, I’ve arranged membership for you.”

I didn’t know what to say. When I recovered myself, I sputtered, “But the initiation fee!”

“Taken care of. Your able assistance is more than worth that pittance. Trust me on that. My brother agreed,” Holmes said.

I should have liked to have heard that particular conversation.

The trappings of the Diogenes Club have been shared to excess, but for those who prefer firsthand reports, allow me to sketch out the classic façade, the limestone stairs, the heavy mahogany front doors with the brass door knocker, the cool marble foyer, and the quintessential butler (or in the club’s parlance, manager) who greeted us like long-lost friends of his. Although, he did issue a reminder to write our names in the guestbook. We requested a table and a meal, and the manager promised that after a short wait, one would soon be ready for us in the dining room.

In one of the meeting rooms, a lecture had been scheduled. These events were open to nonmembers who could attend as guests, and under the aegis of Sherlock Holmes, I'd been able to enjoy the opportunity to hear various commentaries. Today, whilst waiting for our table, we were lured to the lecture room by the prospect of listening to one S.A. André, a Swede, who held forth the correlation between the simultaneous variations of aero-electricity and geo-magnetism. A striking man with a massive physique, André reminded me of a Norse god. His blue-grey eyes, large nose, and handsome features set him apart in a room filled with men. The explorer was so calm he barely seemed to be alert. André travels through Europe in the hope of uncovering inventions that would be useful in ordinary life. In that manner, he is rather like an evangelist for science, because although his demeanor is unflappable, the force of his personality is immense. Holmes and I listened whilst our table was being prepared. At one point, Holmes leaned close enough to whisper, "I have heard that André plans to explore the Artic."

"On foot?" I whispered back. Such expeditions were known to end in tragedy.

"By hot air balloon."

A porter tapped Holmes on the shoulder as a silent way of saying we should come to the dining room and be seated. We were led to a delicate Queen Anne dining table set for two in the midst of a sun-soaked dining room. A server quickly appeared. With a flourish, he opened our napkins and fluttered them into our laps. The place in front of me was set with eggshell-thin white china, emblazoned with the club's crest. The elegance was calculated to soothe members after their weary travail in the world beyond these walls.

Soon we were enjoying a savoury cream of leek soup, followed by sliced mutton, Wesleydale cheese, and hearty slices of bread. When our repast was finished, Holmes raised a jaunty eyebrow and said, "I believe a visit to Mycroft is in order."

"Indeed," I said, by way of answer. 'Though we had not been flatmates for long, Holmes and I had easily and quickly fallen into those habits of communication that are oft associated with married couples. To wit, we had only to sketch out our thoughts before moving ahead, forgoing long and exhaustive explanations.

From the dining room we followed a clerk to a doorway tucked under a set of stairs and leading downwards along yet another staircase. At the end, we transversed a hallway into a space where desks were arranged in a cheek-by-jowl fashion. Those who have read more recent adventures will note that this haphazard floor plan has changed much over the years, but at the time represented here, the subterranean offices of those who work behind the scenes to run our government was more like a convention of confused moles than a finely tuned apparatus. Today, Mycroft occupies a glass-encased office in the midst of a hive of industrious worker bees, but then, he was yet to climb to his present lofty heights of favour with Her Majesty.

Even so, from his first days at his post, working for our government, Mycroft was marked for greatness. As a matter of fact, I have it on strictest confidence that he and Sherlock both were recruited for jobs in the administration after they distinguished themselves in their studies. Of course, their father's abilities and their mother's intellect had early marked them for greatness, along with a family crest that was impeccable. But Sherlock chose to forge his own path while Mycroft agreed to toil along a well-trod road. I believe that was a pressure point where the two brothers' ambitions and goals diverted, and one could never fully understand or appreciate the choice of the other.

So it was that Sherlock was not impressed or cowed by his brother's climb up the ladder of political life and Mycroft similarly felt no exceptional glow of appreciation when tallying up his brother's achievements. Thus, these impressive surroundings did not deter Holmes in his task. He approached his brother's desk with an alacrity in his step that precluded others from interfering with our advance. Mycroft heard his brother's footfalls and glared up at us from a daunting pile of papers. "What is it?" he said, in the most unwelcoming tone possible.

"We need to talk," Sherlock said, and then we waited. If Mycroft thought he could fob off his brother by ignoring us, he was sorely mistaken. After what seemed like an interminable wait, but was probably only a couple of minutes, Mycroft tilted his head, using his plump chin as a pointer, and motioned us towards a closed door without any signage on it. The twin heavy oak panels formed the bottom two-thirds of the door while a glass window through which a roll-down shade could be seen filled the rest of the space. Rather than lead the way and walk ahead of us, Sherlock stood still as a statue, indicating that his brother must get up and escort us, lest we find ourselves twiddling our thumbs while Mycroft did some trivial act to prove his importance. Recognising he had been outplayed, Mycroft gave a grunt of disapproval and slammed down his pencil. Then, snorting like a quarrelsome bull, he heaved his bulk to his feet and headed for the closed door.

Once inside the bleak room, which was empty save for a rickety table and four uncomfortable wooden chairs, we paused to watch Mycroft bolt the latch and lower the shade, signaling the room was occupied. This was not a place designed for comfort, or so I found out when I lowered myself onto the unyielding wooden seat. "No one will ever get drowsy here," Sherlock said to me sotto voce. "Too blasted miserable by half."

Mycroft dragged a protesting chair away from the table and sat down. Glaring at his brother he said, "Out with it. You are interrupting my work."

"Yes, and you interrupted my day by sending Lestrade to ask me to visit the East End," said Sherlock in an even tone. "I am wise to your tricks, Brother. Furthermore, I brought along the good doctor, which wasted his time as well."

"Indeed? And why was it a waste?" Mycroft sniffed.

"Because Lestrade's governor showed up and warned us away."

A myriad of emotions crossed Mycroft's pudgy face. Although they only paraded past for a half second, I registered them.

Holmes persisted. "So what's your game, Brother?"

Mycroft's smile did not reach his eyes. His fleshy face showed a slight resemblance to that of his brother, but Sherlock's hawklike nose gave him a piercing quality that Mycroft could not manage. Quick-witted as he is, Mycroft often seems caught flat-footed by his younger sibling. "What? You accuse me of sending you on some fool's errand?" Mycroft asked. "I should think you encourage quite enough of those without my able assistance."

"Do not parry with me, Brother. Why did you want me to see that poor woman but not to do anything about her tragic demise?" Sherlock persisted.

"I had hoped you might help the local constabulary, but shortly after sending you that note, I was instructed to keep you out of the investigation," Mycroft fairly hissed, despite the lack of sibilant consonants in his words. "The exact phrasing was, 'Keep your meddlesome brother and his crippled sidekick out of this! Or else!'"

"Crippled sidekick?" Sherlock repeated with incredulity. "That is what you call war heroes these days? Such patriotism you and your cronies display. Such gratitude! I wonder what the families of so many dead troops would say if they heard how little you value their sons' valour!"

I badly needed a nap after our large meal and the edifying but lengthy lecture, and I found this petulant tête-à-tête insulting. "Stop it. Both of you. Say what you must, Sherlock, and let's be gone," I said. "If your brother has so little respect for my efforts as a soldier, then perhaps *he* can serve during the next national skirmish. Until then, I shall remove myself. I have been called worse by better men."

Mycroft's jaw dropped and his mouth fell open. My insult had hit the mark. However, I will admit he recovered admirably and apologized for insulting me. I waved his insincere groveling away. "Tell us plainly, Mycroft, what it was you hoped to accomplish by asking Lestrade to send Sherlock to the East End and then ordering us to stay away," I continued.

Deflating a small bit, he said, "I had already issued an invitation to my brother when word came from on high that you were to refrain from investigating."

Sherlock and I exchanged looks of disbelief and puzzlement. Sherlock said, "From on high? What exactly does that mean?"

"It means exactly what it means," Mycroft mocked his brother. "Those whose positions are above mine have sent down an edict, an order if you will, demanding that you stay clear of the investigation into the deaths of the young women over in the East End."

Positions above mine? There were so few that could qualify as having governance over Mycroft that this shard of commentary stuck in my brain.

"Who would that be? And why would they do that?" I mused. "Why are we precluded from trying to help? What a lot of rubbish!" I leaped to my feet. "I say, this old cripple won't stand aside and allow a monster to roam our streets. Even if the prey are women of ill-repute or of low standing, they deserve better. You and your kind should be ashamed of yourselves! How dare you laugh at me and tell me not to get involved when you care not one whit for those poor creatures!"

"Restrain yourself, Doctor," said Mycroft, "and keep a civil tongue in your head. There are reasons behind the request for you to leave off, and I have no doubt they are good ones. There are times when one must allow those in charge to do as they will. Surely, as a military man you are well aware of this!"

Sherlock rubbed his chin. "Then you are saying that you want us to stand aside because someone else, someone more highly placed than you, has instructed you to do so? Or are you making this choice of your own volition whilst hoping your superior will stumble and fall? Is this a game you are playing, Brother of mine?"

"But what of the women?" I demanded. I had not yet sat back down so I lifted my chair and slammed it into the floor as a way of emphasising my point. "While you and your betters play games, they are condemned to death!"

"Not at all," rejoined Mycroft. "In fact, I can assure you that your staying out of this will bring this mess to a speedier conclusion than it could possibly reach if you get involved. There are forces at work here, and those forces need to be carefully managed. If you scare them off, if they catch your scent on the wind, you will force them to seek shelter, to run to ground, and I'll never flush them out."

Aha, I thought. Mycroft slipped up. He said "I'll never" rather than "we'll never." So he was in this for himself!

This made a bit of sense. Not much, but enough to assure me—and assure Sherlock Holmes—that we were not being warned off for an entirely spurious reason. Sherlock shot me a pleading look that asked me to back down. My response included a silent challenge: only if you promise justice will be done.

At the end of the day, that was the best resolution we could hope for.

❧ 3 ❧

Outside the club, Holmes and I spoke little to each other as a result of our individual thoughts. My friend hailed a cab coming our way. The cabman pointed the strutting bay to the kerb and the vehicle's door opened. Out popped Lord Reginald Hyslop, the Secretary of Defence, and Captain Jonathan Pickering, a maritime officer well-known for his hawkish views of English sovereignty. Although I've never been introduced to either man, their images have appeared regularly in *The Times*. In the event, Hyslop was more rotund than I expected and his balding pate was covered by a felt hat of a style called a bowler. Even though he was wearing a fine jacket and slacks, one could tell his physique was more fat than flesh. In short, he was the visual opposite of a man fit for battle. Pickering was muscular and held himself with an attitude of command. His face was decorated with long, perfectly trimmed sideburns that flowed into a mustache curling up at the ends. His eyes were so hooded that the pupils that showed were shaped like knife slits. What little of his mouth one could see was set in a grim expression that suggested cruelty. Both men moved in such a manner to announce, "We are very, very important!"

Hyslop cast a curious glance at Holmes and me before deciding we warranted none of his time or attention. Hyslop seemed to recognise Holmes as he strode past us.

"Hyslop is an old acquaintance of my father's," Holmes muttered. "Curious. I wonder what business brings them here? They missed the lecture and it is past the time for luncheon. I don't remember seeing their names on the membership roster."

The notion that Holmes had unlimited access to the roster and that he obviously scanned it regularly should not have surprised me. Yet it did, even though I recovered quickly. In a sly tone, I whispered back, "Should we go and see if they are welcome here?"

"Capital idea," said Holmes, indicating to the cab driver that he should go on by. Once the street was empty, we scurried around to the back of the august building that houses the Diogenes Club. Slipping behind the edifice, I followed Holmes as he rapped on the door to the kitchen. A startled waiter stuck his head out and drawled, "Yeee-eees?"

"I am Mycroft Holmes' brother, and I was visiting him in his office downstairs moments ago. I left my walking stick at his desk. Give way, please." Holmes proceeded to step forward in such a way that the man had very little recourse, indeed.

For my part, I was content to follow closely in my friend's wake as we pushed ourselves past the astonished staff. The delicious fragrances of cooked onions and herbs wafted around us as we hurried through the swinging door used for delivering meals. No doubt we were being treated to a preview of this evening's meal. We hurried through the hallway, dodging servers carrying trays of drinks and nibbles. The sight of Holmes moving stealthily down the hallway would have been comical in other circumstances, but given the oddity of what we were about, I did not dare laugh. Instead I mimicked my friend's actions until we found ourselves right outside a meeting room, such as those where the lecture by the balloonist had taken place, only much, much smaller. Carefully, we edged up to the door and cupped our hands over our ears so we could hear better.

"Can you assure me, Mr. Holmes, that your brother will not meddle? This is a matter of national defence, after all." Hyslop demanded this of Mycroft.

"Secretary, if you would lay bare your reasons, I might better allay your—" Mycroft began.

"His reasons? Holmes, are you daft? He is the Secretary of Defence, not some underling. You are not in a position to ask for his reasons. Your job is to take orders and obey!" shouted Pickering.

"And I will do. I am simply explaining the difficulty of my task as it regards my brother, who is a civilian."

"Holmes, this is a matter of national security. Are you questioning me? Or my decisions? Or that of Our Sovereign?" the Secretary of Defence sputtered. "Do you have any idea of the problems we might encounter—" The rest was lost as a server dropped a pot that rang out with all the rounded tones of Big Ben up close.

Mycroft responded with a tut-tut vocalisation. "I assure you, Secretary, I have done all you asked and more, and since you insist on ordering me to withhold information, I cannot promise you any joy, sir. You are directing your orders towards a private citizen! As you might well know, my brother has a habit of, shall we say, involvement? While I have successfully steered him away from the deaths, I cannot oversee all of his actions at every turn. Therefore, assuring you that Sherlock will not interfere is clearly beyond my remit."

Sherlock and I were sharing a spot outside the door in our attempt to hear and not be seen. Now my friend turned wide eyes to me. I felt equally shocked. Mycroft was simultaneously acting in an obsequious manner and chastising the Secretary of the Defence of our Nation! This exchange was rather extraordinary on a variety of levels.

"See here!" Pickering raised his voice. "The Crown will not be best pleased with your lackadaisical attitude, Holmes. If your inept response to my request casts aspersions upon this operation, then what follows will be on your head. Do you hear me? Your head! I shall not step in and try to save you, even if you drown in the foul waters of your own twisted ambition."

But Mycroft was not cowed. He spoke in a voice as smooth and unruffled as the surface of a pond on a still summer day. "That is a consequence that I am willing to accept, Captain Pickering. Short of denying a citizen of this realm his liberty, I repeat: I have done all that

I can. Now if you'll excuse me, I have more pressing matters to deal with."

Sherlock and I nearly tripped over each other as we headed for the end of the service corridor. Our fleet action proved important because we emerged at a door at the end of a carpeted corridor just in time to watch the Secretary of Defence and Captain Pickering hurrying away towards the opposite end. They were walking in in sullen manner. When they were midway down the hall, we saw Mycroft come out of the meeting room. Fortunately, his broad back was to us, and he was wholly unaware that we might be skulking around. He continued down the hallway.

After creeping back to the kitchen and through it, Holmes and I exhaled loudly when we were both out of doors and safely so.

"The Secretary and Captain Pickering do not seem to trust your brother. In fact, I would say that that neither is kindly disposed at all!" I said.

"There is more to this," Holmes replied, apropos of nothing.

Once we were on the street, he hailed a growler.

Of course, he was right. There was more to the situation, just as one only sees the tip of an iceberg whilst the treacherous portions are hidden under water. But at the time, we had no way of knowing how right he was or how the consequences of Mycroft's actions might impact our lives. Even as we climbed into the vehicle, I reflected on my grave misgivings. Perhaps my military training gave me adequate rationale to side with the Secretary, and therefore, I tended to blindly take his side. But there is another more likely reason, and 'though I am sad to write this, the truth must come out. I did not and I do not trust Mycroft Holmes. There! I have made a clean breast of this sentiment! If Sherlock reads this and does not know these to be the sincere words of a loyal friend after all these years, he is not the man I think he is.

THE SPLENDID LUNCHEON AND THE HEIGHTENED EMOTIONS OF THE crime scene left me feeling somewhat depleted, as I was still recovering from my time in Afghanistan. 'Though my injury had healed in theory, soft tissue takes longer than bone. Add to that the dysentery I'd suffered and the general deprivations so clearly a part of military life, that 'though I looked quite fit to all I encountered, my fatigue put the lie to that. Holmes and I climbed into another cab. Once the driver headed for Baker Street, my friend turned to me and said, "I regret that I got you involved, Watson. My brother's words were ungenerous. Allow me to apologize on his behalf."

I laughed. "Your brother is perfectly able to apologize for his own actions. We both know that. I am not hurt by the fact he spoke the truth. However, I am angered by his flimsy deception. It's clear as crystal that he is warning us away because he figures some member of the peerage is involved."

A normal person would have responded with a sharp intake of breath, but not Sherlock Holmes. Rather than show chagrin or try to reason me out of my position, he only nodded. "You are right. That's the only mitigating force I can think of. If it's not the peerage, it must be one of the Secretaries, and I doubt that sincerely. No, they are all jockeying for position. Have you ever seen the Palio? The race in Siena, Italy?"

"I have not, but I have heard about it. The races have been held since medieval times, right?"

"Yes," Holmes said with a nod. "There are no rules. The race takes place in a square in the center of the walled city. All the different neighborhoods hope their animals and riders will be chosen to compete. On the day, there is extensive pageantry. Every competing neighborhood waves its flag and places bets on being victorious. Musicians in costumes and various workers' unions as well as city officials march 'round the course while onlookers hang over balconies looking down at the spectacle. It takes many attempts to line up the horses so that their noses are all touching a rope. The entire race takes less than two minutes. And here is the point I wish to make: Once the horses are off and running, jockeys can whip each other, strike each other, or do anything they want to assure a victory. That's how it is for men who work in the service of the Crown. In their race to the top, they can—and will—do any number of underhanded tricks. I can well imagine that either someone is covering for a member of the Royal Family or someone thinks he is covering for a member of royalty. Either way, the end result is the same. We were warned away from investigating the deaths of the young ladies because someone thinks there is something to gain—and that our discovery might embarrass the Heir. The lives lost mean that little to those who are competing for high stakes."

Holmes sighed. There was so much he did not say because he did not have to say it. The elongated mourning period of Our Queen had sent our Country into a tailspin. Queen Victoria did not run our government, that is true, but to our nation and its people she was the rudder on our great ship. Without her, the ship sailed 'round and 'round in aimless circles. Her withdrawal had left us to our own devices, and that simply had opened the door wide to those without purity of purpose.

I considered other remarks that Holmes chose not to share. Although the late, dearly departed Prince Albert had initially been laughed at for his German accent, His stodgy ways, and his too-serious bearing, over time the British people had seen his total devotion to his wife. We knew he was a diligent worker who cast himself headlong into acts of improvement, whether it was saving money in the palaces by not tossing out candle stubs or inventorying the royal linens. We saw how devoted he was as a father, this man whose own father had sent him away when he was just a boy. None of us could challenge his affection for his wife, Victoria, or his eagerness to fulfill his role as the head of the Royal Family.

His son was another matter entirely. Back when I was in the service of the Crown, various rumours had circulated, regarding the temperament of the young heir to the Throne. Bertie was the cuckoo who was slipped into the Royal Family's nest and who managed to sour all the good works by his parents and siblings. A few wild oats were expected to be sown, but Bertie sowed them by the bushel and watered them with his Mother's tears. How an apple could fall so far from the tree was frankly bewildering. At first we heard vague rumblings of mischief in the nursery. Then came stories from visitors who were shocked by the boy's rudeness. Now, as he stood on the brink of manhood, all of us hoped for young Bertie to come to his senses. Instead he grew more and more outrageous with each passing day. His interest in amoral women could be traced back to his Mother's uncle, George IV, his Mother's father, the Duke of Kent, and his Father's father, Duke Earnest I. Yet all of us held out hope that his Father's strong hand and his Mother's position as a morally sound sovereign would bring out the best in the lad.

It did not. Nothing did. Year after year, the Royal Family suffered one dramatic incident after another as Bertie became involved with unsuitable women. When he married Alexandra of Denmark, we hoped that the love of a good woman would keep Bertie on a short leash. Regrettably, that did not happen, and he managed to add new vices to old ones, including getting caught up in a scandal at a baccarat game, when he was accused of cheating.

Given Bertie's sordid history with married women, women in the theatre, and prostitutes, it did not require a stretch of the imagination to conjure up images of him frolicking in the East End. Of course, he'd already been named correspondent in one divorce case, so the public knew him to be incorrigible when it came to romantic liaisons. Was it possible he had killed women to keep them silent? I did not know. What presented itself as the more likely proposition was that women had been killed on his behalf in an attempt to keep them quiet.

In either case, Mycroft Holmes' brother could pose a threat if Sherlock Holmes sniffed out the truth and exposed it. Demanding that Mycroft warn his brother off would have been a smart move on the chessboard. By taking Sherlock out of play, an embarrassing situation could be dealt with quietly and swept under the Aubusson carpet. Keeping Sherlock and me at arm's length would insure that we did not cause problems for the Crown, problems that might reflect poorly on Mycroft. When on the scent of a case, Sherlock proved himself heedless of political stratagems. Instead, he concentrated on the task and the people who might shed light on his inquiries. Whether those people were highborn or low-class made no difference to Sherlock Holmes. He had an amazing ability to home in on the important features of a crime and move towards a resolution regardless of the obstacles in his path.

Someone out there, someone very powerful indeed, considered Sherlock Holmes to be an obstacle and had decided to make sure that

Sherlock did not ruin his plans. As they fiddled, so did Rome burn! Clearly Lestrade did not have the mental acuity necessary to solve a case like that of Jack the Ripper. The man also lacked the sort of single-minded intensity that Sherlock Holmes brought to his cases. I could almost imagine Lestrade metaphorically washing his hands of the murder (or murders) in the East End, thanks to lack of ambition, which coupled with his laissez-faire attitude and topped off with the spectre of embarrassing the Crown, would have been more than enough to put the man on his back foot.

I watched the streets of London pass by my window and reflected that a long nap might be just the ticket. The day was rather warm, the scent of horse manure had been awakened by the heat and the traffic, and the quiet coolness of our rooms sang a siren's song to my senses. However, repose did not await me.

Our day of surprises was not over. Indeed, we were met at the door of 221B Baker Street by a distressed Mrs. Hudson, who was wringing the fabric of her dress. "Gentlemen! I have a fellow in my kitchen. He says he's here for you, and I would have sent him away, but, well, there are reasons. May I send him up to you after you have a few minutes to get yourselves sorted?"

"Of course," Holmes called over his shoulder as he was halfway up the staircase. As we entered the flat, he continued, "You might have told me if you were expecting someone, Watson. I would have hurried our endeavours along accordingly."

"But I am not expecting anyone!" I protested with some little degree of natural irritation at being denied my nap. "Rather more likely, this is a poor sad soul seeking the great detective powers of the wonderful Sherlock Holmes."

My tone was a tad dismissive, but one must remember that back then, I was not as fully cognizant of Holmes' incredible abilities as I am today. Yes, I had seen him work his magical deductions on strangers, and I had been a firsthand witness to his astonishing ability to perceive, discern, and interpret minute details. But the fuller scope of his talents was not as obvious to me then as it is now, and I freely suggest that is in part, because Holmes was still blossoming into the genius he currently displays at every opportunity.

Once inside our sitting room, he merely huffed a response and showed a wise decision to keep his retort under wraps, so to speak. His choice proved prescient as a timid knock on the door to our flat alerted us to the visitor. But before I could cross the room to answer the rapping, a smell so powerful and disgusting that it harked back to the murdered woman came near to overpowering me.

"Gads!" I said, yanking a clean handkerchief from my pocket and pressing it over my nose. This protective action waylaid me, and Holmes rushed past to unlock our door.

4

"Begging your pardon, sir," said a deep voice with a North County twang. "You always told me to come if you was needed, Master Holmes, and by all that's holy, I'm standing here today because I don't know where else to turn! The coneys been torn up fiercely, and whatever it is, it killed a dog, too. An Irish wolfhound named Othello. He was torn from stem to stern, and we ain't got the slightest idea what we're dealing with here, so I told my friend Ducky that I'd bring it on to you."

This fast-paced recitation confused me. "Othello? Ducky? Coneys?"

Holmes smiled in a way I've only seen him do half a dozen times since we've met. His face took on an indulgent expression of concern as he calmed our guest. "Slow down, please, Landover. I am rather at a loss here. Best to start at the beginning. I thought you'd retired from Musgrave Hall."

I needed no explanation for that. Musgrave Hall was the Holmes family's ancestral estate.

"That I did, sir. Five years ago. See, I been visiting my friend, Ducky. That's John Duckworth, and he's the gamekeeper for an estate not far from Windsor Castle, you see. We've been pals since we were in short pants. This morning we were going to do a count of the rabbits and we stepped out to the pens and found this mess. Well, don't you just know, Ducky ran and got his master, and Mr. Johnston, Esquire, said, 'My word! Ducky, what is the meaning of this? This must stop!' and he charged my friend with putting a stop to this, but how can he? He don't know what sort of trap to set, or how to bait it, or whatever! In all my days, nothing's given me a turn like this. Ducky was beside himself, I tell you. Never seen him so het up. So I says to myself that I ought to ask young master for help. I reckon if Mister Sherlock Holmes can't tell me what's what, no one can."

If I could have spoken without gagging, I would have suggested that Landover turn 180-degrees and hie himself hither with a bit of spring in his step. Whatever this old man was selling, I wanted no part of it! One glance at his flat cap, his grizzled and unkempt beard, and his shabby attire convinced me that he might be the source of the appalling odour assaulting my nostrils. Yet, that was not true! And I learned as much in short order when the old man thrust a canvas sack towards Holmes and the movement awakened every stench I'd once associated with bodies on the battlefield.

"Let's take this outside, Landover," said Holmes in a voice as courteous as a courtier greeting the Queen.

"Right you are, young master," the old man agreed.

Before following our guest down the stairs, Holmes paused long enough to add, "Watson? Your knowledge of anatomy might be helpful, if you will indulge me."

"Does he carry a human in that bag?" I asked, while pinching my nose closed.

"Doubtful."

"Then what?" I said. Admittedly, I'd only partially listened to the old man's lament because I'd been concentrating so hard on keeping down my luncheon.

"A rabbit or two and the dog he mentioned, I suspect," Holmes answered.

"Then my education will be of little use. I can do my best, but doubtless another with specialized training would be vastly more helpful." I pondered this for a tick. "I say, there's a young man I know by the name of Flower. Met him at a lecture. Shall I send for him? Flower seems a fine enough chap."

"Just the thing!" Holmes' face brightened. "I'll whistle for Thaddeus Wiggins. Watson? You can entrust a message to the boy, while I get Landover to release his prize to me. It's probably best that we carry this sack around back. I believe Mrs. Hudson still has that icebox, does she not?"

The thought of our kindly landlady offering up her icebox for whatever foul carcasses Landover hauled about in his canvas sack brought on a fresh wave of nausea. My expression must have belied my disgust because Holmes quickly interceded with, "Come now, Watson. This is not the time to be squeamish. I'll buy the good woman a second icebox if need be. Landover would not have traveled all this way if he did not have a good reason."

"You are acquainted with this man?" Whilst I'd told myself my friend's mysteries were his own, his strange and varied colleagues never ceased to amaze me, as Holmes gathered sources the way a bookseller searches out rare tomes. He seemed to know one person in every occupation there was! By no stretch of the imagination were these people his friends, but rather, they functioned as feeder streams do to a mighty river, collecting rainwater and runoff and funneling it into one source: Holmes.

"I've known Landover my entire life," Holmes hastened to explain. "He's was the gamekeeper at my family's estate, Musgrave Hall, for as long as I can remember. There's not a kinder, gentler man on the face of God's green earth. Now, please write a note and send for Wiggins running."

A word about Thaddeus Wiggins: Never have I seen a more motley excuse for a child than Wiggins, a young ruffian of the first order who is entirely devoted to Holmes. The boy lives in a boardinghouse not far from us with a rowdy crew of other street children who really should be under the care of a responsible adult. When his face is clean—and that's a blue moon sort of occurrence!—the boy has regular features spaced in a pleasing manner that would lead one to assume his parents must have been nice-looking people. His eyes are an ever-changing hazel, which I believe would match his brown hair, but I cannot swear to the colour of the latter since I've never seen it washed clean. When the boy first popped up, he was scrawny and obviously malnourished. Since then, he's thrown his lot in with Holmes in the oddest sort of alliance imaginable, and 'though the child still lives as a city rat might, he is better fed, thanks to Holmes. At first glance, Wiggins could pass for a moving pile of rags, but I have reason to know that Holmes makes sure the child has warm clothing. The shredded and tattered scraps that hang off of Wiggins are what the boy calls "me disguise." And lest his mangled English fool you, the child is exceedingly bright and a mimic of the finest order. He can speak as eloquently as any scholar when he puts his mind to it.

On this day, Wiggins must have been 'round the corner because he came skidding into 221B and fairly bounded up the stairs. He would have knocked me over in his exuberance to be of service if I did not have one hand on the door casing. "Take this note," I instructed him. "See the address? Please wait for an answer." I tossed Wiggins a coin. "There's a good lad."

"Aye, aye, mon capitane," he said in a voice so serious I could not help but smile.

Shortly after Wiggins left, Holmes and Landover returned. Holmes afforded Landover the use of his washbasin after procuring a clean jug of water for the gamekeeper. To me, Holmes explained that he and Landover had moved the icebox outside and deposited the bag's smelly contents inside said appliance. "I have high hopes the cold will mitigate that ghastly smell," Holmes explained.

Once Landover had freshened up, or at least attempted to make minor adjustments to his toilet, Holmes invited the man into our sitting room and offered him a glass of cool water. Landover gulped it down thirstily. Whence that was done, Holmes asked me to take notes while he interrogated the man gently. "What did you bring me, Landover?"

"Like I was saying, two coneys and what's left of Othello." Here the man wiped his eyes with his sleeve. "Not much to the dog, there ain't."

Holmes narrowed his eyes as he retreated to that marvelous mind of his. "Othello was an Irish wolfhound, I believe. Is that right, Landover?"

"Yessirree. Ducky got him as a pup. He loved that dog something fierce, he did. I was terrible fond of the dog myself. He were a good one."

"Terribly sorry," I said to the old man. His tears now flowed freely down his face and rested in his beard like dewdrops on the morning grass. "Sounds like a tragic loss."

"Aye, it was that for sure."

I asked, "What is a coney? I've heard the term."

"A rabbit," explained Holmes. "A Belgian hare bred for eating. The fur is used for felt. At Musgrave Hall, Landover keeps rabbit pens, a warren. We've been known for our excellent breeding stock for years. The enclosure is large and secure. Two feet up from the ground, with louvers that can be closed at night and mesh wrapped around the pens for extra protection. I assume the setup is similar at Ducky's place, right, Landover?"

The man nodded.

Holmes asked, "Say, Landover, did you and Ducky hear anything the night the rabbits and Othello were attacked?"

The old man breathed in deeply as if it hurt him to recall. "Aye, you've heard it, too, my boy. That long loud cry, the squeal the rabbits make when they're in mortal danger. I heard it over and over, but I convinced myself I was dreaming because as you only just described it, no one and no thing could get entrance into the rabbit warrens. Leastways, that's what I was led to believe. Now I'm saying to all and sundry that I know different!"

Holmes kept up his questions, asking particulars such as the number of rabbits in the warren, the exact time the cries were heard, and so on.

"Sixty years Ducky has cared for those coneys, and this is a first. He had thirty-six breeding rabbits. Now he's down to ten. Ducky ain't never seen nothing like this."

"Kitten?" I was confused.

"Baby rabbit," Holmes explained.

"But nothing like this, ever. And the dog! Such a fine animal! It never entered my mind that Othello could be brought down. That dog must have weighed as much as you, young master!" Landover's voice trembled with emotion. "It's Ducky's job to protect the livestock, and his master is so angry, I fear he'll let poor Ducky go without notice or reference."

Fortunately, we were saved more of Landover's despair by the tripping of small feet on the stairs. Wiggins pushed open our door.

"Thaddeus!" Holmes wagged a finger at the boy. "What have I told you about knocking?"

"Sorry, sir. They're about a block away. Thought you'd want to know."

"They?" repeated Holmes. "I expected Flower to come."

"Right you are, sir, but this friend of his was visiting and the friend got so interested that Mr. Flower asked him to come along. Begging your pardon, Mr. Holmes, but the old guy with Flower seems sharp as a thumbtack, he does. Flower was asking him all sorts of questions on the way here. I was never so happy to be running alongside the carriage, was I. Those questions, they was powerful hard to answer."

Holmes let his eyelids drift halfway shut. This was his usual manner when he was deep in thought. With a start, he sat up and said, "Wiggins and Watson, will you bring up the icebox? I left it out in the alley behind the building. Our new guests will want to see what Landover has brought us. I hope the cold properties of the box will have reduced the stink."

I went with the young man through the kitchen and out the back door. The icebox was easy enough to locate since 221B Baker Street, like so many houses of the time, had a kitchen one storey beneath the first floor. At the front of our building the visitor was greeted with a choice between two sets of stairs. One went up to the first floor (which my American friends call a ground floor) landing, and the other led down into a subterranean floor consisting of the kitchen, the larder, and laundry facilities. Of course, the icebox had been in the kitchen proper, until Holmes and Landover had moved it out of doors. The wooden structure now destined for our sitting room was a well-built, tightly-constructed box on short legs. A door at the front could be locked with a small drawbolt. The inside of the box had adjustable shelves, and these had been taken out and set aside to open up the space. The tiny cupboard was lined on the inside with iron and could hold three pounds of ice.

Several times a month, Mrs. Hudson would go to the ice depot at Kings Cross and buy a block of ice from the circular building that was filled and refilled by barges coming from Norway. Those canny Norwegians did a booming business, using a free natural resource as their product. Since the introduction of iceboxes, we could enjoy meat and salmon from Australia, as well as the pleasurable treat, ice cream. For a while, iced drinks were all the rage at parties, but that trend had mercifully died down.

Holmes and Landover had barely managed to stick the contents of Landover's bag inside the icebox. The last bits of ice had been crushed with a pick. On them rested Mr. Landover's canvas sack. I slid the bolt closed on the door to make sure things did not fall out as we transported the box. On the count of three, Wiggins took one side and I took the other. The wooden cube was more awkward than heavy. Holmes had been prescient in sending both of us, Wiggins and me, because we had to maneuver this way and that to move it out of the kitchen and up the stairs. Even as we carried the case, the smell roiled out and formed an odiferous miasma in the air. I could not imagine Mrs. Watson ever wanting this particular icebox again! And even if she did, there was no way I would eat foodstuffs that came out of it.

Back inside our flat, Holmes had been joined by two gentlemen, who had evidently introduced themselves. Of course, I immediately recognised Mr. Flower and we greeted each other warmly. The other visitor was deep in conversation with Holmes whilst Landover sat in one of the overstuffed chairs, looking as miserable as I've ever seen a man.

"Set the icebox there." Holmes turned away from the anonymous guest in order to direct Wiggins and me to our table. I did not let go of my end of the contraption as I warned, "Holmes, if you think for one minute that you are going to put the contents of this on the same table where we eat—"

"Oy, can't we set this down afore you argue over it?" asked Wiggins.

"All right, all right," I said, and with a jerk of my chin, I indicated a place in the middle of the room.

"Wiggins? Take this." Holmes slipped a couple of coins to the lad and Wiggins fairly skipped away.

"Watson? Don't be so precious about the furnishings," said Holmes. "See here? I have the very thing." Reaching into the bottom drawer of a cupboard, he pulled out an oilcloth and unfurled it with a flourish. When draped over the table, I had to admit the surface was completely protected. I also noticed he had lit several candles here and there, one with a sandalwood fragrance that went a long way towards disguising the disgusting smell emanating from the icebox.

"Introductions need to be made," Holmes said, once he'd finished admiring his contribution to our project. "Watson? You know Landover and Flower. Landover? Meet Mr. William Henry Flower, a friend of Watson."

Holmes did not introduce the other guest. I found that curious.

Landover uncurled himself from the chair that had become a refuge for him. Once he was standing, his eyes darted around the room before studying the tips of his well-worn boots. An intricate shuffling of his feet followed as he dithered, trying to decide whether to bob his head or offer a hand for a shake. Given the stench of the parcel he had brought us, I rather hoped he would refrain from offering skin-to-skin contact. As if reading my mind, the poor man settled on a quick nod of his head.

"Mr. Flower is a scientist," I explained. "We met when I heard him lecture at the Diogenes Club."

But Holmes still did not introduce the other guest, the man now studying our bookcases, which as always were untidy and overflowing. I thought his behavior rather peculiar. Although when absorbed in a case Holmes can be distracted from social niceties, he has been raised as a gentleman, and therefore, is unfailingly polite. Yet, he did not offer to put a name with the face of our visitor.

Nor did Flower. As a matter of fact, Flower turned his back to our other guest, almost pantomiming an ignorance of the man's presence! This was extraordinary. And yet, I dimly understood that Flower and Holmes were acting with purpose. To what end, I could not say.

Briefly I entertained the thought of asking the fourth man his name, but in the event, I decided against it. Life with Holmes has convinced me to accept that which is out of the ordinary without wondering why. With that philosophy in mind, I've come to relish whatever life tosses my way.

"Flower?" I said, since we'd all decided to ignore the unnamed guest who was now pulling down books and examining them. "I have yet to congratulate you on becoming the director of the Natural History departments of the British Museum in South Kensington."

"How very kind of you," he said. "My wife suggests it is not a job at all. Rather, she thinks I'm like a child in a sweets shop. She may well be right. I cannot imagine a better way to spend my life than working to preserve what I can and share what I might. There is much to do, admittedly, but I am full of zeal for doing it!"

"Holmes, did you know that Flower read his first paper before the Zoological Society of London at age twenty? They immediately named him a fellow," I explained. Turning to Landover, I added, "If anyone can name your predator, Flower will be that man."

But Flower raised a staying hand. "Dr. Watson, you do me honour that might be undeserved. Why not wait and see if I can fulfil your requirements as an expert?" Turning towards our mystery guest, Flower continued, "Speaking of experts, this is my friend and mentor, Charlie."

He did not give "Charlie" a last name.

Charlie turned from the bookcases to give us a nod of acknowledgement. That was all. My sideways glance towards Holmes assured me that he knew the full provenance of our mystery guest, and that perhaps the best course of action was to let the man retain his anonymity.

Charlie was much older than Flower. Both men wore the bushy beards and long sideburns popularized by Prince Albert. Whereas Flower had a military bearing, his erect carriage a tribute to the pride of our nation, Charlie was hunched over. Nonetheless, when he faced us, Charlie's eyes sparkled with intelligence, so his lack of good posture was of little relevance. Even now, as he caught sight of the icebox, Charlie seemed captivated by the mystery that lurked within.

"Let us see what you have here," said Charlie, with a nod towards the icebox.

"Landover? Will you assist me in lifting out your exhibit?" asked Holmes. "Watson, please hold open the icebox door."

I did as asked, 'though I held my breath throughout the exercise. Holmes and Landover withdrew the canvas bag, place it gently in the middle of our table on the oilcloth, and slowly rolled down the sides of the bag to expose the contents. The matter inside the bag looked all the world like fur and flesh run through a grocer's mince grinder. Grabbing a pair of metal tongs from his work station, Holmes sifted through the remains. Lifting out one rotting piece of flesh and then another, he carefully positioned the sinew and pelt pieces on the table, giving each offering a bit of room so it could be examined fully.

Concentrating as I was on not getting sick, I had not noticed when Charlie withdrew a small notebook from his coat pocket. With a pencil, he rapidly sketched the items in front of us.

"Landover? Tell our friends what you told me earlier. They need to know what you heard and saw," said Holmes gently, as he handed the tongs to Flower. Addressing both Flower and Charlie, Holmes explained, "Gentlemen? A portion of these remains belongs to Othello, an Irish wolfhound. The dog was owned by Landover's friend, Ducky, but both men watched the animal grow from a pup. Naturally, this carnage is more distressing to Landover than it might otherwise be if it were only rabbits that had been slaughtered."

"So sorry," said Flower, clapping Landover lightly on the shoulder. "I grew up with foxhounds and Scottish deerhounds. Recently I was asked to distribute prizes to schoolchildren for their kindness to animals. Seeing a creature harmed in such a manner as this plucks at my heartstrings, and knowing this particular animal was a boon to you in life, makes the pain even worse."

I confess that I found Flower's remarks to be most generous, especially under the odd circumstances. After his lecture, I'd overheard several members of the Diogenes Club praising Flower for his 'good heart.' At the time, I wondered exactly what that had meant. Seeing this man live up to his reputation sealed his favorable impression in my mind. Ofttimes a person with a scientific mind lacks an emotional connection with the world, but Flower clearly claimed both intellectual capacity and humanity. With great delicacy, Flower used the tongs passed to him by Holmes and sifted through the flesh and fur. Charlie moved closer to his friend. The two men conferred in hushed, nearly reverent tones, remarking on the gashes in the pelts, and the manner in which one of the rabbits had been devoured.

"Concerning the rabbit, the blow to the throat or spine would have disabled the animal immediately," said Charlie.

"Organs look to have been eaten first," said Flower. As he lifted a shredded strand of flesh, a fresh wave of odour was released into the air. He must have been examining the digestive tract because the smell of faeces was nearly overpowering. To Landover, he said, "Tell us again. Did you hear the squeals of the rabbits?"

Landover screwed up his face. "See, usually a rabbit'll cry out in pain, and then, that's that. But this must have gone on for an hour or more. I heard it over and over, but I convinced myself I was dreaming. No one and no thing could get entrance into the rabbit warrens. No, sir. The coneys are secure. Or so we was thinking. I can't explain this. It's a real head-scratcher!"

Holmes kept up his questions, asking particulars such as the number of rabbits in the warren, the exact time the cries were heard, and so on. Of course, he was trying to provoke Landover's memory, knowing full well that approaching the incident from a variety of angles might encourage a more fulsome response.

"Sixty years Ducky has cared for those coneys, and this is a first. He had thirty-six breeding rabbits. Now he's down to ten. To be sure, the occasional fox would chew on a dangling foot or a weasel might pull a kitten through the mesh, but Ducky ain't never seen nothing like this."

"Could you have dreamed any part of this?" asked Charlie. "Particularly the length of the cries? It would be very easy to do so."

"No, sir. There was a clock next to my bed. I noticed it when the cries started and then I watched it. Must have been more than an hour that the noise continued." Landover dropped his gaze to a spot on the carpet. "Blame myself something fierce, I do. I should have gotten up and checked on the commotion."

He cuffed his eyes with his sleeve. "Truth to tell, I'm getting a bit long in the tooth for this work. I was too tired to roust myself, and for that, I feel terrible ashamed."

An embarrassed silence followed as we all pondered Landover's self-flagellation. Who among us does not harbour regrets for things done and undone? Large and small, our deeds do haunt us to our death.

"I hate to ask, but did you bring us everything from your friend's dog?" Flower wondered. "Were there other parts that remained uneaten? I'm thinking maybe this was just a sample that you chose to share with Mr. Holmes? Knowing that would help us form a conclusion."

"No, sir." Landover's eyes welled up. "That's all that's left of Othello. Poor Ducky looked high and low for more of him, because we aim to give him a proper burial, you see."

Picking up the bits of rabbit, which were largely connected, Flower worked the tongs at the dog's pelt. He did his best to spread it flat. "Do you have a ruler, Holmes?"

Of course Sherlock did, and he delivered it to the scientist. Flower and Charlie took a few measurements. When they finished, Flower shook his head sadly. I expected to hear him announce he could not help us. Instead, he said, "Charlie? Stop me if I speak out of turn or if you find my conclusions to be unfounded, but...I believe these animals were destroyed by something other than a dog and certainly not a fox."

Charlie agreed. "The prey is eaten from the inside out, beginning with the organs and moving to the pelt. That's not usually the case with dogs. Also the measurements of the bite, from tooth to tooth, on the hound's pelt are consistent with the span of the teeth of a much bigger predator. Furthermore, to take down an animal the size of an Irish wolfhound, the predator would need to be both strong and large. Therefore, we can rule out foxes, weasels, and other small mammals. Had your friend's pet been attacked by another dog, we would have found bite marks on his front legs from a struggle. But we have here a portion of the legs and there are none."

Flower gave Landover a nod acknowledging the gamekeeper's sadness. "Again, I am sorry for the loss of your friend's companion. It's a dreadful thing."

Landover agreed to take the wretched-smelling animal remains with him as he left. Bundling up the grisly bits of fur and flesh did not take long. All of us thanked Landover for sharing with us what he knew. Holmes spoke to the man in low tones, and I saw the gleam of a coin pass between them before my friend clapped the visitor on the shoulder and sent him on his way.

We thanked Flower and the mysterious Charlie for their time and promised to share any new information with them. After all our guests had departed, Holmes and I slipped on heavy leather work gloves so we could use carbolic soap and scrub down the icebox and the oil cloth.

"Holmes, you alone seemed to be entrusted with Charlie's last name. Who was that man?"

Soap suds covered Holmes' gloved fingers. While there was a hitch in his scrubbing, he did not stop entirely. "Think, Watson. The man is a scientist. He's a close friend of Mr. Flower. He's old, nearly ancient. He's familiar with taxonomy. Who else could he be but Charles Darwin?"

"My word! You mean to say that Charles Darwin visited us and I didn't know it! How disappointing! I have a thousand and one questions to ask about his book *On the Origin of Species,* and now I've missed my chance. Why didn't you alert me to this honour?"

This time Holmes did stop. He quit what he was doing to peer up at me with an expression of mild annoyance. "Because if Charlie Darwin wished to visit incognito, I was not going to spoil his visit by unmasking him. From all I've read—and I am sure you've read the same—poor Darwin is hounded at every turn for his supposedly anti-religious views. I would not doubt that the poor man ceased sharing his identity long ago as a way to move through society without being heckled at every turn. The vitriol visited on him by the British people is a rather good example of how folks can claim to be religious without acting the part!"

We still intended to toss the wooden chest away, but we thought it prudent to sluice it down, removing any debris that might attract those large and predatory rats that swarm the streets of London as they search for victuals. Once we finished the cleaning, we carried the icebox out and set it in the dust bin for the removal man. Tired from our efforts, I repaired to my bedroom to wash up and Holmes did the same. Shortly after, I heard him ring for Mrs. Hudson. She responded with the good cheer she's always exhibited. Despite our strange doings, the woman remains a paragon of good humour. Through my door, I heard Holmes apologising to her for the requisition of her icebox and promising the good woman that he would buy her another. Since I had refreshed my appearance, I joined them in time to hear her ask what we might like for our supper. After all the blood and mangled flesh that Holmes and I had seen, we both agreed that a ploughman's lunch would be just the ticket.

"Then I shall bring up your meal at the usual time," she said sweetly. "I take it that you've removed whatever was the source of that awful smell?"

I blessed the woman for her patience while Holmes apologized. "It was an unusual case, Mrs. Hudson. "Extremely unusual. I regret if it bothered you, but to ease your mind, yes, we've removed the offensive articles."

"That's all right, Mr. Holmes," she said. "As long as you haven't brought a dead body here, all is well."

I bit my tongue rather than blurt out that Holmes had done exactly that, even though the carcasses belonged to animals!

5

A week and a half went by. Holmes was no closer to discovering what had happened with Ducky's coneys and poor old Othello, but I was gratified to learn that my friend wrote a long letter to Ducky's employer explaining that the attack on the coneys had been an extraordinary occurrence. "Through no fault of Mr. Duckworth," was the exact wording. I heartily approved. Sherlock Holmes went on to stretch the truth, "As near as we can pin this down, the predator might have been another dog. A large one, possibly rabid." He included the measurements of the teeth marks. He also shared the name of Mr. Flower as an expert witness who concurred with Holmes' speculative resolution of the problem.

"Do you think that will be enough to save poor Ducky's job?" I asked.

"How would I know?" Holmes said.

He was in terrible need of a new case. When he had nothing to engage his mind, his energy twisted and turned and tortured him. This much is true: rooming with one of the most remarkable minds of our time afforded me the privilege of chronicling many of our exciting adventures. But as many of my readers are well aware, Holmes could be churlish and disagreeable when there were no cases to challenge his keen mind.

It was during a particularly cruel and spiteful lull in London's crime rate that I reluctantly found myself asking Holmes to double-check my work regarding the samples I had taken from Mr. Wren in the Bethlehem Hospital. To this day, I do not know why I approached my friend with those samples, as I had come to my own conclusions about them. My results should have been the end of it.

But a niggling impulse compelled me to involve Holmes. I had examined all of the contents of the glassine envelopes under the microscope that Holmes kept on the desk. Thomas Henry had secured small clots of blood and faeces, as well as grass clippings and a sliver of hay from his sickly patient. As for the odious liquid I had extracted from the boil, there were no parasites swimming in it. One packet of detritus I had found particularly vexing. The substance looked like ground up sand, although it wasn't. No tiny bits of quartz appeared in my sample. Its true nature continued to baffle me, even though I had shared other information with Thomas Henry in a letter two days after he'd given me my assignment.

Since then, I had heard nothing. Not one word. I knew that Thomas Henry had received my note because the courier assured me that he had personally placed the missive in Thomas Henry's hands. But that was the end of my communication, even though I had expressly asked my old friend to let me know what he thought of my discoveries. Thomas Henry's lack of gratitude—he had not penned a note of thanks, much less a response to my research—had done nothing to lift my spirits.

Indeed, I felt very badly used. Thus, I had little patience with Holmes' petulant and mean-spirited disposition. This being the tenth day after I'd shared my findings with Thomas Henry, I hailed a cab and made the journey to Bethlehem, only to be turned back rudely at the main door when I arrived. According to the matron on duty, my old colleague was in the middle of a meeting and could not be disturbed. Furthermore, he had no time for me, and she suggested I try to make an appointment for several weeks in the future. I found the entire episode to be disconcerting. Now, having returned by cab to 221B

Baker Street, I had no other desire than to rid myself of the foul stench and oppressive mood as I hung my coat on the back of the door.

Holmes lay sprawled on the sofa, browsing the papers. From the mess of discarded pages scattered about the room, it was obvious that he had not found any article to his liking. When he turned in my direction, his expression confirmed my fears.

"Ah, Watson," he remarked, swinging upright and tossing the remaining papers in the air. "I trust you had an enjoyable outing?" There was a sarcastic tone to his query.

"Not now, Holmes! I'm in no mood to —"

Ignoring my words entirely, Holmes continued to rant, "Has the Queen offered a proclamation, placing all of London's criminals on holiday? There's not one hint of scandal or conspiracy brewing in any of these rags!" In a fit of tantrum, he punted the newspapers into the air, scattering more of the fluttering sheets about the room.

"My word, Holmes, must you?"

Ignoring my pleas, he continued, "I must admit, up until today, there was a ray of hope on the horizon. I've been following a case that held some promise of excitement. But today, there's nothing at all! Not a mention of the missing agent! I declare, Watson, has my mind become so addled that I find even this curious?"

Holmes angrily thrust one of the crumpled pages in my face, jabbing his long, bony finger at a particular story. "An outbreak of vicious attacks by an unusual-looking dog," complained Holmes. "Read it yourself. Oh, never mind!" he said, thwarting the intended flight of the badly abused page. "I'll read the pertinent facts to you."

Holmes painstakingly pressed the page flat, using the heel of his hand, scanning the article again, and spearing his finger at the point that so annoyed and offended him.

"Several witnesses stated," he quoted, in an exaggeratedly breathless tone, "sightings of a particularly gruesome and vicious-looking dog in the vicinities, just prior to or after the attacks."

His narration continued, "Have I come to this then? Am I now so addicted to the chase that I seek my escape into a higher plane by chasing down ill-tempered dogs?"

"Perhaps you should. It could be the same animal or animals that bedeviled your poor old friend, Landover." I tried to be as sincere as possible, but I was feeling rather put-upon myself and in no mood to coddle my flatmate.

Rising from the sofa, Holmes angrily paced the floor. His hands were clasped behind his back as he swept his foot across the mounds of newspapers, sending them into a storm. His temper continued to flare. "A crime! A crime! My kingdom for a crime!"

"Stop this foolishness, Holmes! If it's crime you want, then investigating Bethlehem Hospital should be your opiate. There you'll find the most heinous crimes being committed. That place is a scourge on humanity," I said.

Holmes' glowing eyes dimmed, as he stopped pacing and looked at me with an ashen face.

"Oh, I'm sorry, Watson. Today was your visit to the asylum. I saw the note you left me. Very kind of you. How did it go?"

"Not well. I was turned away." I sighed and tried not to seem like the piteous person I felt I was.

"But you presented your colleague with the results of your explorations beneath my microscope, didn't you?"

I nodded. "Yes, I sent my findings to Thomas Henry via a letter the day after I brought home the samples."

"And he responded?" Holmes raised an eyebrow.

"No," I said. "As a point of fact, I found it rather odd. He didn't send any sign that he saw my results."

"May I see your slides and samples?" Holmes asked. "I am curious as to what you found."

"Of course." I rose from my seat to accomplish his request. If Holmes wanted to see the detritus, then so be it. I had no desire to quarrel with my friend, nor did I feel like forestalling his interest since keeping Holmes busy was rather like keeping a child out of mischief. One might not like the intense scenes but the blissful moments of peace that followed such an engagement was worth all the trouble. With this in mind, I went to my room. Finding the small glassine envelopes with the detritus, I brought them into the sitting room and made them available to my friend. Holmes brought over a notebook and pencil. With great enthusiasm, he slid the first glass plate under his microscope. He made notations. He repeated the process with the second glass slide, and so on. Holmes was still turning the viewing handle with excitement when he let out a powerful shout. "Ho! Did you see this?"

He moved aside and let me check out the powdery substance on the slide. "Yes. I concluded that the poor man had been rolled around in some sand—"

"Yes, but do you not see it?"

"See what?" I asked wearily. I had already had determined what was there. Holmes' repeated questions merely annoyed me.

Peering into the tube, he slowly turned the knob, bringing the sample into focus.

Humming softly to himself, Holmes raised his head and furiously scribbled notes. Suddenly, he stopped. The great detective stepped back, placing his hands on his hips as he stretched his neck backwards and closed his eyes. A tight smile played across his lips before he opened his eyes, turned to me, and winked.

Walking back to the table, he removed the slide and placed a new one in the microscope. He reached for the tweezers and lifted a fragment of the seashell, placing it on the glass rectangle. Again, he studied the specimen for some time before his head snapped up. Walking to the bookshelves, he surveyed the many tomes, texts, and monographs that cluttered the area.

Running his fingers along the tops of each book, he pinched the one he wanted between thumb and forefinger and removed it from its sanctuary. Holmes took his accustomed chair and thumbed through the pages. It wasn't long before he found the text that he was looking for.

"Cirripedia!" he exclaimed. He pulled himself to his feet, hurried over to his desk, peered into the microscope and glanced at his notes.

"Pardon?" I thought he had meant to say, "Eureka!"

"Barnacles, Watson! Barnacles and sea salt." Holmes swung round, smiling triumphantly.

"Barnacles?"

"Yes."

"Why would this man, or any man for that matter, be covered with barnacles and salt? After all, he was found in the middle of London!" I asked.

Holmes' reaction to my question suggested that it troubled him, too.

"I suggest that we ask Mr. Wren," he replied calmly. "This seems like the perfect time to poke around."

"No, Holmes! I'm not going back into that horrible place! Only the mad can withstand it." I admit that I was still disappointed by Thomas Henry's cavalier attitude towards me and my efforts. Not even a note!

Holmes gave me a sly look. "That's it, Watson. I am, indeed, mad. Madder than a hatter. At least for a short while, I shall be. If you will not validate my madness as my medical doctor, then I will go in alone. If you won't certify my insanity, then I must ask for your assistance in helping me gain entry. The authorities most assuredly will not allow me entrance on my own to conduct my own investigation. Watson, I don't like the possibilities that are unfurling before me. I fear that there's more to this than meets the eye."

"This what? What are you talking about?" I had lost the plot.

"This mix of barnacles, sea salt, and all the other strange materials that were stuck to this poor man."

"Poppycock! You know little to nothing about what I found."

Holmes said, "I know exactly what you found. You wrote two drafts of your note to Thomas Henry. The first you pitched in the bin after blotching his address. I fished it out of the trash and read it."

"Good grief, Holmes. What sort of man stoops to reading his friend's trash?"

"The sort with a curious mind, Watson. That's all there is to it. And now I have decided there is something terribly wrong in Bethlehem. Something having to do with your Mr. Wren and his recent escape. There must be a reason the man refuses to talk."

I shook my head. "No doubt it has to do with his poor condition. Holmes, you have not seen him. His skin, where not mottled and bruised, is an odd shade of yellow. His eyes are swollen shut, both of them."

"All the more reason to ask him what his history is. Obviously, someone has committed a crime or two against him."

Sherlock Holmes could be incorrigible. "Holmes, you are so patently transparent. As usual, your brain is seeking a client, when there is no case."

"Perhaps, but what if you're wrong? Hullo, we have company, Watson!"

A quiet knock confirmed the arrival of an unexpected visitor. How Holmes had known someone was approaching was beyond my remit.

"Enter!" Holmes shouted, as I went to greet our guest.

Upon opening the door, I said, "Thomas Henry! What brings you here?" And I count myself as very generous because I did not add, "When you were too busy to meet with me just a few hours ago." No, I caught myself before hurling accusations, but his worried look suggested that was an avenue I should not pursue.

"What is it? What's happened?" I hurriedly ushered him into the apartment.

"John, he's gone!" Thomas Henry staggered into our flat.

"What are you saying? Has Mr. Wren escaped again? How on earth did he manage to free himself and get out?" Reflecting on the strait-jacket I'd seen Wren wearing, the man must have had help. Rather a lot of it, in fact.

"I have no idea. All I can tell you is that he's gone!" Thomas Henry replied as if that was an answer to my question. My old colleague managed to collapse in the chair closest to the door. "This time he didn't run off. They've taken him!"

"They who?"

"Mr. Wren!" Thomas Henry groaned, placed his elbows on his knees, and covered his face in his hands.

"No, Thomas Henry. I meant who are the 'they' you speak of?"

Holmes poured Thomas Henry a glass of brandy and placed it in our guest's trembling hands. Then Holmes stared at the agonized man intently. "Dr. Knopf? Now, start at the beginning and tell us what has happened."

Thomas Henry's body tensed noticeably. "Pray, forgive my lack of good manners, but I came here to have a word with John. This is something that must be kept confidential." Thomas Henry's words were impassioned, but his countenance displayed just the opposite emotion. In fact, his face held no expression at all!

I could not hold my tongue. "Whatever you have to say to me, Thomas Henry, you may say in Holmes' presence. Remarkably, we were just discussing Mr. Wren before you arrived."

Thomas Henry swung his head in my direction. A look of annoyance was evident and that irritation was aimed at me. Ignoring it, I took the chair immediately across from our guest. Holmes acted like he hadn't caught Thomas Henry's irritated expression. Instead, the detective walked over to the bookcase and leaned idly against it. "Dr. Knopf? Why don't you tell us what has happened?"

Taking a sip of the brandy, Thomas Henry wiped his brow with a handkerchief. "Where to begin?" he sighed, resignedly. "This has me at a loss to explain."

Finishing the brandy in one swallow, he reluctantly forged ahead. "Watson? I received word from the matron that you were visiting and hoped to see me. I explained to her that I was in an important meeting, and that I could not see you. Not at the time, at least. After you left Bethlehem, I finished my meeting. Then I retired to my room and had supper brought in. I was making notes in my journal whilst I ate, and I recalled a remark made by Mr. Wren that puzzled me. Putting aside my dinner, I returned to his cell to question him further. But when I arrived, I noticed that the door of his cell was unlocked! Knowing that I had secured immediately upon leaving him, I grew alarmed. Although I entered the cell, I had no idea what awaited me. You see, I still hadn't determined whether Mr. Wren was dangerous or not. My precautions proved unnecessary, as the chamber lay empty."

This made no sense. I knew it was a firmly ingrained habit for Thomas Henry to lock the door of each cell after visiting his charges. I had seen him do so countless times. "You mean Mr. Wren wasn't there?" I asked.

"I mean that *nothing* was there. Everything was gone. It was as if the cell had never been used. It was scrubbed clean!"

"Continue," Holmes remarked. A flutter of his long fingers indicated that I was to take notes. Rising from my chair, I went to the desk and retrieved paper and pen before resuming my seated position. Notes seemed appropriate, whether this would rise to the level of a case or not. Often, I've learned that the smallest divergences in our lives seem to fan out and abruptly come back, circling 'round to have more meaning than what we'd originally assigned them.

Thomas Henry kept on with his recitation. "Thinking that in my fatigue I had entered the wrong cell, I checked the two adjacent ones. The morning before, they had been occupied by two other patients. These chambers, just like Mr. Wren's, were vacant. There was no trace of the previous tenants. Every evidence of his occupancy had been meticulously eliminated."

"What do you make of it, Holmes?" I asked, looking over at my friend. Holmes still leaned against the bookcase.

"Continue, Dr. Knopf. You have a captive audience," said Holmes, ignoring my question. Curiously, he sniffed the air.

"Please, as I told you before, I don't stand on protocol at this hospital, Mr. Holmes. No one calls me doctor there. My name is Thomas Henry. In fact, everyone at the asylum calls me Thomas Henry, even the patients. To continue, I sought out the warder responsible for Mr. Wren. I found him, the warder, in the utility closet, unconscious and trussed up like a Christmas goose."

While Thomas Henry continued speaking, Holmes walked behind me. The detective watched as I jotted down Thomas Henry's words.

"The warder had a nasty bruise on his head, but he eventually came 'round and told me what had happened. He said he was making his rounds and checked in on Mr. Wren, who appeared to be sound asleep," Thomas Henry said.

I interrupted, "Holmes? A point of clarification. In order to check the patients, it is not necessary to go into the cells."

Holmes nodded and moved to the desk where his pipe rested in its stand. From the desk drawer, he retrieved a match from the matchbox he keeps there. The match sputtered to life when he struck it against the sole of his boot. The head glowed with a hellish light that reflected red in Holmes' eyes. The great detective soon disappeared behind a cloud of smoke. Knowing him as I do, I could tell he was thinking, thinking hard.

Thomas Henry felt it necessary to expand on my explanation, "All the attendant has to do is slide the viewing plate to the right, and he can peer into the cell. One never needs to go inside.

"After checking on Mr. Wren, the warder proceeded to the other cells. The patient in the first one also appeared to be sleeping. As he came upon the last cell, he saw a shilling on the floor and bent to retrieve it. According to him, as soon as he stooped, the door swung violently open. An assailant conked the warder on the head. I'm afraid that's all he remembers." Thomas Henry sighed as if to punctuate the end of his commentary.

Holmes paced the room until he stood directly behind Thomas Henry. The great detective froze whilst staring down at my old colleague's shoulders. Holmes deftly removed something from our visitor's jacket sleeve without Thomas Henry's knowledge.

"Oh, one more thing, Mr. Holmes," said Thomas Henry, craning his neck to look backward at Holmes. "I'm not sure what it means, but the attendant was quite emphatic about something rather odd. I'm sure he was mistaken, but..."

"Yes, what is it?" I asked. I hoped to distract Thomas Henry from the fact Holmes was almost breathing down his neck.

"A dog." Thomas Henry said those words reluctantly, as if he regretted having them come out of his mouth.

"What do you mean *a dog*?" I asked. This was really too much. Twice in one month a dog, that most valued domestic companion, had appeared during the commission of a crime. Of course, that assumed one counted killing coneys a crime. I'm sure Landover and Ducky saw it that way.

"The attendant swears that just before he blacked out, he saw a strange-looking dog scurrying up the stairs.

"Yes, what is it?" Holmes asked. After completing his circuit behind Thomas Henry, Holmes had turned to complete yet another lap around the divan.

"A very large dog." Thomas Henry reddened. "His report is incredibly hard to credit, is it not? We've had attendants who are known to take a nip from a flask at night, so I cannot promise that this man was not prone to exaggeration."

This was disturbing but not surprising. London is infested with animals. Dogs, cats, and rats roam the streets. They feed off of the garbage, the offal, the horse manure, and whatever detritus they find in the tunnels that run under the city like a giant honeycomb. Whilst the building of the Embankment has vastly improved our city's sanitation, that is only one aspect of the problem. Without a centralised effort to pick up trash and haul it away from London proper, there will always be scavengers. Always.

Thomas Henry prattled on. "The attendant swears that just before he blacked out, he saw this large, strange-looking animal, fairly galloping up the stairs. He is most probably mistaken. After the knock on the head, I'm sure that he became confused."

"Did he mention the dimensions of this...creature?"

Thomas Henry's face reddened. He coughed into his fist. "It's hard to credit, but he swore the, um, animal was as big as a man. Rather like an excessively large dog."

I found this report shocking, but it bothered Holmes not one whit. He returned to his favorite armchair. Sprawling out, he covered his eyes with the crook of his arm and quietly slumped there. In fact, he remained in that pose for so long that I thought Holmes had nodded off. Thomas Henry and I stared at each other, perplexed. I shrugged my shoulders and settled into my chair.

Suddenly, Holmes swung his feet to the floor. "Doctor, have you yourself seen animals in the hospital?" Holmes hurriedly walked to the microscope. From my vantage point, he seemed to be holding a specimen between his thumb and index finger. Possibly whatever he'd plucked from Thomas Henry's shoulder. Placing this sampling on a glass slide, Holmes casually eyed it through the lens.

Thomas Henry laughed nervously. "Small creatures, to be sure. I've seen evidence of their cohabitation. One of the warders brought in a cat to abate the mouse and rat problem. The cat had the run of the hospital. During that time, I noticed fewer rat droppings, and I recall the cat leaving a dead mouse near the desk of that particular warder. As a tribute, if you will. But that is life in the world's largest city, is it not?"

Holmes and I did not answer his rhetorical question. Thomas

Henry continued, "But nothing so large as a man! Since this peculiar occurrence reported by the warder, I have specifically ordered the groundskeepers to set traps and check them religiously. As you are well aware, no one can stop rats and mice from traveling around and seeking food and comfort. Dogs are much smarter admittedly, but in truth, I seldom see those. In fact, I'd say I've only spotted a dog inside the hospital twice in as many years."

"I see," Holmes remarked, ignoring Thomas Henry's words. A sly smile formed on the detective's long face. Once again, Holmes took up pacing the floor. "What a pity you don't allow pets in your hospital. There are studies that claim that domesticated animals are remarkably effective at calming quarrelsome patients. By the way, do you own a dog? Or a cat?"

"Do I own a dog? Or a cat?" Thomas Henry parroted back to my friend.

"Come, come, doctor," said Holmes. "I have no time to parry words with you! And I do so hate repeating myself. It's a straight enough question—a simple yes or no will suffice."

"I'm sorry," Thomas Henry replied, tightly. "I was not being clever with you. In response to your question, the answer is no. No, I do not own a dog! Or a cat, for that matter. If you must know, I have a physical aversion to them. That is one of the reasons that warder's report of seeing one was so distressing to me!"

"What do you mean? In what manner were you distressed?" Holmes asked. Walking over and crouching in front of Thomas Henry, Holmes continued, "Are you afraid of animals with fur, or is it physiological? I myself suffer from the latter. In fact, if I get near them, I suffer endless fits of sneezing."

That was news to me! There had been numerous times when that Holmes and I had both come in close proximity to dogs. I've never observed any such bouts of sneezing, as my friend had just described.

Startled by Holmes' closeness, since the great detective was now practically on top of the doctor, Thomas Henry pushed himself back in his chair and smiled weakly. "I know what you mean. I've the same problem. I can't get near them, either." He shook his head and laughed with self-deprecating humour.

"Yes, of course," Holmes replied tartly, returning to the sofa. "Tell me, Doctor. Did anyone hear any noises last night?"

Thomas Henry nodded. "Funny you should ask. One of the gatekeepers reports he heard a loud, shrill cry. He said it was like someone had pinched a baby. Very odd. Rather like a yodel. He said he heard people yodel once during a German festival."

"Indeed." Holmes' expression was bland.

Curiously, Thomas Henry smiled, and I wished that I knew what it was between the two of them. It was as clear as glass that they did not like each other. Since they had only just met, I could not help but wonder why this hostility had sprung up. Holmes is typically aloof and remote unless a subject piques his interest, but he is far too well-bred to ever stoop to overt rudeness. I've observed my friend being disinterested, even when the subject is quarrelsome or irksome, and then hurrying out of the flat when an idea tickled his interest. Yet this obvious dislike was a new aspect, one I'd never noticed and didn't particularly like. Holmes was practically glaring at Thomas Henry and the detective's body language suggested that he was highly irritated.

Holmes changed the direction of the conversation, "It would seem that Mr. Wren is either very important to someone and must be kept alive, or they needed him out of the way and quiet. Whatever the answer, Mr. Wren is most probably in mortal danger. We must find out who he really is, and what this case is about. I must get into that ward. Perhaps, we may learn something. Can you get me in there, Dr. Knopf? I do best when I am at the scene of a...disappearance. I have trained myself to see that which other men overlook."

Again, Holmes refused to call Thomas Henry by his first names. An unsettled feeling rose up in my gut. *What was going on?* I wondered.

"Of course, Mr. Holmes," Thomas Henry replied, looking agitated. "Surely, we can do that. But it might not be right away. I shall have to get permission from the board of governors. It's a lot of trouble especially when I don't see what that will accomplish. As I explained to you, the cells are absent of any clues."

"Perhaps." Holmes cocked his head at an odd angle. "At least, that is what you think. Who knows what you might have missed?"

That seemed to conclude Thomas Henry's strange visit. I stood to see our guest to the door. That's when I asked, "Are you not curious as to what we found in Mr. Wren's clothing and on his skin?"

"But, of course!" Thomas Henry said, as if he was shocked that I hadn't shared this information earlier.

Holmes gestured with his chin towards his microscope. Thomas Henry joined him in bending over the eyepiece. Withdrawing the glassine envelopes from a toast rack that Holmes had "borrowed" from Mrs. Hudson for this exact purpose, Holmes prepped the slides and put them in the slide-holder for Thomas Henry to view.

When they got to the last slide, the one with the bits of sand and barnacles, Thomas Henry suddenly sat upright. His eyes were round and wide, as if in fright. He pushed away from the desk and mopped his brown. Spinning on his heel, his arms flew out—and his elbow bumped a pile of books on nautical crimes and knocked them all to the floor.

"Dreadfully sorry," he muttered as he stooped to retrieve the volumes. But when he read the spine of one of Holmes' books, Thomas Henry moaned. His face turned pale. But he quickly recovered and shoved the title onto the surface of the desk. As Holmes and I watched, the doctor grabbed one book after another and stacked them where they had been. Once that was done, Thomas Henry fairly ran to the door and announced, "Look at the time. I really must be going. I have taken up too much of your day. Please forgive me."

Thomas Henry had one hand on the doorknob when Holmes said, "Don't you want us to help you search for Mr. Wren? These slides suggest—"

"No!" snapped Thomas Henry. "I was remiss in my responsibilities. I should never have shared such personal information about a patient. Ever. I cannot believe I said what I said, and I can only plead with you to forget it! Remember that I was shocked to the core, especially with the news about a man-sized animal, and therefore I raced here, taking leave of my senses. Pray, forget I was ever here, and I beg you, do not speak of my visit to anyone. Anyone!"

With that, my old colleague threw open the door and flat out ran down the stairs.

As the sound of his footsteps faded away, I asked, "What was that all about, Holmes? Between you and Thomas Henry, I mean?"

The venomous tone of Holmes' voice made me flinch. "If your friend Dr. Knopf is allergic to dogs, then would you kindly explain the dog hairs on his jacket?"

"So that was what you lifted from his shoulder. Really, Holmes, a single dog hair doesn't mean anything. You're making wild speculations and jumping to conclusions."

"Watson, if you learn nothing else from me, learn this: I never speculate wildly, and never, never do I jump to conclusions!" His voice, loud and angry, shocked me to silence. "How did it escape you, Watson? That man had enough hairs on him to knit another animal. And the smell! All the medicines, chemicals, and ointments in the world could not mask the singular odour of an ill-kempt dog. There was something else. There was another odour that mingled with the dog's. I've yet to put my finger on it, but it's familiar to me. Time will bring it out. No, Watson. Thomas Henry Knopf, or whatever his true name is, is not unaccustomed to being 'round dogs. There's more to your friend than meets the eye. I knew he was lying, and he knew I knew he was lying."

6

The next few days meandered past lazily, and without any effort turned into three whole weeks. More and more households on Baker Street planted window boxes. As a result, the minute we opened our windows, heady floral fragrances perfumed the masculine air of our flat. Especially when mingling with Holmes' pipe tobacco, I found the spring scents enjoyable. This morning, they were overtaken by the delicious odour of the generous rashers of bacon that our kind landlady had sent up as part of our breakfast.

Glancing at the plate that had held the rashers and was now empty, I said, "I do believe I could eat bacon every day of my life."

Holmes said, "I concur."

"Well, my friend, what cases have come in the mail?" I asked. This was a common opening salvo between us. I would ask Holmes for news about interesting cases, and he would indulge me. Since I was rarely called out to serve in my real capacity as a doctor, I was often able to lend my friend a hand. This had two purposes: 1.) It interested me and stimulated my mind. 2.) It generated a small amount of pocket change, and that was a most agreeable addition to my retirement pay. Of course, there was a third benefit, and that was my ability to keep tabs on Holmes. Over the two years that we had roomed together, he proved himself to be a wholly mercurial sort of chap. Keeping one eye on him was vastly preferable to having him disappear for days or turn up after staying out half the night. Really, I enjoyed our congenial status as flatmates. I didn't want to lose him! Therefore, keeping one eye on him was perfectly acceptable to me.

"Hasn't come yet," said Holmes in a testy voice. "That postman —Kieran?—

seems to bring our mail later and later every day. I find it most irritating."

I happened to know that old Kieran was struggling with a terrible case of rheumatism that made his rounds as a postal worker extremely trying for the old man. The steep stairs leading from the first floor on the ground to our second floor were particularly trying for Kieran.

"Yes," I agreed, as I struggled to find a way to explain the old man's problems, but I needn't have worried because Holmes interrupted me.

Holmes shouted, "Come in, Mrs. Hudson!"

I had not heard Mrs. Hudson's approach. Yet there she was, opening our door. Our landlady entered and handed Holmes an envelope. "I'm sorry to bother you, gentlemen. Mr. Holmes? A man said it was urgent, Mr. Holmes, and he's waiting for an answer. He was most insistent and terribly rude."

"Thank you, Mrs. Hudson!" Holmes answered. "Now, what could be so urgent?" Holmes tore open the envelope and unfolded the note inside. "Short and direct!" he remarked, reading its contents.

"What does it say, Holmes?"

"It seems we have a missing fiancé," came the reply. "The matter is so urgent that the writer didn't even wait for the post."

I clucked, disapprovingly. Inwardly I groaned. Missing lovers were two-a-penny. Men emulated Prince Albert's exemplary behavior as a husband only so far. The late Prince Consort had proved Himself a loyal spouse in every way, but there were sadly, those men who saw the constancy that he exhibited in his marriage as German prudishness and not a sign of true love. As women became more and more delighted by Prince Albert's monogamous behavior, men grew increasingly angry. One of my old army chums said to me, "Good old Albert sets a high bar, He does, and the rest of us pay for it. My missus is always chatting me up about how remarkable the Prince is! I'm fair sick of it, I'll tell you. Just because He and the Queen are happy as two lovebirds in their nest, doesn't signify that I can't have my head turned by a trim ankle in a boot."

As it happened, women expected more now than ever before, when it came to good behavior by the men in their lives—and a few members of my gender openly chaffed at the guide reins, proving in their own minds that they would set the terms of their marital union and not consider their wife's wishes. The upshot was that many a young man who had once looked forward to marriage lately found reasons to doubt he could fulfill the expectations of the role. We'd had more romantic runaways, more disappearing daddies, and more deceitful soon-to-be-wed men than ever. Or so it seemed. Perhaps people simply were not bothering to hide their problems as they once did.

Holmes continued as he stared at the note, "I wish them all to go to an agony aunt and leave me alone! Their petty problems bore me silly! But I should not be so quick to dismiss this as the rantings from an hysterical woman because, in actuality, this missive comes from her father, and fathers in general do not succumb to hysteria. Perhaps the author of the letter may be of some interest to you." Holmes handed me the note.

I read the letter to myself: *Our future son-in-law is missing three weeks. Require your services, immediately! As per your brother, M. Holmes. Will await your arrival this evening. Please come. Colonel Garnet A. Caldwell.*

The name was familiar, as Caldwell was a decorated hero who had distinguished himself in the Queen's service whilst fighting in the Sudan.

Holmes and I shortly found ourselves in a hansom, traveling towards Kennington. "Mycroft's imprimatur," said Holmes, "indicates my brother has a particular purpose for wanting me to get involved. I wonder what that is."

I said nothing. I knew better than to get between Sherlock Holmes and his brother, or any two brothers, for that matter, and yet I did not maintain a similar level of trust such as Sherlock Holmes had that Mycroft acted with good intentions.

The house on Kennington rose up before us, a white clapboard mansion, trimmed in brick and surrounded by a black wrought iron fence with spikes jutting from the upper edge. Holmes requested that the hansom driver wait for us. A short stone walk separated the garden from the street, and mercifully, the gate was unlatched, so Holmes and I hurried towards the front door where a butler greeted us with sonorous tones. From there we were ushered up the stairs into a man's library. A rosewood desk, a very fine piece, dwarfed all other furnishings. Indeed, the piece was nigh unto absurd, given its size and dominance. Two club chairs faced the desk, but these chairs had clearly been an afterthought. I admit I always find situations such as this an opportunity to acquaint myself with what other people are reading, so as Holmes settled into a leather club chair and did his strange faraway meditation on the day's events, I eagerly moved from bookcase to bookcase and availed myself of various titles that I was unfamiliar with.

The door opened behind that preposterous desk and a man with a ramrod-stiff carriage came in. He wore a crisp white collar and an old-fashioned suit of very good material. I could imagine that with his years in the service, the colonel had no call to wear his civilian clothes until now. Colonel Caldwell's eyes were clouded with cataracts, but there still glowed a daunting intensity from behind those clouds. The way he dragged one leg suggested he'd been grievously injured or even that his leg was a prosthetic device. With great difficulty, he made his way to the desk and practically fell into the desk chair. Since I was already on my feet, I offered my hand and introduced myself. Holmes quickly joined me.

Caldwell did not bother to offer us refreshments. The troubled expression he wore suggested that such niceties would have been unusual in the best of circumstances, but extraordinary in this one. The colonel seemed to chew on his thoughts before finally saying, "Dash it all! Dash it twice over!"

Holmes had retaken his club chair as I'd taken the only other seat. Coolly my friend said, "If you could start at the beginning,

Colonel, I would have a better shot at following you and helping you."

The colonel let his head sink into his hands. From how awkwardly this was done, one could only surmise that the man was rarely given to such extremes of emotion. Gathering himself, he jerked up his chin in a gesture that clearly suggested he'd mentally chastised himself to "carry on."

"Yes, yes, of course," he said. "My only daughter Ennis is the light of my life, gentlemen. I would do anything, anything at all, for that girl. She's twenty-two, and I'll admit that's late for her to be considering marriage, but she's a very particular young woman. Not at all frivolous. Perhaps because of my career, she understands the gravity of a life with purpose. As a matter of fact, her mother and I thought she might never marry. That would have been fine by me, as I very much enjoy having Ennis in the house.

"During a fête to raise funds for a local public boys' school, she chanced to meet an alumnus, Walter Benson. Benson has a curious history, a gap in his whereabouts, and he's only recently returned to the school as a teacher of geography. The attraction between Benson and Ennis was obvious and instantaneous. Soon Benson was asking for my daughter's hand. I gave him my blessing immediately, as he's part of the Bensons, the family that owns mills up in Lancashire. I knew that Walter could provide for Ennis, and more importantly, I could see how happy he made her.

"All was as it should be, and the plans for their nuptials moved along quickly. They were to be married this coming September. My wife, Agnes, thought it prudent for Ennis to spend time with Walter's family at Brookhaven Manor and get to know them, as one's in-laws can make a marriage blissful or an ongoing nightmare. I also thought this wise, so when Walter's sister, Gillian, invited Ennis up for a weekend, all was well. According to Ennis, the visit was going nicely, and then..."

"Then?" Holmes prompted the colonel. Our host's ruddy colour paled as he reached the climax of his story, so I was pleased Holmes encouraged the man to continue.

"During a walk in the woods, Ennis twisted her ankle. Badly. Gillian and Walter helped her back to their house and the Benson parents quickly took charge. A country doctor was called and came right away. He thought it rather more than a sprain and prescribed bed rest for Ennis. A couple of weeks at least. This was awkward, to say the least, because the Benson parents were due to go abroad in a matter of days. However, Gillian and a houseful of servants would be there to chaperone, so all seemed to be in order." Here the colonel sighed deeply. "For the rest of the story, I shall rely on my daughter."

Holmes said nothing. I felt my eyebrows shoot up with surprise at this abrupt turn of events. Taking my cue from my friend, I sat there silently as did he while the Colonel rang the bell. A parlour maid appeared.

"Is my daughter ready?" asked the Colonel, speaking to the maid. After assurance from the maid that his daughter was expecting us, Caldwell continued, "Gentlemen, let us repair to the conservatory. Ennis is there. She finds it...soothing."

Holmes and I followed the stiff old warrior as he led us through his beautifully appointed home. From the front or street-side, we traveled to the back. The sunlight was blindingly bright as we stepped into a glass building open on three sides to the world at large. The colonel wove a path around various stands of pots and we followed him. Hanging above us were large pots of plants. Around us, woven wicker stands upheld more plants, but these I recognised as various ferns, and they no doubt loved the moisture that was gathering on the glass windows. Personally, having served in similar climes, I felt uncomfortable. A strange crawling sensation had taken over my body, and if I didn't know better, I would have said I was being swarmed by termites such as we often saw on our jungle forays. Beyond that, there was a prickling at the back of my neck, a harbinger of alarm, and although I had every reason to ignore this animalistic impulse, I clamped my arms tightly to my body so that I could feel my pistol. This somehow bolstered my sense of security.

Our entry into the conservatory brought us up behind what is called a peacock chair, a rattan chair with a fanned-out back that mimicks a peacock's tail. The Colonel gently cleared his throat.

"Ennis? Darling, I have brought you the consulting detective and his friend."

Holmes moved with the stealth of a cat. I did my best to emulate him. We faced the young woman. Ennis was tiny, perhaps five feet tall, and slender. One foot was propped up on an ottoman. The ankle was wrapped securely as befits the treatment for a fracture.

Ennis Caldwell had her father's piercing manner of appraising us, but her grey-green eyes were clear and perceptive. Her light brown hair was piled on top of her head. There are those who would not have found her attractive because her features were rather strong, but I admired the sense of character that they suggested.

The Colonel, Holmes, and I took chairs opposite the young woman. The colonel introduced us and then explained how far he'd gotten in his story. "Carry on, please, darling girl," he encouraged his daughter.

She seemed unable to meet his gaze. In fact, she looked everywhere but at her father. Those quick introductory glances at us that she'd managed had been enough to convince her that we were worthy listeners, but not enough to put her at ease. Her father sensed this and rang the bell.

When the maid appeared, he said, "Bring us a fresh pot of tea, please. Peppermint and lemon balm."

"Ennis?" This time her father's voice held a warning. "Mr. Holmes has torn himself away from other cases to come here. It would be rude to waste his time."

With downcast eyes, she nodded. "I am—was—promised to Mr. Walter Benson. An invitation to his family home, Brookhaven Manor, was tendered. The house is not far from here. My visit was exceedingly pleasant. Near to the day I was scheduled to leave, I took a walk in the woods. I tripped over a rock hidden in the brush. My ankle was fractured. The doctor looked at it, bandaged it, and said I was to stay in bed and limit my movements. So I did. At first, all was well. Then, Walter suddenly turned strange. I have no other words to describe it. He was solicitous, to be sure, but there was a pent-up air about him, as if he was guarding a strange secret. But not a happy secret. Nothing like a birthday celebration or the like. No, whatever it was, it was not lighthearted. This was a burden that rested heavily on his shoulders. When he came to sit with me, I'd look up from the needlework I was doing to see him..."

She paused.

"Pray go on," said Holmes in as gentle a tone as I have ever heard from him.

"He was watching me in the most peculiar manner! Please do not think badly of him, sir! I could not bear it if you did. I do love Walter! He is a wonderful man, and I thoroughly enjoy his company. The Caldwells have a conservatory attached to the house. I should say the size of this glasshouse is easily twice the size of ours. Walter dotes on exotic plants, particularly those that grow in the tropics. There he introduced me to flowering specimens such as I have never seen. And the fragrance? Intoxicating. But that's not all, Walter knows so much about the natural world that to walk with him in the forest is a treat beyond all else! He points out where animals are hiding. Every creature in the wild is known to him. I could not bear it if I brought shame to such a good man!"

Holmes shifted his weight. "I understand your desire to keep his reputation blemish-free, Miss Caldwell, but hear me plainly: there might be some issue with your young man that he was too embarrassed to share, but that has bedeviled him and caused him so much pain that he is in hiding. The more candid you are with me, the better I can assist you in finding him. You do want him to be found, don't you?"

"Oh! Assuredly, I do!" She swallowed hard.

"Once you and he are reunited," said Holmes in a voice that promised such a reunion would be imminent, "you will be free to tackle any problem that presents itself."

Ennis nodded and continued, "Let me put the description of his behavior aside for a moment. I promise I shall return to it."

At that juncture, the maid returned with a tea tray. There was a fine selection of teas, as well as a plate with a full complement of biscuits plus scones with clotted cream and a selection of jams. Ennis thanked the maid for bringing us our refreshments. The maid left us, presumably to do her duties.

"Several times I overheard Walter asking his father if perhaps I could be taken back to my home by carriage. Or even if he could move out of the house! His sister Gillian seemed worried, too. Walter's parents had acted like cats on hot coals since my arrival, so their skittish actions were not surprising. I wondered if there was some bizarre sense of propriety that was making Walter and his family uncomfortable. And the night before his parents left for Bermuda, where they own a plantation, I insisted on being carried downstairs to the dinner table. Once there, I was astonished to see that Walter dined on raw meat to the exclusion of all else! To be sure, the footman served him vegetables and consommé that completed the menu, but these helpings seemed to be a mere formality."

"No one said anything to you about this odd dietary preference?" Holmes asked.

"No," Ennis answered firmly. "The next morning after Walter's parents had gone, I determined that I must ask him what was bothering him. Fractured ankle or not, if he'd decided against marrying me, I needed to hear the truth from his lips. I said that if he told me he'd found me wanting or unsuitable, he must say so. This would be the best resolution for both of us."

"Indeed," I interjected quietly. I thought this young woman to be a rarity. Most young lovers in the first blush of a relationship see no faults in each other. The fact that Walter was concerned and that Ennis Caldwell was smart enough and brave enough to ask him about it, told me that this was a mature young woman, a woman who would make any hapless man into a lucky fellow.

Ennis continued, "Asking him so plainly what was wrong seemed rude, but I gave it a lot of thought. Eventually I decided that if we were to be man and wife, difficult conversations would be part of sharing our lives. After all, only those with truly boring fates never face adversity. So I plucked up my courage. The night after Walter's parents left, I waited until Walter poked his head in my room to tell me goodnight. I said, 'You seem to have an aversion to having me here. I realise I have overstayed my welcome, but you'll allow that's not my fault, won't you?' He agreed that this was through no fault of my own. None. I continued, saying, 'I do not want there to be secrets between us. Whatever it is that has caused you distress, please share it with me. If

I have done something egregious, you must let me make amends. If you have decided I am not the woman you thought I was, then let us agree to part ways. If you have turned your heart against me, you need to let me know.' And then I waited for his response."

What a brave young lady. How forthright she was! What a fine helpmate she would make some lucky man. As she warmed to her subject, her cheeks pinkened and her eyes sparked with the fire of her emotions. The intensity transformed her from plain to stunning.

☙ 7 ❧

"Walter responded to my questions by turning pale and trembling," Ennis said. "His shaking became violent. He stuttered that I was wrong, and then he corrected himself. He vowed that he loved me, but he also said he was worried about my safety. When I asked why, he said that since his family estate was surrounded by dense woods, and their grounds harbored many species of animals, he worried about them getting into the house. According to him, that might frighten me. Cause me to cry out."

She picked up her cup of tea and sipped to fortify herself. "I thought this was rather queer, indeed. I am not an overly nervous woman. I have never subscribed to the idea that to be womanly, one must shriek and act like a fool. Walter's concerns seemed out of proportion to the situation at hand. So I asked Walter if Gillian was not at risk. After all, she lived in this house, too. He told me she was, but that she had learned to protect herself. And I asked, 'From wildlife?' And he said, 'Yes.'"

Holmes nodded. "Did he specify which animals worried him? Did he say if this had happened before?"

"Probably bats," I said confidently. "As a doctor, I've seen more than my share of stray bats and the havoc they can cause. You say

Walter lives on an estate? That makes perfect sense to me. So many of the old sheds and lean-tos built to accommodate livestock do become infested with bats. Once one gets into a house, it can be the dickens to hunt down."

Ennis was trembling. "Doctor Watson, you are a clever man. I thought as much, also. I've seen other girls at school carry on like they are insane when confronted by a little brown bat. They used to fly in through the windows at night in the summer. I recall one evening when a senior girl went after the bat with her field hockey stick. But when I put it to Walter, he said bats were not a problem. I even wondered about mice and small shrews as they are inclined to wriggle their way into buildings. But when I brought up those concerns, Walter shook his head and seemed more agitated. He said, 'I only wish to heavens that we were speaking of small creatures that could be crushed with a cricket bat or under the heel of a boot, but sadly, we are not.' And then he made me promise that two days hence, I would bolt my bedroom door at night, as well as the sliding the bolts on the windows. I assured him that I could easily do so. By that time, you see, I'd somewhat mastered the use of crutches, so I could hobble from my bed to various spots around the room without much trouble."

Ennis poured a second cup for all of us. The fragrance of mint lingered in the air, and the medicinal properties of lemon balm had gone a long way towards calming the young lady. She continued, "A day later, Walter asked me if I remembered my promise regarding the bolts. I said I did. He told me that two of his school chums would be visiting. They were Frank Donnelly and George St. Ledger. Since Walter had spoken of both men frequently with affection, I felt as if I knew them."

She paused to gather herself. "When they arrived, Walter brought his pals upstairs to say hello to me. It was all perfectly civil. After they left my room, I could hear the three friends' voices drifting up the stairs as they talked and laughed in the billiard room because it was directly below me. Gillian seemed to have withdrawn to her room, and still the men laughed and the balls clicked. It made me happy that Walter had such good friends! And then, perhaps because I was enjoying the sound of their laughter, I drifted off to sleep."

"You forgot to bolt the door and windows?" Holmes asked for clarification.

"Exactly so," Ennis replied. "Around midnight, the grandfather clock in the foyer struck twelve times and went silent. The gongs must have awakened me. My room was strangely illuminated, and I couldn't understand why. That is when I realised that I had forgotten to pull my drapes shut and the light of a full moon was streaming in. I grabbed my crutches and got out of bed. Relying on the sticks, I made my way to the window, planning to rectify the state of the drapes. Immediately I noticed that the moon was not only full but it was as close as I've ever seen it! I swear to you that it's never been so near or so big as it was on that particular evening."

Now we were at the nub of it, and a light sheen appeared on the girl's upper lip. She was perspiring due to nerves. Her hand shook violently and her tea sloshed out of the cup. Her father, who had been watching her carefully but saying nothing, jumped from his chair. Putting an arm around her shoulders, he drew her close and confronted the poor child. "There, there," he repeated as he stroked Ennis's hair.

After what seemed like an eternity, Caldwell let go of his daughter. "You must tell them what you saw, my darling. Otherwise, all of this has been for naught."

Dabbing her eyes delicately with the edge of her napkin, Ennis nodded. "Yes, Papa. You are right. I must continue. Mr. Holmes? Dr. Watson? You will think I have gone crazy, but I could swear I saw three large dogs dancing under the moon. It was very peculiar because they balanced on two legs like we do! They threw back their heads and howled. I leaned against my windowframe, struggling against my warring emotions. Simultaneously, I was terrified, intrigued, and enchanted. Then I heard footsteps in the hallway outside my door. I did my best to hobble to it, but before I could get there, it flew open.

"Gillian marched in. Curiously, she wore a necklace of tropical flowers strung together. The perfume totally enveloped her, and she would have looked quite dreamlike in her white lawn nightdress and loose hair, but her face was blazing red with anger. I've never seen anyone so furious! She stormed past me, moving directly to my window. In one quick motion, she locked the window, using the metal bar. Raising both arms, she jerked at the curtains and pulled them shut. 'Get in your bed, you silly girl,' she said. 'You were told to bolt the door and windows! Now see what you have done! All for the sake of a dream. A dream! You are having a dream. Do you hear me? This is all a dream. Now go back to your bed!'

"I did as ordered. Once I was snug under the covers, Gillian carried my sticks to the far side of the room, which meant I could not rely on them, as they were at the farthest point away from me. 'You won't need these for the rest of the night,' Gillian said. A sense of panic rose in my chest. The sticks had allowed me to maintain my sense of independence, and having them placed so far from me so violently was yet another frightening aspect of the evening. But I sensed that Gillian was not herself, and that she would not take kindly to any questions from me, so I pulled the covers up to my chin and pretended to succumb to sleep. I must have done a passable job because she left soon after."

"Is that all?" Holmes asked gently. I was impressed by the way he had modulated his tone. Usually he gets agitated when hearing a story and his voice projects impatience. Not with this young lady!

"No," Ennis Caldwell said with a sigh. "I only wish it were. My door was still unbolted, because it could only be latched from the inside! I suspect that Gillian forgot about it in her fury. She had closed the curtains, assured herself I was asleep, and left my room. But I hadn't forgotten about the unlocked door. I stared at that open latch bolt and I felt fearful. Eventually, I puzzled out how to leave my bed without relying on my sticks. I scooted to the edge of the bed and performed a series of gymnastics that were definitely not ladylike, but that resulted in me sitting on the carpet. Next I maneuvered myself to the bedroom door. Once there, I pulled myself up, using the handle hardware to help me gain my balance. Whence that chore was accomplished, I locked the bolt, of course, and I would have gone back to bed, but the scent of the flowers around Gillian's neck served to warn me of her presence and her departure. She hurried down the hallway and past my chamber.

"A part of me said, 'That's enough. You've seen plenty. Go back to bed and do your best to feign sleep.' But the questions that ran through my mind concerned the man I was in love with! I had to know more, and no matter what happened next, I needed to see this through. So I hopped from one place to another by using the furniture to steady me. Slowly, I made my way around the room. When I found myself back at the drapes, I opened them once again, but this time, I kept myself hidden behind the cascading folds of fabric. It took my eyes a while to adjust and parse what I was seeing. Presently a shape in a white dressing gown floated across the grass. I recognised it as being Gillian! Still wearing those flowers! And she looked to be carrying a canvas bag. My heart was in my throat as I wondered what she was doing and how those three dogs would react. Even worse, the dogs had disappeared, and it occurred to me that she might be attacked. For what seemed like an eternity, I stood frozen and unsure what I should do, and if I should do anything!"

During this recitation, I'd moved to the edge of my seat. So stirring was Ennis' description of these events that my body reacted with that familiar sensation that commonly occurs before going into battle. All of my senses were on high alert. Time slowed down. Intellectually, I knew that this young woman had prevailed over the adversities that might come. After all, she was sitting there in front of us. But on a visceral level, her story had impacted me greatly and a glance at Holmes told me that he, too, had been affected by this unusual tale. When Ennis paused, I struggled not to urge her to go forward, realizing she was in an altered state and that any interference on my part would only delay her recitation.

Sure enough, she slowly said, "But when Gillian walked outside, she was not attacked. She actually whistled! Not a tune, mind you, but a shrill whistle such as you do to call a dog. I unbolted my window and leaned out far enough that I could see clearly what was happening. Gillian whistled again, and this time, all three dogs came running. They were exceedingly large and furry and although they snapped and snarled at each other, they did not try to hurt Gillian. As a matter of fact, she opened the canvas bag and to my great shock, she reached in and hauled out a chicken! A live, squawking chicken with its wings fluttering wildly around its head and oh! the thrashing and the feathers flying! And with a toss, Gillian heaved that chicken up and into the air. All three dogs leaped in unison, snapping and snarling as the bird tried to escape, but of course, that was useless. One of the dogs snatched the bird right out of the air, and as that dog trotted off with his prize, Gillian repeated the process with another bird. This time another dog was the victor. Rather than trot off, he rested one huge paw on the bird and methodically shredded it into smaller bits, even as that poor bird squawked and clucked for its life."

Closing her eyes, Ennis took a shuddering breath. "I don't guess I need to tell you that the process was repeated. All three dogs ate their fill. I could not move from my open window because the scene was so riveting. There was much growling and snarling and tearing of flesh. A rabbit in a nearby pen squealed with fear. I could smell the blood and the droppings wafting up from the grounds. The foul odours filled my room, and although I've never been to war, it reminded me that my father had, and I wondered—"

Her eyes fluttered open. "I hope you do not think me another sort of animal. A shy kitten afraid of her own shadow. It is true that a sense of revulsion was keenly upon me, but I admit I was still intrigued. I could not tear my eyes away. The activities were hard to see and yet I both thrilled to them and felt repulsion. I know full well that death is part of life. Men go to war and give the ultimate sacrifice for our Country. Every meal on my platter derives from either a dead animal or a dead plant." She hesitated, "Save for a rare few, such as an egg or grain or fruit."

Her eyes flashed with flint-like steel. "But I had never seen such as this! It was more brutal and disgusting by far than anything I could ever imagine. And when the animals had finished eating, all save Gillian, wore dark banners of blood soaking their fur. Who knew that any animal could bleed so much! But now I've seen the proof. When I thought I could safely relock the window and go to bed, just as I was withdrawing my head and shoulders since I'd been leaning halfway out of the window to get a better look, at that very moment, I lost my balance! I fell out of my bedroom window with a shriek. Of course, I could easily have died, and in fact, I should have, except that my nightdress caught on a protrusion, part of the ornate ledge. That bit of artistry broke my tumble. For seconds, I hung there with my hair covering my face and my entire being disoriented by being upside-down. Only then did the terrifying thought hit me with full force—that I was plunging into the midst of those wild dogs and their feeding frenzy. Nothing could save me! I would be as helpless as one of those chickens. Or so I feared."

My heart raced and I could scarcely breathe. Holmes was similarly struck by her amazing story, and he managed to glance at Colonel Caldwell. I did the same and was not surprised to see the old man very much unsettled by his daughter's strange tale. Did he realise that she needed to be institutionalised? I wondered. Would this be the manner in which our meeting would conclude? Would we load this girl into a hansom and take her directly to Bethlehem Hospital?

Ennis Caldwell continued, "Gillian had seen my tumble. She raced over to give me assistance. Whilst gripping my shoulders, she coached me to hook one foot and then another into the lattice that ran up the side of the building. I did not exactly walk down the ivy trellis, but I managed to move ever closer to the ground, thanks to Gillian's strong arms. Later she confirmed to me that she loved rowing, and I thanked the Lord above that she was a rower because her intervention kept me from a headlong fall to the ground."

"And the dogs?" I asked.

"They seemed to have vanished. Gillian kept telling me that I'd had a dream. A bad dream. Kind Sirs, I wanted so much to believe her! The scene I'd observed made so little sense that of course, it had to be a dream. When she helped me hop up the stairs, Gillian left me for the briefest of moments. She came back with a small bottle of laudanum and poured me a spoonful. Over the successive days, she dosed me liberally. I'll admit to you both that the drug has had a deleterious effect on my memory. What was once clear to me is now shrouded in mist. It does now seem like more of a hazy picture than a real event."

"Is that what you believe now?" asked Holmes.

Ennis gave him a bleak look. "Now? No. Walter has gone missing. How could I believe that he's fine when he disappeared shortly after I dreamed a nightmare about three dogs? I don't know what to think! I am worried about him!"

Holmes spoke in low tones. “What would you have me do, Miss Caldwell? Drag him back to you?”

“Holmes,” I warned. I thought his query rather harsh.

“Drag him back to me?” she scoffed. For the first time her eyes snapped with anger. “No! I am not even sure I want the engagement to continue. All I want is to know that he is all right. Then perhaps with time, I can forget about Walter Benson. As clearly, he has moved on without me!”

8

Holmes asked Ennis a few more questions. Typically, I listen carefully when my friend conducts an interview because I have found Holmes to be the most penetrating thinker I have ever known. His ability to see past the confusion and uncover the facts never ceases to amaze me. One point of clarity: Holmes does not ignore the random and indistinct portions of any adventure. No, no, no. But unlike some, he does not allow those to toss a distorting veil over the truths they often hide. Holmes has this uncanny way of taking everything in, excluding nothing, and still picking out those vague lines that link one curiosity to another.

I, on the other hand, "see but do not understand." Or so he says. Perhaps I am simply a different sort of examiner. To me, the grief that Ennis exhibited was frightful. That poor girl was torn between happiness that she had escaped a fearful event and profound sadness that the man she loved had run away without a word. I could sense that Ennis would not be able to trust anyone for a long, long time. Indeed, if I were a betting man, I'd put down a crown that the poor girl would never marry. She was that shaken by the events that had occurred around her. Holmes went over these events repeatedly until he was satisfied that he knew how she would respond. Her story never wavered.

Holmes signaled it was time for us to go. His getting to his feet surprised me as I'd been absent-mindedly staring at a fern frond and thinking of other climes and tragedies. One of the doctors who treated my wound told me that he's seen such reactions before from men who have been in combat. There's a shift that happens in my thinking without my knowledge, and I move from this time and place to another, a location much more dangerous and threatening, despite my good intentions. Often the result will be a restless day culminating in a bad night's sleep. Today this malaise manifested in a sense of detachment. I could well imagine the way the chickens fought for their lives. I'd seen men do as much on the battlefield.

Holmes and I thanked the Caldwells for their time and their hospitality. Although I had reckoned Holmes to be unmoved— because he finds emotion to be a distorting element— my friend thanked Miss Caldwell for her courage and her candor. We adjourned to the hallway. There Caldwell and Holmes worked out the details of their arrangement in regards to reporting and such. As instructed, our hansom driver had waited for us. Holmes and I climbed into the conveyance gratefully because what we'd heard had come as a shock. The story we'd been told had a profound impression on me. I've always been drawn to the fantastical and this recitation delivered such in spades.

"Watson? Watson?" Holmes snapped his fingers in front of my face. The gesture could have been taken as rude, so he immediately apologized. "You went away, old chum. Far, far, away. I have been prattling to you for a while now, and you've been sitting like the Sphinx with its frozen visage and no outward signs of life."

I shook my head to recoup my wits. "I'm sorry, Holmes. That story was strangely affecting, was it not?"

"It was. The problem that I have concerns whether to believe Miss Caldwell."

"She's not a liar!" The words flew out of my mouth.

"No, indeed, she is not. She believes every word she said. But that does not mean that she saw what she thinks that she saw. Does it?"

Holmes spoke in a calmly reassuring voice. There was not a hint of chastisement. "Remember, she was given laudanum."

"After she nearly fell from the window," I interjected.

"Ah, but who's to say she did not ingest a drop or two sooner? Let us hypothesise, shall we? What if she was given a dose before she saw the three dogs? Might such a drug cause hallucinations? Yes, indubitably. Perhaps she did see three dogs, but isn't it equally possible these were normal-sized animals and the drug served to enlarge them in her mind."

I shrugged. "If you do not believe her, then there is no case, is there? I assume we are headed back to Baker Street."

"Not at all. I decided that we must drive to the Bensons' estate without delay."

"Really?"

"Of course. If you were a young man, turning your back on your intended, would you not head for home?"

I slapped my knee. "That's the problem, Holmes! You are assuming that he has severed his ties with Miss Caldwell. Perhaps he did not. Perhaps he simply left the house in a hurry and did not share a forwarding address. Perhaps he was called out in the night by one of his friends, and there was trouble, and mayhap he's cooling his heels in a gaol cell somewhere!"

"Perhaps. That is why we will call upon Lestrade when we get back to London. He's sure to know if Walter Benson has turned up dead. At the very least, Lestrade can search the morgues and the police logs. Benson is a missing person! In the meantime, I pin my hopes on Brookhaven Manor."

"Brookhaven Manor," I repeated. This was the first time I'd heard the name and I knew, deep down, that I'd missed it before because I'd been adrift mentally.

Rather than explain to Holmes why I'd been so distant, I leaned my head against the back of our seat. Despite the numerous bumps and swerves, I managed to doze off for close to an hour. As the hansom slowed down, my eyes snapped open and I realised we had turned onto a country lane. This route took us over a hill and through open fields of rapeseed, yellow as the sun and ready for harvest. A stand of trees ahead announced a formal drive to a country manor. Indeed, I soon found myself staring up at an imposing edifice of limestone and brick. I could not name the architectural style, having no training in that arena, but later Holmes told me that the country home was in the Jacobean style. In short, it was more of a palace than a house. As had been told to us, a large glass conservatory was attached to the building.

Holmes strode up to the oversized front door, lifted the door knocker and dropped it twice in succession. The size of the place encouraged me to think that perhaps no one would answer. By my reckoning, there were well over a hundred rooms to this monstrosity. Since I had no expectation of being granted entry, I simply waited and stood by our carriage. "Oy," said the driver. "That's a sight you don't see every day. I ain't been out of London in so long that I forget how powerful blue the sky is."

The man was right, and I joined him in staring up at the wondrous spread of cerulean over our heads and the sheep-like clouds that wandered past. A swallow swooped down from one tree and glided to the next as effortlessly as a cloud might float past. The cabman and I must have made an odd sight when Holmes came rushing back to tell me we'd been invited inside. A butler allowed us entry.

Not surprisingly, the interior was as opulent as the exterior. We walked on marble tiles, following the butler into a sitting room with a thick Aubusson carpet, comfortable wingback chairs, a leather chesterfield, and a fireplace set for a blaze when the weather turned chilly. Around the room were the sort of trinkets that underscore the fact a family has money. On the mantel, a Chinese vase, an alabaster obelisk a foot high, a lovely clock with gold trim, and heavy candlesticks. In each wingback chair there were a multitude of needlepointed cushions, and over the backs of the chairs were draped lap blanket made with some sort of needlework or another. I lacked the education in these fine skills to recognise the manner of contrivance. What I did note was that all of the lap blankets seemed to be crafted by loving hands. In one corner of the room was a large stuffed bear that had been mounted in an upright posture and with bared teeth. This creature sent a chill down my spine. In this way, the room was a curious mixture of soothing and unsettling. Added to the odd décor was a tension, a frisson that I assumed was my imagination working too hard. What would we learn about the missing young man? His family had not requested Holmes' help. Was it possible we were due to be turned away without answers?

I'd no more than concluded this would be the case when light footsteps echoed outside the room. The young woman who joined us was tall, with an erect bearing and eyes of a light amber colour. Although her features were regular, she was not pretty, and I cannot explain why this was so. Instead, she seemed competent, oddly so. There was a brisk air about her as if she wanted to get on with whatever was happening in her life, and therefore, getting rid of us was a priority.

Holmes introduced himself and me. We all shook hands in the most civilized of manners. Then my companion explained how we'd been called upon by the Caldwell family to inquire regarding Walter Benson's whereabouts. During this recitation, Gillian Benson, for that was how she styled herself, kept her eyes resolutely glued to a spot on the carpet about ten feet from where she was sitting. Although her face turned pale, I did not detect any other signs of distress. No, there was only one symptom that the woman was suffering and that was the way her shoulders slowly drooped. There seemed to be a tremendous burden placed on this girl, and I call her that because I judged her to be about nineteen or so.

"I must ask you plainly, do you know where your brother is?" Holmes asked. His piercing eyes had never left Gillian Benson's face.

"Not exactly," she answered.

"Could you be more specific?" Holmes pressed.

"No."

"Are you being truthful?" Holmes asked.

"Yes."

Holmes went silent. These were not the answers he had expected. Nor were they answers that moved our investigation along. While I didn't sense the girl was lying, clearly she was highly reticent to say more.

My friend pondered this. He went silent. Finally he said, "I do not wish to distress you, Miss Benson. The purpose of my visit is not to cause you pain. You have met Ennis Caldwell. She appears to be...shattered. Her love for your brother seems genuine to me. I notice you are all alone in this house. You should know that you can confide in me and Dr. Watson. Think of us like two priests. If there is something that burdens you, perhaps we can help. If not for your own comfort, have a care for Miss Caldwell. She's unsure what to do next. She does not want to forsake your brother, but she's not confident that he will return and—"

"Oh, sir!" The girl could take no more. Her hands flew to her face. For a heartbeat, I thought she might tear at her hair. Her body sagged with misery. Her wail was long and so full of pain that I winced.

"Oh, please, oh, please, help me!" Gillian Benson cried. "Ennis was so smart to locate you and request that you involve yourself. Truly, I do not know where to turn or how to proceed! My parents have gone to Bermuda to oversee one of our plantations, and they do not expect to return for several months. That leaves me to make decisions—and I cannot! I fear my mind is slipping! If I knew exactly what to make of all that has happened, perhaps I could move forward, but I do not. All I know is that I dearly love my brother. We were all so delighted to have him back, and then when he found the position at the school, we thought his troubles were at an end. Of course, Ennis is a gem! And I was looking ahead with joy at having a sister such as her. Now I don't know where to turn or what to do! I don't want to worry my parents when they are not in England. Other matters require their attention, and they've been through so much. They would be brokenhearted if I wrote to them and shared my fears."

"Been through so much?" Holmes repeated.

Gillian nodded. "I take it you do not know."

"Know what?" Holmes asked.

"Your brother's résumé has five missing years, does it not?" I asked.

"Y-y-y-yes, nearly six," she said in a voice much like the air hissing out of a tyre.

"What happened during that time?" I persisted.

"I am not at liberty to say." She paused briefly to catch her breath. "Because my fears seem so outrageous and so without merit and lacking good sense that I am certain my parents would laugh at me if they were here. And yet they are not. Not here. So I am all alone and vastly unqualified for the dilemma that bedevils me."

"Then allow us the privilege of helping you," said Holmes

"Miss Benson, you are clearly in distress. As a physician, I suggest you allow us to advise you," I said sternly. What a pair we made! Holmes and I had swapped our typical positions.

The girl twisted her hands this way and that. "But if I trust you, can you swear it will go no further? Because if word of this is bandied about, my family will be ruined. My parents will never forgive me. Nor will Walter or Ennis, I am sure! And frankly, if my fears have any merit at all, I probably should pack up this place and move. Leave the country! Flee to America or Australia! Or our plantation in Bermuda! Change my name and—"

"Pray start at the beginning," said Holmes. "If you share with us every piece of this problem, or at least every piece that you know, mayhap we can move forward together."

Gillian wrung her hands again and squeezed them as if they were face flannels. The girl's violent emotions worried me. She was teetering on the sharp edge of insanity.

"Miss? Perhaps a cup of tea might settle you. As a doctor, I find tea to have wonderfully revitalising effects. Might you ring for some?"

With a nod, she reached for the bellpull. When the maid appeared, the two conferred. I wanted very much to speak to Holmes in private, but I feared that a diversion might stall the progress we'd made, so I bided my time.

"The tea will be forthcoming," Gillian began. "And I have come to a decision."

My heart lurched. Would this young lady renege on her decision? If so, we'd find ourselves back at the Caldwells' with nothing to share for our efforts. I did not dare look at Holmes. This was too worrisome.

Gillian rose slowly from her chair, but she kept one hand on the back of the seat as an aid to her balance. Her unsureness reminded me of an elderly woman, which led to the reflection that whatever her brother had done, he'd wounded his sister terribly. With great effort, she moved past me and then Holmes, and finally, she paused in front of one of those ingenious cabinets that house both a bookcase and a small desk surface. Fiddling about in the pocket of her skirt, she withdrew a tiny key and used it to unlock a drawer. Inside the drawer was a small book bound in scarred and scuffed leather. A length of leather tied the warped and foxed pages so that they did not spill out. Gillian clasped the book to her chest. Then she handed the book to Holmes. "Would you be so kind as to read this aloud? I don't think I am able. So that you understand it better, this journal was given to my brother on his fourteenth birthday, nearly six years ago."

With that, she slowly moved back to the chair she had vacated. When she sat back down, it was with such an air of exhaustion that I was troubled. "Have you spoken to your family doctor?" I asked. Holmes glanced up at me, but most of his interest was centered on the book he was gently prying open.

Gillian's smile flickered. "You are very kind, Dr. Watson. Our family doctor says I have suffered a severe shock to my system. He prescribed a tonic with laudanum. I've tried it, and whilst it seems to do me some good in quelling my agitation, it also provokes bad dreams. I think I am more tired than poorly."

The maid appeared with a heavily laden tray. Gillian poured the tea and encouraged Holmes and me to eat heartily of the tiny sandwiches, egg salad with crisp watercress, cucumbers and cream cheese on rye, and thinly sliced ham on toast with mustard. Only after she judged that we were sufficiently refreshed did Holmes ask, "Shall I endeavour to read this? The handwriting is faint in areas."

Of course, the answer was yes.

9

What follows is a remarkable text that I am sharing in its entirety. As an author myself, I found the diary to be remarkably well-written, especially for a young boy. That said, I did take the liberty to correct a few grammatical errors for ease in reading. –JHW

From the journal of Walter Charles Benson, this being his book and a gift from his godfather, Charles Williams Benson, Esquire.

23 September 1887

Father is angry with me again, and it all started with a silly joke.

I cannot stomach Mr. Hamcot, our teacher. He is incredibly boring and a mean fellow in all respects, and his breath stinks something foul. His clothes smell of boiled cabbage and spoilt mutton. He is always cruel to me. I am far ahead of my classmates in reading and writing. As for maths, I shall never comprehend sums. *Ever.* It is pointless to try.

Mr. Hamcot accused me of blotting my copybook, so when his back was turned, I did pour ink all over my papers—and that made the old man furious. Father was so angry when he heard that he sent me to bed without any supper.

I hate school. I hate it.

I want to be a writer. That is why my godfather gave me this journal. I love to read and I have read nearly every book in Papa's library. But Papa says I am to be an accountant. I try to tell him that the numbers get all scrambled in my head, but he does not believe me.

25 September 1887

Today Mr. Hamcot accused me of being cheeky, only I wasn't. He was talking about *Julius Caesar* and quoted Shakespeare as having written, "Let loose the dogs of war." But I corrected him. It's "Cry, 'Havoc!,' and let slip the dogs of war."

That made him powerful angry. More so because I am right and he is wrong, but he will not admit it. Instead, he slapped my hand with a ruler and made me stand in the corner. I don't mind that too much because I make up wonderful stories in my head whilst there, but I did miss some of the maths class and I am already behind in that. Perhaps I should not have said anything, but I knew the teacher was wrong.

26 September 1887

I brought in Papa's copy of *Julius Caesar* and showed Mr. Hamcot the line. He said I was mistaken in that which I thought he said. I only stared at him. He is a liar and we both know it. There was a hateful look in his eyes and I can tell he will now do everything in his power to make me pay for embarrassing him.

In front of the class, he laughed and said that I was wasting my time reading Shakespeare because he knew for a fact my father wants me to be an accountant. He said I would sit all day staring at numbers, and wouldn't that be a fine way for me to spend my miserable life? "Your big vocabulary shan't do you much good when you are calculating sums!" he said.

I said nothing. Books are my escape, but numbers are my enemies.

27 September 1887

This was a rare clement day in a month of rain. I am so very, very bored of school! To be mean to me, Mr. Hamcot makes me do sums all the time. He refuses to let me read or write. I have only this journal as a place for my thoughts. Therefore, I have determined to be exceedingly honest in all that I put down here.

Instead of going to classes, my friend Dudley and I decided we would ride the train into London. Our plan was to be back by dinner. To be sure, we had the most marvelous time. London is ever so wondrous! There are Punch-and-Judy shows. Jugglers. Strolling musicians. Even an organ grinders with cunning monkeys wearing a red velvet vest and matching hat with a gold tassel.

Dudley had a bit of pocket change, and after a bit, we were powerfully stricken with thirst, as we walked around in Covent Gardens. The lemonade seller was a hag with rotted teeth. The cider man told us to go away. There was a pub, the Royal Oak, and Dudley said, "We are nearly old enough for a pint. What do you say? Do you fancy one?"

One pint led to another. When the time came to pay, we didn't have the money. All I can guess is that a pickpocket stole Dudley's wallet. The barkeep was awful angry and he sent for the constable. In the end, Papa had to send one of his London friends to pay our tab. Papa said he's never been so humiliated in his life.

I didn't mean things to get so bad. I swear we never meant to do mischief. We were only having a bit of fun.

It wasn't just this incident either. I've had a streak of bad luck, I have. Mr. Hamcot says I cheated on my writing exam. I did not. He says none of his students are smart enough to have written so eloquently, but he is wrong. I wrote everything myself. To make matters worse, last week I didn't revise my maths, and so I did rather poorly on the exam. As I have said, I hate maths. The headmaster tried to whip me, but I grabbed the cane from him and broke it over my knee, afore he could. The headmaster was angry and tattled on me to Papa.

As angry as my father was about the cane, he was more upset that I am having trouble with maths. He has his mind made up that I should be an accountant.

That will never work.

October 1887

Papa has decided to send me to Anton, a boys' private school. He says it will be the making of me. I think he wanted this all along, on account of, he's brought up Anton before. Mama begged him not to. She was crying. I heard her through the door but she doesn't ever go against Papa. I think she's scared of him. I was shaking when he told me. I never stayed overnight anywhere or slept anywhere but in my own bed. I'm going to miss Gillian so much, because she's ever so little and growing up fast. Somedays she's a pest, but mainly I like having her around. I told Papa I did not want to go. His mind is firm on this, he says, and when he gets like this he doesn't budge. No, sir. He tells me that if I want to drink and go to pubs like a man then I can live away from my Mama like a man.

This is my first night at Anton. I am writing this by the light of the moon and doing my best not to cry. I stole a linen handkerchief from Mama's dresser and I hold on to it, tightly. Already I can tell that I won't get on here. The headboy doesn't like me. His name is Bertrand, and he's bigger and older than the rest of us. Bertrand shoved me into a wall and my nose began to bleed. The headmaster says I'm behind for my age. "Behind what?" I asked and he smacked my fingers with a ruler for being cheeky. I can't do sums. I never could, and today I had to wear a dunce cap and a slate that said, "Cannot do his sums." To show me what was expected, I had to go to bed without supper. I'm powerful hungry. I miss my Mama. I miss Gillian.

. . .

December 1887

This morning, Bertrand pushed my face into my bowl of hot porridge. Lucky for me, it weren't good and proper hot, but I didn't like that anyway. Yesterday, he tied all my shoestrings into knots so I couldn't put on my shoes in the morning. I had to choose between missing the morning line up and wearing my shoes, so I went in my stocking feet. The headmaster was angry with me and made me go in my socks all day, which gave me chillbains because it's miserable cold outside. Christmas holidays are coming up, but Papa says I'm not to come home because the headmaster gave me a bad report. I am trying! I swear I am!

Bertrand told the other boys not to let me have a turn at bat when we are playing cricket. Then the headmaster called me into his office and asked me if I thought I was too good to play with my schoolmates. When I tried to tell him no, he said I was cheeky and that he needed to bring me down a peg. Then he caned me across my backside. I never been struck like that before, and I swear it was worse than I could have imagined and now it hurts so much I can hardly sit, but my teacher says I must. I am so lonely! I didn't get dinner again tonight. But I was lucky because Frank, another new boy, brought me a piece of cheese and a leftover bit of bread after dinner.

Franklin Donnelly and George St. Ledger are my only friends. The headboy is always mean to us. He tripped Frank when we were playing cricket, and then he stepped on Frank's hand and broke his little finger. The headboy pushed George out of a tree and we thought George had maybe broken his arm, but he didn't. The doctor said his shoulder was dislocated. When Bertrand isn't being mean to us, his friends are. Another sixth-form student dosed my soup with extra pepper yesterday. I coughed and could not get my breath. The teacher yells at me all day. I try but I cannot do my sums like he wants. Not yet. It is all very new to me.

. . .

February 1888

Frank and George and I have decided to run away. Yesterday the cook served some sort of soup with bits of gristle floating in the broth. It stank badly. I haven't had a good meal since I came here, and that's the truth. When I'm hungry, I can't concentrate on my schoolwork, but my teacher says I'm bone lazy and he raps my hand with his ruler. My fingers are all swollen so it hurts me to write but I am determined to keep up my diary. Last week, Bertrand smacked Frank's head with his geometry book. For hours, Frank was sick at his stomach and he couldn't see properly. Frank and I are not the only two who are in pain, George has marks on his back from where the headmaster took a whip to him.

It's not only the punishments for bad behavior that are troubling us. The boiler broke and the headmaster decided we should all start the day with cold showers for our health and our stamina. This is nonsense. I think he finds it too dear to replace the boiler, that's all. It is so awful cold here during the day with the draughts. Then ice freezes over our washbasins at night. And when I wake up and have to take a cold shower, I shiver and my teeth chatter all day. Then comes the evening and I can't sleep thinking about how miserable I am! And I don't get any mail because the headmaster says I'm too naughty. The other boys get sweets and nice letters from home. I'm still not caught up with my sums, but I am trying hard. So I cannot stay here. I think this place will kill me.

March 1888

Frank and George and I climbed down the tree outside our window and ran away from Anton. We found an old hay wagon, loaded with dried grasses for the market, so we burrowed underneath it and wouldn't you know? We were warmer than we'd been at school! The waggoneer drove to town, and all of us were surprised when we hopped off. This place is by the sea! We did not know that before! There are boats and boats here. Then we tried to get hired on, but we were told we were too young. We didn't have any money, and we were hiding behind boxes on the dock when we heard a man say, "You ain't seen three boys, have you?" Lucky for us, the other man didn't see us at all. Frank and George and I had a parlay. We decided if we stayed here, we'd go hungry or we'd get sent back to Anton. One or t'other. Instead, we've decided to stowaway on the Matilda Briggs. She sets sail first thing tomorrow morning. That means we have to find hiding places on the ship tonight. I think it's smart for us to each find a place rather than huddling all together. George and Frank think so, too.

April 1888

I am writing from the Indian Ocean. This is a place I never thought I would be, but I am here, and I am on my way to where I do not know. The ocean is much bigger than I thought it would be. When I look out at it, I think this ship is the only thing in the world—and maybe England does not even exist!

The first ten days at sea were awful bad. I was sicker than I have ever been in my life. Like we had planned, George and Frank and I all hid in different spots on the boat, but the sailors found us that first night because of all the noise we made retching. George in particular was laid low. At first I thought the captain might throw us overboard because he was that mad, but then we came upon rough weather and he didn't have time to mess with us, he said. A couple of the sailors took pity on us. They'd started crewing on ships when they were young, too. Since the captain was so busy keeping us from capsizing, one of the men, a father with boys our age, saw to it that we had enough food and water to stay alive. I wonder what the captain will do with us...

April 30 1888

The captain isn't even waiting for a proper shipping port. No, sir. He wants us off his ship. The plan is to put us in rowboats and dump us on land and then take the small boats back to the Matilda Briggs. I wonder if he'll even spare us provisions. At least it won't be just me and

Frank and George. Captain also decided to get rid of the cook, because Chen the Cook is Chinese and the captain doesn't like Chinamen much. He says they can't be trusted. I don't know for sure, but Chen seems like a good sort to me. He's always slipping us food, 'cause we're growing boys. I tried to ask the captain why he brought the Chinaman in the first place, since he approved all the folks on board. It didn't make any sense to me, why he'd bring someone on and then treat that person so cruelly. I say cruelly because the Captain had the Chinaman whipped with a cat-o'-nine-tails a few days ago. He said the Cook was stealing food, but I ask you, how can you steal food when you are on a ship in the midst of the ocean? What would you do with it? I said as much to the Captain and then another sailor pinched my arm hard so I shut up. Later I heard how there's a junior cook and he's family to the captain, don't you know?

❧

So here we are, on a deserted island, and I got to admit that I cried as the ship sailed away from us. I never intended for this to happen! I am sitting under a coconut tree and writing this, as all I brought with me was my journal and a pencil. My friends tease me about my diary but I tell them that one day when we tell our own boys about our adventures, this book will help us all remember every detail. George said, "If we live that long." He's probably right. While George and Frank are exploring this place and trying to catch crabs for our supper, I am writing this. I don't think we will starve. Chen can't hardly hobble around because his back is covered with open cuts from the cat-o'-nine-tails, but he's still trying his best to take care of us. Chen showed us how to crack open a cocoanut, and he brought with him matches when we were put overboard so we can light a fire. That's good because we do not know if there are any wild animals here! I have to say the fire here didn't smell like the fires back at home. Owing to the wood we used, I wager. Here it smells wet and fishy.

Month unknown/ May?

Been here ten days. I get a little confused about which months have thirty days and which have thirty-one, so I don't know much right now about dates. I do know I'm getting sick of fish, even though Chen does his best with it. Each day, two times, Chen soaks his back in the salt water. I've got to admit his skin is healing real fast.

I guess I ought to be thankful, as we could be starving to death, and we aren't. We fixed a little lean-to that first day. It's basically two support poles with a cross pole, and then we covered the surface with palm fronds. After that, Chen told us to add more poles to pin down the palms so they don't blow away in a stiff wind. See, we don't have nails! But Chen's idea worked fine. We split open a lot of branches and shrubs until we found one that was stringy inside so we could use it as twine. George found a bunch of green vines and we used them, too. So we lashed down the poles that were laid over the palm fronds, fixing the poles so they hold the palms in place and can't blow away. Doesn't sound like much, but it is better than nothing, and it proved that last night when a bad storm kicked up. Rain was blowing in, but we huddled together with our backs to the wind and it wasn't too bad. Today we plan to make a free-standing wall to cover the open end and shelter us.

May

We were finishing up our wall of palm fronds when George screamed. I figured he'd cut himself on the sharp edge of a branch, but he was yelling because people were coming our way. Only they weren't people like the people you'd see in London. No, sir. They were mostly naked and they carried spears and bows and arrows. I knew right away that if they didn't like us, we would be dead. George and Frank and I thought about running, but that didn't make no sense, as there must have been thirty of them and three of us. Besides, Chen Wen, that's the cook's full name, started talking to them and pretty soon it was clear they didn't mean to hurt us. That was good because we never thought about making weapons or anything like that. We had spears for fishing, but only six of them. We would not have survived a fight.

The leader and Chen talked and talked. Finally, Chen said, "No

Dutch! No Dutch!" and the leader smiled. I guess the Dutch have been trying to take over this island. Peppercorn trees grow a little ways from here. I haven't seen them yet, but Chen told us the spice sells for a lot of money all over the world, and the Dutch want all of this island for themselves. That means they are fine with killing the natives so they can do what they wish with this place. Thank goodness Chen was able to convince the scouting party that we were not Dutch or they would have murdered us on the spot!

Instead, they decided to take us to their rajah. A rajah is a sort of king. I was worried that we would be sacrificed to the rajah, but while we were walking single-file towards the village, I asked Chen and he said our lives had been spared because we are English. Everyone knows the English and the Dutch are enemies.

We walked a long way. The village was built on a defensible bluff that overlooks the water. To get down to the sea, one must climb down several perilous sets of stairs, so we had a long hike going up the stairs to see the village proper. But once we arrived, the natives shared food with us. At first I wasn't too keen on the fruit they call bananas, but the more I ate the more I liked it.

When we got to the village, we were pushed into a tent. That scared me lots, and I wanted to cry. I figured they were rounding us up the way you round up sheep before you slaughter them. Worst of all, the sailors had told us tales about how brutal natives could be. The seafarers even said that some tribes eat human flesh! George thought this was a lie intended to scare us, but Frank and I thought it might be true. I could see my friends were doing their best not to burst into sobs. I bit my lower lip so hard that I could taste the blood.

But Chen told us that we were fine, and we were. There was a guard at the tent but we could look out and watch the women preparing food while the men talked. A little later, the rajah came to inspect us. His name is Kiawonka, and he is very tall and thin with huge earrings in his ears that dangled to his shoulders. On his forehead there is was a scar shaped like a rat, and it looks like it was burned into the flesh. Around his neck were many, many necklaces. He wore a headdress made of feathers such as I have never seen! It is glorious!

Like the other men, instead of britches, he wears a small skirt. But the rajah also wears a cape sewn from a variety of fine furs. Kiawonka barked out a few questions to Chen. I really wished I could follow their conversation, but I couldn't. At one point Chen looked horrified. He even cried out and said, "No, no! You can't do that!" but we could only stand and watch and George whispered, "Don't look frightened. We want to look like we aren't a threat. Like we're passive, but we don't want to look like babies." George is almost a year older than Frank and me so we listen to him a lot.

Sure enough, Kiawonka decided we were all right.

That night there was a party like I've never seen before. Natives played the drums and a sort of whistle. Everyone danced. I even tried to! All the women had been cooking all day and my friends and I ate and ate. Some of the food seemed strange to us, but it all tasted good.

After the meal, there was a ceremony. The rajah sat on this throne and nodded to three men. They disappeared and came back holding three huge rats. At least, that's what the animals looked like to us. These rats were almost three feet long! These animals had faces more like pigs than rats. One by one the rats were held up to be admired by the crowd. The natives bowed deeply to the three rats and threw up their hands and shouted in a chorus. It was very peculiar, but George seems to think it has something to do with their religion.

The next day, Kiawonka took us to see the sacred ones. That's how Chen translated the words, at least. First, all the natives got into line and walked quietly, like they were in a wedding or graduation ceremony. We followed. They took us to an elaborate structure of pens, like rabbit pens only excessively fancy and painted in bright colours. Inside were the pens were more of these animals. Chen called them "sacred rats." They were very well tended, I think. All of them had shiny coats. One was red and white, one was tan and white, another solid black and that was the one the natives seemed to worship. We were cautioned that we should never try to touch them, but Kiawonka picked up one and cradled it in his arms. Chen couldn't understand everything, but he told us later there was talk of how those big rats had saved the natives. He says they are very much revered. In fact, according to Chen, those rats are all that stand between the natives and their many enemies.

We wondered who the natives' enemies were, but Chen could not say. He didn't have the words to explain.

Chen said that tomorrow the rajah will show us the peppercorn trees. That's what the Dutch want so badly.

❧ 10 ❧

Month Unsure

We saw the peppercorn trees that everyone was fighting over, and plantings of other spices as well. Chen whispered to us that we were gazing at a fortune if we could get what we saw back to Europe. George laughed and said, "What ho? Do you really think that we will ever see our homes again? I find that jolly amusing."

Whilst I am sad when I think of my sister, life here is not all bad. The rajah has been good to us, and therefore, so have all of his people. George said something queer the other day. Maybe because he's the oldest of us, he asked, "Can you imagine how our families would have greeted one of the Sumatrans? I don't think my father would have hesitated to shoot one, much less feed him and put a roof over his head." That was a sobering thought indeed, and as far as I can tell, the honest truth.

One of Kiawonka's four wives is teaching Chen how to cook like she does. He thinks that if we ever get back to England his new skills will be very much in demand. I doubt that, but it makes Chen happy. After a fashion, we have all adapted to life here. Frank, George, and I are learning to use a bow and arrow. We're also getting good at making and using spears. At first, the native boys laughed at us a lot, but when they saw we were willing and happy to learn, they changed. They are also showing us how to use slingshots.

Frank and George and I made a pact that we will be ever so helpful and keep the natives happy. After all, they might still kill and eat us! So far we have done a good job of pleasing them, I think. Every day we learn something new, although I suppose these are not the sort of skills that Papa expected me to get while I was away. I wonder what he would think of me now! My skin is as brown as a chestnut. My hair reaches to my shoulders. I wear a small skirt to cover my privates, and although it took some getting used to, it is much more practical than trousers could ever be here in the tropics. I wonder if I shall ever see Papa or Mama or Gillian again. If I ever get home to England, I will try so much harder to be a good chap! Papa meant to teach me a lesson and he has, even though I heartily suspect this is not the lesson he wanted for me.

Date Unsure

We have been here with the natives for nearly a month now and last night was the oddest night of all. Last night before it got dark, they brought cages into the center of the village. They pulled on ropes and hung huge bamboo cages from the highest limbs in the banyan tree that sits in the middle of their village. That banyan tree is massive, and it grows in a way such as I have never seen any tree grow, with roots extending to the ground after starting at the uppermost limbs. Thus, the mass of roots forms fascinating configurations, even creating chambers below where the upper branches sprout. Through Chen, the natives explained that this tree is sacred. I could see that by how they treated it with reverence. Three natives climbed up the tree and looped ropes around highest branches. Even though Chen asked a lot of questions of the natives, the only answer he could get was, "She is coming. She will come. There will be blood."

Naturally we were very frightened. I reckoned that they meant the Dutch were coming and that we might be killed or taken hostage for money. But if that was the case, why put us in cages? Surely the Dutch could climb up the trees, undo the knots, and get to us?

And if the Dutch were coming, why couldn't we see their ships on the horizon? It was very confusing. We pondered all of this for a long time. Frank wondered if the Dutch and the natives would clash and the victor would own any prisoners in the cages. That put a fright into us!

When we told Chen about our fears, he laughed until tears rolled down his cheeks. "You rich boys! Have you not seen slave markets? That is what might become of us. We will be stripped and stared at and sold like mutton."

That made even George whimper with fear.

I still shiver as I write this. The very idea turns my stomach.

Around dusk, the cages were lowered to the ground. The doors of the cages were opened. First a group of women entered. They brought with them strands of flowers and wound them around the bars of the cages. Then the women walked out and rejoined the other natives who stood off to one side, watching and talking among themselves. One of the tribal elders told the three of us to go inside one of the larger cages. At least we had each other! Chen had his own cage. I could tell he was trying to stay calm. My friends and I did our best to act bravely, but it was terribly difficult. I am not ashamed to say that I cried. I think Frank and George did, too. I could not understand why the natives who had been so kind to us had suddenly turned on us, because surely they were intending to give us to the Dutch! Or kill us! Maybe even eat us!

As the sun started to go down, the natives began to chant. Chen translated, "She is coming. She will come. Blood will be spilled."

As I pondered on these gloomy thoughts, the natives surprised me yet again. Three young mothers with little babies assembled at the base of the banyan tree. At the back of the parade, a group of men carried another cage like ours. The three mothers were given flowers to put in their hair. Their cages were decorated with flowers like ours were. I believe I have seen this plant in Grandmama's conservatory.

She called it a plumeria. The fragrance of these blossoms is extremely potent. Once the women had tucked blossoms into their hair, they carried their babies into their cage. None of the women seemed frightened for themselves or their babies although they did kiss their husbands in a manner that suggested they were saying farewell. The mothers and babies were hoisted into the air like we were. All of the cages are tied about thirteen feet high to limbs of the banyan tree. You would have to be a skilled climber to reach the knots. Each of the cages dangles freely so that none of the sides touch the tree or the ground. Their cage was also tied to a spot high off the ground. Thus the rope would serve to keep the cage suspended from all except for a skilled climber.

Slowly, the sunlight began to fade. All the while, I found myself growing more and more confused. The women held their babies and seemed very calm. It was as if the cages had been designed to protect us. But from what? This made no sense at all! Why make us hang in the air? How would that protect us?

Here's what made it more confusing: The women were holding their babies and I have seen that the natives care about their children. I had seen them cuddling the babies (and older children) and kissing them. Were all of us going to be sacrifices? Were the babies and the women going to be sacrifices, too? George and Frank and I discussed the matter among ourselves and could not feature an answer that would fit the scene unfolding before us. What was the reason for such singularly strange behavior? I couldn't imagine it.

As the last rays of the sun disappeared, all of the natives gathered in the central area right below us. There were men and women and the older children. They stood side by side with their heads held high. Kiawonka came striding through and everyone bowed to him. He was wearing a headpiece six feet high with feathers in colours like the rainbow. Around his shoulders he wore a fur cape. In his hands was one of those sacred rats. He held it up high overhead. The rat's body was easy to make out in the moonlight. Then the rajah handed the rat back to a warrior who ran off with it.

What I am going to write next will be hard to put into words. Very hard. I can scarcely believe it myself. By now the moon was full and bright and shining down. I'd been focusing on the warrior who had run off with the rat, but suddenly I heard groans and whimpers and cries and yips like a dog makes. These noises were coming from the natives. At the same time, some horrid force seemed to hit them all at once because they pitched forward onto their hands and knees. George and Frank and I watched the natives writhe and twist as if in pain. All of them! Every one of them, including the children. The only exception were those three women with the infants in the cage. They watched calmly as the spectacle unfolded. The groans and cries continued, echoing into the night. From our place in the cage, the moonlight offered illumination, but not so much that we could see all clearly. The cries and yips and moans grew louder and louder and then, surprisingly, fell into silence. A change seemed to come upon the natives, but what that change was, we could not tell at first.

All we could do was watch in awed silence, trying to parse what was happening. I think Frank was the first to speak, "Look! Can you see it? They are turning into wolves!"

Date unknown

When the cold light of day returned, I wondered if this had all been a dream. True, I was in a cage, but I was unharmed. So were my friends. The natives gently lowered us to the ground. They seemed genuinely happy to let us out of the cage. The mothers and babies were released, too, as was Chen. We waited until the natives were not about and then we asked Chen if he had seen what we had seen. I shall never forget his response: "There must be very powerful magic in the air."

I am very confused

Oddly enough, the ritual was repeated one month later. Again, this occurred when the moon was full and at its apex. The entire village except for the mothers and their babies made this amazing transformation from human to wolf and back again. I am sure that anyone reading this will think I am insane or that I need to be taken to Bedlam and locked up. That would be fine by me, because the hospital is in London and not here.

If I did not keep a journal, I might have cause to disbelieve what I saw last month. But from the first, I decided that this book would be my record. In it I tell naught but the truth. It is possible that the natives deceived us, me and my friends, but I am certainly not the deceiver. And if this was a deception, it was one that happened regularly!

Like thirty days before, we were forced to enter cages. Again, the cages were hoisted into the air. The tethering rope was tied off high enough that none of the animals that roam this area could reach the knot. Only a human could climb up the tree and untie it. As happened before, we were provided with sufficient food and drink before the sun went down. Flowers were woven into the bars. Chen had his own cage, as did the mothers with babies.

This time Frank became very agitated, more so than the first time. We were in our bamboo cage, swaying above the meeting place. The women and babies were in their cage, and Chen was in his. Frank suddenly said, "What if this time, they eat us? They seem to be wolves. I saw one once in the London Zoo. They are vicious predators. I think we are going to die."

"Of course, they are wolves," George said. "That's patently clear."

"But isn't this a lot of trouble if they plan to eat us?" I asked. "Why not leave us on the ground?"

"I don't know the answer to that, but I can say we are fatter this month. They have fed us better than what we got at Anton," Frank said. "What's the reason for that?"

"Maybe they aren't cruel or miserly like the headmaster at Anton," I said.

George agreed. "Food is plentiful here, as long as you help catch or prepare it. So why would they bother to eat us? Besides, we are being very helpful. All of us are learning their skills and applying them. When we arrived, we knew nothing."

"But maybe they've lulled us. Maybe now they'll eat us," Frank said. He was truly worried, although we could not figure out why.

We turned to Chen. "Tell us truly. Do you know? Are they planning to eat us?"

Chen stood up, gripped the bars, and leaned his weight on them. "What do you think? Do you think they would tell me? A Chinaman? If that was their plan? I think not! I ask you, smart boys. You went to school. Did they teach you these things? I am only a poor man who likes to cook! You tell me. Tell Chen, are they men or are they wolves? If they are hungry, why put us in a cage and make it hard to get to us?"

George was angered by the taunt. "You speak their language, Chen. You could ask! Why don't you?"

Chen spat. "You think I have the words to say this? You think they tell Chen everything? You are a funny boy. You make a joke. I see what you see and I am surprised, too. In my culture, we have many creatures with special powers, but none who become wolves."

"No, Chen," George interrupted. "I mean you speak the language of the natives! Have you asked them about these wolves? What do they say?"

Chen turned his face away. George tried repeatedly to get the cook to speak, but he refused. Frank whispered to me, "I would bet you a shilling if I had one, that Chen knows more than he tells us. I think he likes to see us suffer."

"Why?" I asked.

"Because other white people have treated him poorly," Frank said. "This is his chance at payback."

Frank is correct, in that we have seen such churlish behavior towards the Chinaman, especially on the boat, but I did not see any reason that Chen would be unkind to us. We were outcasts just as he was.

Twenty-eight days later

As we approach another full moon, we talked to each other about the transformations. Were they real? How could we be sure?

George suggested several experiments. He asked that the day after the full month, each of us might draw what we saw during the change.

So we did. After the next full moon, the three of us boys went as a group to the beach. We stood with our backs to each other and, without watching what the other was doing, we used sticks to make images in the sand. The pictures we drew were very, very much alike. Especially given the limitations of our artistic abilities.

Frank had another idea. He suggested that we not to eat or drink all of the day before the full moon. In this manner, we were able to confirm that our visions were not induced by some strange drug. Once again, when the full moon came around, we abstained from food and drink. The day after the changes, we compared impressions and discovered what we experienced was the same.

This time, I pointed out to my friends that there are signs of the transformation that linger after the night of the full moon. Frank wanted to know what I meant. I said you need but to look around carefully. There is the blood-soaked sand in areas around the camp. George nodded. He said he has seen tufts of fur embedded in tree bark, which he assumes are the aftermath of wolves trying to climb the banyan tree. I pointed out there are always bits of rotting flesh scattered around the huts after the full moon. These are clues, I said. They tell me this must be real and my mind is not playing tricks.

One year later.

Time has passed quickly. My friends and I keep track of the days by creating a calendar of sorts. This has become increasingly important, as you will see. We have cut marks into the poles of our hut. I am unsure of the exact date, but I put my journal away twelve months ago after writing an entry so strange that I could not believe it. Over and over again, I have told myself that I was delusional. However, Frank and George and Chen all confirm what I saw. We were all loathe to speak of it very much in the beginning, as none of us could believe what we'd seen. Frank thought our water had been dosed with a potion that caused hallucinations. Chen has told us there are mushrooms in his culture that no one will eat because they cause such daytime dreams. George thought the natives were wearing costumes. I had no idea what was happening!

For a few months, Frank, George, Chen, and I believed that we had partaken of a strong elixir that muddled our senses. We decided we should be more careful about what we ate and drank. Of course, this would be difficult because we share the same food and drink as the natives. Eventually, we discarded that plan as nonsense.

We looked to Chen for guidance but he said very little. That made us angry. Clearly Chen knew more than we did—or so we thought. He was becoming somewhat knowledgeable in their language and surely he could ask the questions that troubled us all. But if Chen knew what was happening, he kept his counsel. Those first few months, Frank and George and I badgered Chen, asking him one question after another, but he responded by becoming increasingly quiet. He also acted rather brusque with us, and that, too, was a surprise, because overall Chen has been exceedingly kind to us in all matters. I do not know how we would have survived without his assistance.

The others and I discussed our reactions to what we had seen and concluded that the glow of the moon in this tropical clime had fooled us. As with all other aspects of our new lives, we came to a sort of acceptance. That which had once seemed incredible or phantasmic was yet another strange adventure for us to endure.

There is a slaughter each full moon. The hunters who bring down the small deer and rabbits and such on this island are natives who take on the shape of wolves. There. That is the simplest way of explaining what we see each thirty days.

Every full moon, we find ourselves in the cages and hoisted high, watching this odd transformation and hearing the sounds of the hunt. Like all occurrences that begin curiously but continue over time, we have become inured to this strange transformation. After all, the villagers protect us. Isn't that all that matters? If once a month, they give us a magic potion that leads us to believe they turn into wolves, who cares? All that we knew to be true back in England does not apply here. I have despaired of ever going back home to my family's home in Wiltshire. I also care not one whit for manners or for the rituals of society. My appearance has changed. My hair is long. I am growing a beard in patches. No one would receive me, seeing me like this. But what does it matter how I might be received in society? There is no society here. Or if there is a society, we are it. All we have is this life here on this island. If I had not been born in the world beyond, I would have never known about England. That country no longer exists for me. All that matters is that which I can feel and hear and taste and see. The other world, that other life, and all my memories associated with it, are but a fantasy.

Our understanding of this monthly transformation has grown as well. When the natives said, "She is coming," they were talking about the moon. They believe the moon is a goddess who watches over them. The rat is her sacred pet, doing her bidding and watching over the natives. The rajah is the moon's appointed representative on earth. Or at least that's as close to an explanation as I can give, because our language and our cultures are so different.

The reason for hoisting us in the air is so that we are protected from the wolves. Obviously, given that their hands become paws during the transformation, they can't climb up the banyan tree or untie knots. The natives weave plumeria blossoms through the bars of the cages because those flowers have a fragrance that's repellant to the wolves.

Frank and George and I have speculated there is a certain loss of control visited upon the natives once they have undergone the change. Therefore, leaving us exposed to their animal natures would make us highly vulnerable. Fortunately for us, the wolves expend most of the night hunting for food rather than snapping at our heels. I do not understand why the mothers are caged, too, but George speculates that is has much to do with the fact they are feeding their babies. After the babies are big enough to eat solid food, they and their mothers seem to make the transformation into wolves like every other member of their tribe.

Nor are we completely sure what part the rat plays in all of this, beyond being a sacred animal. We don't know if these natives transform into wolves because they inherited this disease or if they drank a potion or what. Maybe they ate one of the sacred rats? We don't know.

Other than this strange occurrence, life here continues in an unremarkable way. More and more Chen has become a wise older brother to the three of us. Yes, on occasion our questions irritate him, but otherwise he takes good care of us. Frank is becoming wonderfully proficient at hunting. He can handle a bow and arrow with great skill and accuracy. George is learning to navigate a boat by the stars. He is also becoming well versed in capturing fish and other edibles from the seas. I am doing my best to learn about the culture of the natives and how to use a slingshot.

In addition to the moon goddess and the rat, the Sumatrans (or so we are told they call themselves) worship a variety of spirits that inhabit the natural world around us. While the society is patriarchal in most aspects, the women have more freedom than I might have guessed. Children are treated as communal property and enjoy a lot of affection from all the adults. As for relations between men and women, they are considered very normal and natural and nothing to inspire shame. (Yet still I blush as I write this.)

It seems strange to think of my father and how he said that I was a child before he sent me off. I was. But I have grown up in many ways. This is a culture where everyone has a job to do. So I do mine, even though that job changes from time to time. Last week, I went with a hunting party to a part of the island where the trees grow so thick that you cannot see the sun. Using slingshots, we shot birds. These we brought back to the women, who prepared them in a variety of ways. Some birds we only wounded, and these we will raise for their eggs. Being included with the other men feels very good indeed! We all work together and everyone matters. I didn't matter back in England. I do here, so I can honestly say that in some respects—most respects—I like this better.

Date unknown

Yesterday, a white sail was spotted on the horizon. Watchers climbed the tallest trees and kept their eyes on that far-off ship. Eventually, they concluded it was a Dutch ship, but it veered away from our island. There was a profound sense of relief.

That same night, Kiawonka told us what happens when the Dutch arrive on an island. He was very small when they invaded the island of his birth. He explained that our island is one of many dotted around this part of the ocean. The rulers of the islands are all related to each other. When his parents realized they would be overtaken by the

Dutch, they entrusted their baby to a pair of caretakers. A boat had been hidden in a cave, expressly for the purpose of whisking the royal baby away. The caregivers took Kiawonka to the cave, loaded him into the boat, and under the cover of night paddled here, to this island. The baby Kiawonka and his caregivers were welcomed by this island's rajah, Kiawonka's uncle. And so Kiawonka grew up among the natives here. When he became a young man, Kiawonka went on a quest, sailing back to this native island. There he learned that the Dutch had killed most of the natives, including his parents, forcing the survivors into slavery, and making them harvest the spices under brutal conditions. Kiawonka observed all of this and only narrowly evaded capture so he could return here.

All of this reminds us how lucky we were that Chen was able to honestly say we were not Dutch! No wonder the natives hate the Dutch so much! These people love their freedom. A life enslaved would be no life at all.

Date unknown

We have now been amongst the natives for nearly five years. Sometimes, when I close my eyes, I cannot even remember my life before I came to this island. Those days seem like a dream I once had or a book I once read. Were it not for this journal, I should dismiss my early years as fantasy entirely.

Will we ever get back to England? I sincerely doubt that we will. So far, we have seen the distant white sails of ships only a handful of times. Never do they come to this island. Either this spot is thought to be worthless or uninhabited or dangerous or all three.

Yet here we are.

I continue this journal for my own education and reference. If one day in the future, someone does read it, I have a request to make of my audience: treat our story with compassion. At the time we were left here by the captain of the Mathilda Briggs, we were twelve, thirteen, and fourteen. As I write this, we've lived a little less than one-third of our lives on this small island. The Sumatrans have welcomed us into their tribe. Had they not, we surely would have perished!

All this leads to a new chapter, one I am reluctant to share. Yet I must. Recently, my friends and I have made a difficult choice. In light of it, others will no doubt judge us harshly—if this journal ever leaves this place and travels to what is generally considered civilisation. Regarding that decision, I must remind you that what one considers in the abstract is substantively different from what one feels compelled to do in the event. Never did we entertain a plan for any of this to happen. Never!

We had accepted our plight, George, Frank, and I. We had given up any hope of returning to England. One by one, we had concluded that our destiny was to live and die here. We discussed our options at length. In the end, we came to believe we had no choice but to act as we did! May God forgive us!

But I digress. I must start at the beginning. Anket, one of the natives, came racing into the village and screaming at the top of his lungs. He had seen a ship approaching. He recognised it as being Dutch. The Dutch tradesmen have made no secret of their desire to take possession of this island and exploit the peppercorn trees that grow here. The elders tell stories of other visits by the Dutch, and how they have come with weapons to kill all the natives. Chen explained to us that the Dutch consider everyone who isn't Dutch to be inferior, especially if their skin isn't white. (This grieves me as I once might have thought the same, but over the years I have learned this is not the case. However, that is a topic for another time.) Therefore, the Dutch are very cavalier with the natives' lives.

Anket's warning set off a flurry of reactions. The full moon is but three days away. George, Frank, Chen, and I have seen how much stronger the natives are in their animal form. The wolf-natives can jump, leap, wrestle, and bite. Their sense of smell is amazing, as is their ability to hear the faintest of sounds. As wolves, the natives are faster than humans and they are able to see in the dark. As for their strength, it is truly astonishing. They work as a group to bring down large prey. First, one of them will leap to the animal's throat and sink its teeth in. As the panicked animal bucks and kicks and fights for its life, the other wolves will bite the legs of the prey, rendering the animal unable to run away. Once the prey falls to the ground, it is mobbed by the snarling, snapping wolves as they tear into the fallen animal's flesh. Curiously, the wolves feast upon the internal organs of their prey at the time of the killing. Only later do they come back for the flesh.

In their wolf forms, the Sumatrans might have a chance to save themselves from the Dutch sailors. As humans, they had none. Somehow we needed to come up with a plan for avoiding conflict until the night of the full moon.

Nature provided one point in our favour: As was common this time of year, there was a lull in the winds. An eerie sort of stillness. The natives said it was an omen. Such odd weather could mean trouble ahead. The Dutch boat was sitting dead in the water.

Kiawonka and the men of the tribe discussed their options. The Sumatrans consider us men, too, so we listened and participated as well.

Chen stood up to speak. He was captured by the Dutch as a young child, and thus began his life as a slave. He hates the Dutch and he would rather die than submit to them. "They are greedy and do not keep their word," Chen said. But he also noted that the Dutch have guns, both large and small, so the natives will not be able to overpower them easily.

The Sumatran men talked for a long, long time. Frank, George, Chen, and I listened carefully. By now, all of us understand their language pretty well.

George is a very logical thinker. He asked, "What if the Dutch are only here to take the spices? What if you told them they could have all the spices they want? Wouldn't that make them happy? Might they not go away after they got what they wanted?"

"And then there would be no fighting," said Frank. By nature, Frank avoids quarrels.

Chen and Kiawonka exchanged looks, reminding me of how my parents would communicate without words. Chen spread his hands wide. "The Dutch might say they want spices, but that is not all. They will want this island for their own. They will want to sell the natives for a profit. Remember, I was one of their slaves. I know these people. When the Dutch sailors come onto this island, they will not come as friends. They will come as conquerors. They will burn down the huts.

They will kill most of the men and the old ones. They will take the women and the children as spoils of war. It will be like a bad dream, except this bad dream will run hot with blood."

George spoke for all of us. "We must come up with a plan to delay their arrival and then we must do our best to defend ourselves. We might die, but then again, if we were in Her Majesty's Service, we would risk our lives in battle, too."

I agreed. There was no place for us to hide. We could only do our best to repel the Dutch. I had never been in a fight, much less a situation such as this. How would I comport myself? I did not know.

In the end, the Sumatrans decided that rather than fight the Dutch, the rajah will make the Dutch welcome. Perhaps that will be enough. Perhaps the Dutch will take the peppercorn trees and go away. At the worst, it is hoped that this appeasement might buy the Sumatrans enough time to change into wolves.

George pointed out that this plan hinges on the Dutch being very lazy—and arrogant. Frank said they must be very prideful if they think other people will simply give them what they want. Chen assures us that they are. They have ruled the trade routes for so long that they think they are invincible which is why they are picking fights with the British. I think this is a rather shabby excuse for a plan, but I know nothing of waging war so I stay silent.

Once the plan had been adopted, the Sumatrans started doing everything possible to prepare in case the Dutch do decide they want to fight. The natives have donned their war gear, and they stage mock battles in the center of our compound. Frank, George, and I are more than willing to fight along with them, as it seems like a jolly adventure, but we sincerely doubt that we can be very effective as warriors. Unlike the Sumatrans, we have not trained for this our whole lives. I am ashamed to say that each and every time we have practiced our fighting skills, the Sumatrans have beaten us soundly. (George suspects that we are disadvantaged because from an early age, we have been told to comport ourselves like gentlemen. Frank sees the problem differently. He says we lack years of training. I wonder if they both are right.) The longer we stay with the Sumatrans, the more I am forced to conclude that we are the ones at a disadvantage, not the natives. This is ironic because in the beginning we thought we were superior in every way!

Given how untrained and unskilled we are, we felt useless, but several of the old men had an idea. They want to encircle our encampment with what they call killing pits. If there is a fight, the Sumatrans will avoid these pits whilst herding the Dutch toward them. So the old men need help digging deep holes. George, Frank, and I volunteer. These pits are six to eight feet deep. At the bottom of the hole, stakes are planted with the sharpened ends in the air. A lightweight net of vines is tossed over the hole. Leaves are scattered on the net to render the trap invisible.

George, Frank, and I put our best effort into digging. We were working on our second pit when Chen came hurrying over. He and the rajah have been talking. They are both worried about us. The rajah is not sure he can protect us from the Dutch.

This, of course, was our conclusion as well.

George acted as our spokesman. He explained that we will do all we can to help the Sumatrans. We were ready to go back to our digging —in fact, Frank had never stopped—but Kiawonka had a proposal, one that he had discussed with Chen.

"You could turn into wolves," said the rajah.

George looked up from the wooden tool he was holding. He turned a scoop of dirt onto the ground beside him. "We could do that?"

Frank stopped jabbing his shovel into the dirt. "We thought only Sumatrans could change."

I nodded. "We assumed it was inherited!"

"No." Kiawonka smiled at us. "Tell them, Chen. You talk better."

"Yes, there is a way for you and me to become wolves during the full moon. But first you must know everything and then you can decide. Some of what you will hear is good and some is not. The rajah wants you to know it all before you decide."

"Us? Only us?" I asked. I worried about Chen being included.

"I have been invited, too," said Chen with as broad of a smile as I have ever seen.

We quit digging and went with Chen into the rajah's hut so Kiawonka could explain the details. Once we were seated, Chen explained that if we chose to become wolf-men, at midnight on the eve of the full moon, two days hence, we would undergo an exceedingly painful transition.

We would have no control over the transformation, meaning that we could not stop the process once it began. This new shape would last until first light, when we would undergo the same transformation in reverse. If we died as wolves, we would stay dead in that form. Kiawonka thinks we will have a better chance of survival if we chose this path, but whatever choice we make, he will honour it and do his best to keep us safe.

Without looking at my friends, I knew they were as touched by this offer as I was. The old ones, the tribal elders, told stories about this sacred power. They have said that the rat god had given this ability to the Sumatrans and the Sumatrans alone. Yet here Kiawonka was, offering to share it with us. Our own families had pushed us away, but these people had taken us in, and now they offered us an unimaginable honour. I am not ashamed to say my eyes were wet and my throat was tight with emotion.

Still we had questions.

George wanted to know the duration of the alteration, as in would we be able to cast off our wolf nature at some date in the future? There are no wolves on our home island, George explained. If we return to England as wolves, surely we would be hunted down and put to death!

Kiawonka was taken aback by this. "Would not your tribe protect you?"

In a chorus, we said, "No."

"What sort of family does not protect its children? What sort of father would not give his life for his young ones? Not a good one! And your mother? Would she not die protecting you? I would do anything for my children." His vehemence turned his face dark red with anger. Kiawonka spat on the floor of his hut, a way of cursing our parents.

Of course, the rajah doesn't know our fathers or our culture, but we were too polite to say as much. More and more, I wonder who the savages are—and who are the civilized people?

Kiawonka told us he considers the three of us his adopted sons. He would respect our decision whatever it was, and if we decided against becoming wolves, he would still do all he could to protect us.

The three of us asked if we could confer by ourselves in our hut as this was a weighty decision. As we were leaving, Chen told us, "I am accepting the rajah's offer. I would die rather than live my life as a slave again. Whether I die here or in England, it doesn't much matter."

Once the three of us were alone, George said, "From what we've seen, this transformation into wolves only lasts for six or seven hours on one night a month. My father used to go to his club in London for days on end. If we ever get back home, we'll simply hide out once a month. That should work, don't you think?"

Frank argued that we could just as easily die here as anywhere else. I expected him to propose that we run away and hide, but he surprised me when he said, "It would be unfair of us to let the Sumatrans fight alone. They have been good to us. Besides, the Dutch are also the enemies of our people back at home!"

As for myself, I had resolved it in my mind that we would die here anyway, one way or the other. I continue to write in this journal with the vain hope that it might be discovered after my demise and afford my family a small comfort to know I thought of them often and regretted any pain I had caused them.

But my family is far away—and they *sent* me away. I am here, and I have learned to depend on these people, the ones who are around me.

I owe the Sumatrans my loyalty and such bravery as I can muster.

I shall make one small admission: When first we ran away from Anton, I took with me a linen handkerchief. It belonged to my mother. Through all my adventures, I have managed to keep it safe. Now and again, when I am alone, I press it to my face and smell Mama's perfume. A mix of lavender and lily-of-the-valley and English roses. At those moments, I struggle not to cry. One time, finding me alone with my nose buried in the handkerchief, George happened upon me. I feared he would jest at my tender emotions. Instead, he placed a kindly hand on my shoulder. "I know it is hard," he said. "I miss my family, too."

I was thinking about that linen square when told my friends that I would abide by their decision. Mama at least would have been proud of me. "We have come this far together. I see no reason for us to go our separate ways now. I could not have survived without all of you. If we die, we die together."

It was abundantly clear what we must do. When we left England, our country was fighting the Dutch. If we had stayed home, by now we might have pledged ourselves to the service of Our Queen. Was that really any different than what we faced now? Did it matter if we fought as in the guise of young men or as wolves? Surely as wolves we were offered an advantage! Then would we not be foolish for taking it? Yes, if we were back in England, the very idea of being wolves would have seemed ridiculous. Horrifying, even. But here we would be among similar-minded creatures. And didn't we owe our loyalty, not to mention our lives, to the Sumatrans? They had treated us with kindness, fairness, and generosity. They had shared all that they had, even though their possessions were meager.

To my way of thinking, there really wasn't a choice. There was only one path to take and we were already on it. As three boys from England, we could not do much. As three wolves, we would be a dangerous force to reckon with.

We were in agreement and there was no time to waste. We left the hut and went to talk to Chen and the rajah. Kiawonka received our news silently. He did not look happy. Chen explained that the rajah knew we had made a difficult decision and he honoured us for it, but the way forward would not be easy—and there wasn't much time.

Chen did his best to explain the process to us as Kiawonka talked him through it. We were surprised to learn that those large rats are carriers of the wolf disease! (I hesitate to call it a disease, but I do not have another word to explain the transformative powers.) That explains why the rats are so prized. The Sumatrans worship the rat because many generations ago, other large predatory beasts roamed this island, and the people could not protect themselves. Changing into wolves gave the natives a way to survive. Since then, the human wolves have killed off the large predators and thus, they are grateful to the rat for this gift.

When a person is bitten by one of the sacred rats, he'll turn into a wolf once a month on the day of a full moon. Otherwise, no one would guess a wolf-human is different from any other person. As I had guessed, the smell of the plumeria drives the wolves away. Young women do not change into wolves until after their babies no longer need their mothers. Otherwise the humans might not continue: there was a possibility the mothers would be overcome by their animal nature and eat their young. That's why we saw three young mothers in cages—the confinement was for their protection, along with the plumeria.

George had an important question to ask, "After the change, do people think like wolves or think like humans?" The rajah said it varied from person to person. Strong persons maintained more of their humanity. However, the wolf urges were also strong. We wanted to know if the wolves only ate meat. Yes, the rajah said. It appears so. Of course, once we were back in human form, we could eat other foods.

Kiawonka cautioned us that this was a serious decision and should not be made lightly. Again, he promised us that if we didn't want to change, the Sumatrans would do their best to protect us from the Dutch.

We thanked the rajah for this opportunity to become wolf-men. We were as resolute as any three boys could be under such trying circumstances. Again, the rajah and Chen pointed out we didn't have much time. The white sails of the Dutch ship were still small out on the horizon, but that could change rapidly. If this was the path for us to take, we needed to take it quickly. Because we are not Sumatran, the rajah worried that our bodies might handle the change poorly or even not at all. Therefore, Chen volunteered to go first. "I am not English, but you will see if the change can happen to anyone other than a Sumatran." We thanked him, but he was not done. He explained that if the rat's bite was deadly, that by his going first, we would be saved.

I must share an aside: I find it most peculiar that I was always taught that yellow and brown people are not civilised like us, and yet at every turn, the danger to our lives was coming from other white-skinned people! The brown and yellow people protected us and treated us kindly. This is curious and I hope to explore this idea further.

Kiawonka signaled to one of advisors to blow the sacred horn. At the sound from the conch shell, the Sumatran people all gathered around. The rajah explained what a commitment we had made. The natives cheered and patted us on the shoulder like proud parents, which is what they were in the oddest manner possible. From there we processed to the pens where the sacred rats were kept. One particular chamber had been built and decorated solely for the purpose of this transformation from human to...what? I could not answer that question.

Chen went first. It was terribly brave of him. One of Kiawonka's wives handed Chen half of a coconut shell filled with salve. She instructed him to smear this on his flesh. I believe it was some sort of animal fat. Certainly, it smelt like the rashers of bacon I enjoyed at home. Chen dutifully rubbed the salve on his legs after smoothing it on his arms. When he was judged to be properly covered with the grease, the rajah droned an incantation and burned a stick that smelled like church on Sundays. The smoke tickled my nose.

The sacred chamber had been constructed with care. A glyph of a rat was burned into the wood trim at various intervals. This symbol was the same one that appeared as a scar on the rajah's forehead. Around the perimeter were peepholes so that onlookers could gaze upon the interior. A heavy door marked the spot of egress and exit for the person. A small sliding door at the base of the wall separated the rat pen from the chamber.

The rajah opened the door to the chamber and Chen went inside. The rest of us were able to stand outside and watch through small peepholes. In the center of the chamber was an altar about a foot high. Fresh orchids, sweet fruits, and small pieces of meat were scattered in small bowls around the altar, presumably as gifts for the rats. The only other furnishings were several plush cushions on the dirt floor. I knew from our time on the island that fabrics are hard to fashion, as all of the thread preparation and weaving is done by hand, so those cushions were symbolic of extreme devotion. The fabric had been dyed in various shades of orange-yellow, which gave me the idea they might be coloured with turmeric, a spice Chen used often.

Once inside, Chen sat down on a cushion. The small sliding divider at the foot of the wall was drawn back and a sacred rat ran inside the chamber. The rodent lifted his pink nose to the air and sniffed eagerly. Then the animal ran over to Chen and suddenly bit his arm. To his credit, Chen did not cry out but he did wince. That rat had such a firm hold on Chen that when the Chinaman stood up, the rat dangled freely from his arm. At that juncture, the keeper of the rats entered the enclosure. By offering the rat a small treat even more enticing than Chen's flesh, the keeper encouraged the rat to let go of Chen. While the rat handler fed the rodent more treats, Chen hurried out of the chamber.

"I feel no difference," Chen said. We'd been eager to hear this, and now we were disappointed. Kiawonka only smiled. "That is the way of it."

Then it was our turn. We drew straws for who would go next. Frank drew the shortest so it was his turn, then George's, and then mine. The procedure was practically identical to Chen's for all of us. George's rat bit him hard on the leg. Frank was bitten on the foot. They both told me it didn't hurt too badly. Even if it did, they wouldn't let on, and I knew they were keeping the truth from me.

I wished I had gone first and gotten the ordeal over. I felt ill and thought that I might vomit. I fumbled with the lard-scented salve, dropping the coconut twice. My nerves had gotten the better of me. Seeing my friends and Chen handle things so well contrived to worry me. I was afraid that I would disappoint them by screaming in pain. It took every ounce of courage I had to put one foot in front of another as I walked into the enclosure. Once there, I sank to the dirt floor and prayed that the rat would come in a hurry before I lost my composure.

I need not have worried. The rat was on me in a flash. His bite was painful, and I guess the rat decided I was tasty because instead of choosing one spot and hanging on, he nipped me again and again. Using all my powers of restraint, I resisted the urge to throttle the little beast. Up close, I had the chance to see this particular sacred animal more clearly and I can confidently report that he looks like most other rats, only three times larger. His fur had longer guard hairs, those being the longer, coarser hairs distinguished from the softer down beneath. His colouration was uniformly brownish-grey, and his nose a soft pink, as was the skin of his tail and the pads of his paws. When he quit biting long enough to stare up at me, his eyes glowed red with such a ferocity that I could only shrink back and then jump to my feet. My haste caused the rodent to tumble away from me. "Let me out!" I screamed, and as soon as the door to that sacred chamber opened, I stumbled from that horrid place and fell immediately to the ground.

Hands lifted me up. Smiling faces greeted me. I had become one of them, whatever that was.

That night passed as if nothing had transpired. Except for the bite marks on our bodies, George, Frank, Chen, and I showed and felt no signs that we'd been initiated into this strange community. At first, I felt disappointed. Then I decided that I was glad to have that particular initiation over.

Date Unknown

The next day everyone woke up early. We had only two days to prepare for the arrival of the Dutch sailors. Attunka, one of the best warriors, came to us. The rajah had asked him to prepare us for the coming battle.

During the brief time we have lived among them, the natives have tried to teach us to defend ourselves, mainly from wild animals. Now this information is deadly serious. I must admit, however, that I found it nearly impossible to absorb what Attunka says. In the cold light of day, the idea of changing into a wolf and then fighting as an animal seems absurd. My friends feel the same. We are hard pressed to contain our giggles. After an hour of this, Chen came over to see how we were doing. He was furious when he saw how silly we were being. He spoke to us in a grave manner. "This is no laughing matter. I have seen Dutch guns rip open a man's belly. His guts spilled out on the ground. The air was ripe with the stink of his waste and his blood. The man cried in agony for hours. He bled and bled and begged us for death, but the Dutch only laughed. This could be your fate. Do not make the mistake of thinking this is a game."

This gave us pause.

Attunka said, "Listen, little brothers. Let me tell you how to stay alive in a battle. When the first rush comes, do not run forward. Let the older warriors go before you. They know what to do: Wait. Watch. Steal with your eyes. See how other warriors fight. You will not have long to learn these methods, but if you are smart, you will see how to kill. Your wolf teeth are long like daggers. If you can leap up, do that and bite the neck. Otherwise, bite the arm where the blood flows near the skin. Bite the groin at the cease of the leg. Pull your man down and go for his throat. Rip it out with your teeth. Keep an eye on what is happening around you. Help each other. Watch out for one another."

After Attunka left, we discussed what he had said. Chen assured us that Attunka was correct. "A battle can go on and on. Attunka was right to say you should look out for one another. That might be your only chance to survive."

These words made a big impression on us. No one had ever talked to us about killing other people. Yes, I had gone shooting with my father or with family friends at various estates. I had seen animals die. My father was always very careful that no animal would suffer needlessly. But what would Papa do on a field of battle? This I could not answer.

Date Unknown

I know all of this will sound incredible (and even laughable) to anyone who might stumble upon my journal. Quite possibly this book will never see the light of day. If that is true, no one else will know about the terrible decision we English boys felt compelled to make.

But if you are reading this, I beseech you to have a care and imagine yourself or your sons in our positions. We had no parents to counsel us. As far as we and the Sumatrans knew, we were the first to be in this odd position of having a choice regarding whether to take on the form of animals. For the Sumatrans, this transformation was an expected part of life. For us, it was highly unusual, beyond the pale.

If my friends and I survive this, no doubt we will be called to account for our decision. I pray that we will not be judged by the rules of English society; those rules do not apply here. We are too far from home, figuratively and literally. As George says, our dilemma is simple: we must do what we can to survive.

In fact, when examined in that light, every action we take—everything we learn—either aids us or defeats us. Thus, decision-making has been pared down to simplest terms.

Tomorrow will be the night of the full moon. The rajah and his advisors have cautioned all of us repeatedly that our plan will only work if the Sumatrans can hold their own until midnight. If the Sumatrans and the Dutch fight each other before the moon is high in the night sky, the spice traders shall surely prevail.

What can we do to delay any conflict with the Dutch traders? That is the question on all of our minds.

❧

THIS MORNING A SKIFF ROWED FROM THE DUTCH SHIP TO OUR shores. Three men were aboard as a scouting party. Chen was sent to greet them as he speaks their language.

After they left, Kiawonka called a council. Chen explained he was told that the Dutch captain sent his men to report on the peppercorn trees. The captain said he wanted a better sense of how many trees there are and their location. But Chen does not believe that. He thinks the captain wanted to know how many Sumatrans there are on this island. The questions were about the Sumatrans, not about the trees. Chen did his best to act confused and to purposefully misunderstand the Dutch. However, he thinks the Dutch plan to come ashore and capture as many Sumatrans as they can, and later sell the natives as slaves.

The scouting party has returned to the Dutch boat. We must hold them off until the moon is properly full! That is one long day away. Otherwise, we cannot defend ourselves. The rajah, Chen, and the rajah's advisors talk among themselves. They have a few ideas. First of all, they will do what they can to disable the Dutch ship. Secondly, they want Chen to tell the Dutch that the natives are planning a big celebration in honour of their visitors. There will be feasting and dancing. Chen thinks the party is a good idea. He has spent much of his life at sea. He says the Dutch men are getting restless. Chen suggests that they are lonely for women.

The rajah has spoken to his wife. She says that the Sumatran women will do what they can to entertain the Dutch men.

George gives Frank and me a dark look. He does not need to say anything. We all understand what this really means. I think of my baby sister, Gillian, and feel sick at my stomach.

Furthermore, as a gesture of goodwill, the rajah has decided to send six of his best men to the Dutch captain. These are a gift. The Captain is free to keep them or sell them as slaves. The rajah hopes this will further lead the Dutch to believe that the Sumatrans mean them no harm.

Chen will go with them (because he speaks both languages) and deliver this message: "The rajah sends his greetings. He knows his natives cannot hope to hold out against the Dutch. He hopes you will accept these men as a gift. Furthermore, the rajah asks you and your men to be his guests at a banquet in your honour tomorrow when the sun goes down. There will be much food, dancing, and beautiful women."

Chen will immediately return to the island with a response from the Captain. (That is the plan, at least.)

George worries that the Dutch won't care. He thinks the party and the offerings will not be enough. Chen explained that not only are the Dutch greedy, but they are also lazy. Besides, what other choice do we have?

The rajah has asked for six volunteers. George was willing, but the rajah and Chen said our presence should remain a secret. Otherwise the Dutch might think there are more British troops hiding on the island. Other men quickly stepped forward to offer themselves. The whole tribe gave them a warm sendoff as they (along with Chen) climbed into canoes to row out to the boat. Attunka was one of the volunteers. Before he left, George, Frank, and I thanked him for his help and wished him well. I was sad to see him go. All of the native volunteers seem very brave to me, but Attunka is one of the finest men I have ever met.

We hated to see Chen climbing into that small canoe, but George, Frank, and I knew he was doing the right thing. After the canoes were shoved into the water, the three of us and a few Sumatran boys climbed to the top of the cliff overlooking the beach. From there we could watch as Chen, Attunka, and the five other men approached the Dutch ship. When the canoes came alongside the boat, Chen requested permission to come aboard. The Captain granted it. Chen climbed the rope ladder and parlayed with the Captain. Their talk must have gone well, because shortly thereafter, the men left their canoes and joined Chen on the deck.

Here's what the Dutch don't know: The Sumatrans have played a trick on them. The natives are marvelous swimmers. They can hold their breath for a very, very long time! Using the canoes as cover, several of the best divers swam along beside the warriors, making their way to the Dutch ship. Once they are close to the Dutch ship, the hidden natives will dive down deep and puncture the Dutch ship's hull with sharp rocks. These holes will not be enough for the vessel to sink, but they should be enough that the Dutch will want to repair their ship immediately, lest they take on too much water. Tonight when dark comes, the native swimmers will return to the island. It is hoped that the "gifts" of slaves and the holes in the hull will encourage the Dutch to delay their arrival on our island until tomorrow evening when the celebration will be held in their honour. We must somehow keep the Dutch from fighting with us until the moon is full! Only then will we have a chance at survival!

Earlier we felt jubilant when the Captain accepted the Sumatran men as gifts and sent Chen back to the island with the empty canoes trailing behind. That elation quickly turned to despair. To celebrate their impending victory—for this is how the Dutch see this, as a great triumph—the Dutch had their own party on their ship. Of course, they are too far away for us to see what they ate and drank, but from the sounds of their voices coming across the water, they must have imbibed in strong spirits. The Dutch sailors grew increasingly rowdy. The songs they sang became more bawdy and loud.

George thought this was a very good sign indeed. "Their defenses will be down," he said. Frank was optimistic, too, because they had let Chen return to the island. My stomach was twisted into a large knot. I thought to myself that I should be very glad when this was over. Very glad indeed.

Frank, George, Chen, and I went back to work, doing various chores. Besides digging more pits, we are busy helping with food preparation for tomorrow's banquet.

I was pounding roots to be turned into a sort of flour when the sentry raced down from the top of the cliff where he had been told to watch the Dutch ship. Then the scout began talking to the rajah very quickly. Only Chen was proficient enough to translate the scout's hurried words. We could tell from Chen's face something was wrong. Attunka's name was repeated by the scout many times.

By now it was a few hours past noon, the hottest portion of the day. Kiawonka's face turned crimson. I thought it might be from the sun, but I was wrong. The rajah and the scout hurried back to the top of the cliff overlooking the sea. The ocean was still quiet and a lovely calm blue. We followed along, and Chen came, too. At the top, the rajah squinted out at the Dutch boat. Just then, I heard a sharp whistle. It was the sound of a leather whip, a cat-o'-nine-tales slicing through the air. The ship's first mate was thrashing Attunka with a whip. Chen turned pale. George poked him and demanded an explanation. Chen explained how leather strips are knotted at the ends. When those bumps strike flesh, they tear the skin away. It is a brutal, gruesome punishment.

Attunka withstood the whipping without making a sound. We watched in helpless horror as the first mate struck Attunka over and over again.

"Why?" asked Frank. He was about to cry. "What did Attunka do to deserve that?"

"Nothing. I believe the Dutch captain is having him whipped for sport," said Chen. "Remember? I told you the sailors were restless."

After a dozen or so strikes, the first mate stopped. The Captain nodded to a sailor who tossed a bucket of saltwater onto Attunka's back. The pain must have been tremendous because our friend's legs buckled. If he had not been strung up by his wrists, he would have fallen onto the deck. As it was, Attunka went limp.

"I shall make the Dutch pay for what they are doing to Attunka," said George. "I swear it." Frank agreed. "Before, I did not know if I could kill anyone. Now I am sure I can. Walter, are you with us?"

"I am," I said, but those were the saddest words I've ever spoken. If you are reading this, you might think that a rat bite changed me into an animal. It did not. What turned me into a predatory beast was seeing and hearing the Dutch torture my friend. I had lived my last day as an innocent. I was hungry for blood, and ready to kill.

But was I both mentally and physically capable of extinguishing a life? Of the three of us, I was the least proficient as a hunter. My friends did their best not to laugh when one of my arrows fell wide of the mark and frightened our quarry away. I was only a little better with a slingshot. If fighting broke out before we changed to wolves—*if we changed to wolves*—would I be of any use on the battlefield? Would I at least acquit myself with dignity? Or would I run and hide?

What abilities might show themselves when I changed into a wolf? Would my animal nature make me braver? Or would I cower and run away? Would I die on this strange island? Did my little sister ever think of me anymore? What would she say if she knew what I was preparing to do? And my mother? Would she be ashamed or proud?

As for my father, I have come to think differently about him. After these years with the Sumatrans, I had decided there was another way to be a father. A path much different than my own father had taken.

All these questions torment my soul.

Date Unknown

If the Dutch captain had hoped to enrage the natives by whipping Attunka, he could not have done a better job. Anger surged in my veins, and I could see barely restrained aggression on the faces of the other warriors. Kiawonka continued to look stoic, as if he were carved out of stone.

The sun seemed to take forever to set. Frank, George, and I climbed the banyan tree so that the Dutch would not see us. Chen reminded us, "If you cannot stick to the plan, many lives will be lost. The Sumatrans are brave; you must be too."

The rajah sent a small party to greet the Dutch visitors. A handful of women carried flower necklaces, noticeably devoid of plumeria. Distinguished men from the tribe also welcomed the Dutch. Everyone pretended that they hadn't heard Attunka being tortured.

The Dutch allowed the women and the ambassadors to walk them into the center of the compound directly below our banyan tree. All of the food was displayed: roasted pig, cooked snake, bananas in sauces, baked roots, berries in coconut milk, breads from roots, pasta from various plants beaten into flour, and much, much more. The Dutch men fell upon the foods like a bunch of starving animals. As they ate, they drink wine. The musicians played and the women danced. Soon the Dutch men started reaching out and grabbing women as they danced by. I could not bear to watch.

When, oh, when would the moon be finally full?

Suddenly all was quiet. I cannot say whether it was because the women were changing and the Dutch men were astonished, or if it was because the women could no longer cry for help. One reason I can't say is because I was changing. And it frightened me.

The transformation was slower than I expected, which was good because it allowed us time to climb down from the tree. Maybe we changed slowly because we were newly minted as wolves. Or maybe it only seemed faster when you were watching and not undergoing the process. Whatever the reason, the change went on and on, seemingly taking hours, as my nails grew into claws. My limbs lengthened. Fur grew so quickly I could watch it sprout from my skin. My body folded and buckled and fought the transformation. My stomach churned and my head shrieked in pain. My binocular vision changed and at first, I could scarcely walk because the alteration gave me vertigo, but that was quickly overcome because my sense of smell became my primary driving force. Whiskers had popped out of my face, on both sides of the area between my mouth and nose. When I dropped to all fours, I realized instinctively that these whiskers would help me map out the world around me. As they brushed against surfaces on either side of me, I knew where I was and where I could go and if I could hide. I ran my tongue over my teeth and reacted with surprise when I felt how sharp they had grown. After the fact, I noted that my tongue had grown exceedingly long.

Of course, there were no mirrors on the island and I could only see my reflection in the water, so my description might be somewhat incorrect. However, I can record how the transformation looked when I glanced over at Chen, George, and Frank.

Hairs sprouted all over our bodies. Frank's thighs thickened and bunched up under his body. His fingers turned into claws and the family ring he always wore looked exceedingly odd on those gnarled and hairy phalanges. George's nose grew longer as the tip thickened into a button-like shape. I looked down in time to see the transformation of my hands was nearly complete as my nails were talons protecting pads on paws. I had dropped down to all fours without realising it. My tailbone ached, as though I had bumped it hard. Then a knot grew at the base of my spine. Before I knew it, I was sporting a long and fur-covered tail, which curiously gave me good balance. Meanwhile, my elbows seemed permanently cocked in a crouched position.

My vision changed. I was seeing the world from differing vantage points, and then I reached up and touched the long snout that separated my eyes.

Finally, it was done.

I was a wolf.

My mind split into two halves. One half was this person once named Walter. The other was a wild animal, an oversized, ferocious dog-like creature. Clearly, the human Walter was so much weaker than my wolf-self. Old Walter wanted to be in charge, but sadly, he could only issue quiet requests.

Slowly, animal instinct won out. Vaguely, I remember throwing myself onto the back of a Dutch sailor. My teeth sank into his throat, breaking through the thin veil of his flesh. His hot blood tasted deliciously salty and rich on my tongue. As a matter of fact, the precious liquid of my victim's life strengthened me and an extraordinary energy pulsated through my body. I cannot tell you how my first kill went, in terms of how long it took, how cruel I was, and so on. I only know that

I prevailed and this glorious feeling bubbled through me, making me more alive than I have ever felt before!

Some wolves attacked small groups of sailors, whilst other wolves chased down their prey. As the moon climbed higher in the night sky, the lunar light added an eerie glow to the strange scene. The Sumatrans seemed to be holding their own.

The doubts that had plagued me vanished. I had not only turned into a wolf; I had turned into a killer.

II

The three of us sat in stunned silence as Holmes closed the journal. It rested innocently on his lap, as though the tattered pages did not tell the most devastating story I had ever heard. I cast about for an appropriate *bon mot*, a witticism, a phrase of encouragement, but my mind was limp as a wet flannel. The world's greatest detective wore the stunned expression of a man who has been treated to a tale too extraordinary for human comprehension. I understood what he was thinking because I, too, was similarly deeply affected by the account.

"Is it possible your brother wrote a fictional account?" I asked Miss Benson.

Her wan face turned to me. Any bit of liveliness had vanished and her tired voice confirmed her nerves were exhausted. "No," she whispered.

"Of course not," Holmes snapped. "This narrative is the only explanation for what Miss Caldwell saw out the window, is it not? Three wolves, three young men turned into murderous canines and cavorting in the light of the moon. You knew your brother would change, did you not, Miss Benson? You wanted Ennis Caldwell to quit this place, to return to London, to be safely tucked away—and yet, you would have allowed her to marry that monster! That creature who was once your beloved brother!"

"Once? He is yet my beloved brother!" she spoke in a voice that rattled the china plates on the serving tray. "Walter will always be my beloved brother! None of this is his fault! My father sent him away. My brother's only fault, if you must call it that, is his loyalty. He was loyal to the Sumatrans and would not stand for them to be killed or sold as slaves. He was loyal to his friends, Frank and George, so when they finally were rescued from that island, Walter did not desert them. The three of them pledged to safeguard their secret—and they made a blood promise to protect the world from their curse!"

"Ho! So you say, and yet, unless I am very much mistaken, they have roamed the hills and fields of this estate and nearby others, killing domestic animals." Holmes leaned forward in his chair, that sharp nose of his quivering with anger.

"And do you not eat meat?" snapped Miss Benson.

Holmes froze in place. She had pierced his armour of illogic.

"See here, Holmes. What are you accusing these boys of?" But then it came to me. I understood exactly what had happened and so did Holmes. This was the problem that bedeviled Landover. This explained what had happened to his dead rabbits. The three wolf-men had tortured and slaughtered the coneys during one of their monthly transitional periods. More than likely it was they who killed the Irish wolfhound.

"Mr. Holmes!" Gillian Benson said forcefully. "You judge these boys and me unfairly. My brother and his friends begged me to lock them up in an equipment shed. I had done so! I even hired a man, a keeper, and I paid him handsomely to see that Walter, Frank, and George could get up to no mischief. Look around you, Mr. Holmes. Do you think that all of this wealth has been accumulated by good deeds? Ha! Not likely, sir, not likely. My brother's problem is miniscule in comparison to all the folly of the generations before us."

Holmes half-rose out of his seat. "You say you were careful. That you hired a keeper. Then explain how your brother and his friends managed to terrorize the countryside! Either you are engaging in falsehoods or you are not being entirely honest with me, Miss Benson."

She drew back in her chair like a cat withdraws before striking out with a paw. "How dare you! They say you are a great man, Mr. Holmes. I do not see it. I see intolerance. I see prejudice. I see pride. Perhaps you do not have a sister or a brother. Mayhap you cannot understand the depth of familial love. But there it is. I love my brother with all my heart. God returned him to me. Yes, it is a trial that he has changed. But men who go to war come home changed, too, or so I have heard. None of us stays the same forever. The test of love is whether or not it can endure change. As you read his honest testimony yourself, this was not Walter's desire. He had to choose between honour and fear. Loyalty and cowardice. Life and death. He could have chosen to be slaughtered by the Dutch. Would that have satisfied your desire for justice? Would his life count so little that you would rather see a man die than a few rabbits?"

My word, but she was magnificent! This firebrand went toe-to-toe with Holmes, standing up for her brother and reminding my friend that his judgement might be impaired by his lack of imagination. Holmes could not visualise Mycroft in a similar situation, and therefore, he could not find a way to understand Miss Benson's misery.

But I was wrong. Holmes had a different motive all together. His thin lips twitched and curled into a smile. "Very well, Miss Benson. That will do. I simply had to know if you believed what your brother had written and if you could truly live with the change in him."

"You dared to test me?" Her voice shook with the indignity.

"I did. I do. First of all, I needed to be absolutely sure you were being honest with us." Holmes steepled his fingertips. "After all, that journal could well be a forgery."

"See here, Holmes," I interjected. "Speak for yourself. I thought that diary to be wholly convincing."

"Watson, one must always gather all the facts before theorizing. You know that. In lieu of seeing this transformation myself, I must turn over every stone, question every assumption, and test every belief. Once I see this change with my own eyes or hear about it from a direct source, I shall feel less hesitant."

"Then you doubt me?" Gillian Benson asked. Twin spots of pink glowed on her cheeks. "You think I am a liar?"

"No, Miss Benson, I do not," Holmes spoke in reassuring tones. "However, I prefer to digest firsthand and not rely on hearsay. That's all you have in this small book. Hearsay. And you cannot prove to me that your brother did not write this whilst under the influence of a mental disorder or of a strong drug. Therefore, I must work with what I have, and all I have is you. Thus, in order to be sure that I am not being taken for a fool, my only recourse is to apply pressure to you, personally. Do you see my dilemma?"

She hesitated. Holmes' words made their impact. Holmes was doing all that he could to make sure the information he'd been given was true. Under the circumstances, convoluted and twisted as this information was, he had no other choice but to test it. It was incumbent on him to eliminate any shadow of a possibility that this situation was a ruse. Since he only had one person at hand, this poor gentlewoman was forced to bear the brunt of his intellect.

As I was growing more and more uncomfortable, Holmes switched tactics, a strategy I'd seen him employ before with great success as it tripped up any unsuspecting prevaricators. He spoke mildly when he said, "Now I know that you, Miss Benson, are a true believer. If I am to be taken as a fool, you will not be the author of my embarrassment."

"Sir, if you are taken as a fool, that is on you. All I know is what I have shared with you, and that which I have seen. I tell you plainly, although I have not been allowed to witness the transition since it would be unseemly for me to see men without their clothes, I have seen my brother and his friends go into a shed on the afternoon of a full moon. I have watched and listened all night, only to quake in fear at the dreadful howling and clawing that sounds like nothing I have ever heard before in my life! With these two hands, I have locked the door so they could not come out."

Holmes narrowed his eyes and looked at her speculatively. "But they did get out. And you say you hired a keeper? They escaped on the evening when Miss Caldwell was here. How did that happen?"

Gillian Benson shrugged. "I wish I knew! I thought the keeper could be trusted, but the next day, he was found drunk in the hayloft. Believe me, I do not know how that happened! To this day, I wonder if I was not diligent enough when hiring the man. As for the shed, my brother and his friends dug their way out. I did not know enough about wolves to foresee such behavior."

"So you were not able to contain them," Holmes said, more to himself than to Gillian.

Gillian Benson covered her mouth with one hand and gripped the arm of her chair with the other. Her knuckles turned white. A moan escaped her. "I thought I was being careful. However, I failed. The bald truth of it is horrendous. I am guilty of ruining my brother's life."

I thought it unwise to point out that her brother's life had actually been ruined some time ago. Such an observation would be cruel and unnecessary.

"Is your brother entirely sure there is no antidote to his problem?" I asked gently. "Did the tribe have any shamans or healers who might have specialised knowledge that the other natives might not know? Would it be possible to contact a person on that island and ask questions?"

She hung her head and stared down at her dress. With the back of a hand, she flicked away a tear. "No. The tribe no longer exists."

"What?" Holmes snapped to attention. "Explain your comment, and do so quickly, Miss."

"Just so," she said. "A few days after the battle with the Dutch, Walter, Frank, George, and the Chinese gentleman were taken off the island by a British ship, the Gregor Valez. The captain had actually been chasing the Dutch ship, the same one that hoped to conquer the Sumatrans. You see, after everyone changed into wolves, they overcame the Dutch and killed them. Then the Sumatrans set fire to the Dutch ship, hoping to hide what had happened. But the British sailors on the Gregor Valez noticed smoke on the horizon. Using the blackened air as a guide, the British headed for the island. The Sumatrans saw this new set of white sails. Once again, they hid. Quickly enough, the boys identified the ship as being British and ran down to the water's edge to meet the newcomers. When the boys were introduced to the captain of the Gregor Valez, they lied and said that they and Chen were the lone inhabitants of that island. The boys spun a tale that the Dutch sailors had fought among themselves and that's how their ship caught on fire."

"What was the captain's name? The man behind the wheel of the Gregor Valez?" I asked. Although I was not in the Navy, but attached to the Fusiliers as a surgeon who was moved from post to post, my experience extended to all branches of Her Majesty's service. I thought mayhap that the captain might be familiar to me.

"Captain Jonathan Pickering," she said without hesitation. "He was the one who personally delivered Walter to our father. 'Though I was not privy to all their conversations, I did overhear a word or two. What I gleaned was enough to convince me that Pickering hates the Dutch passionately. His own son was murdered in the Sudan by a Boer battalion, and Pickering has vowed to give his own life fighting them."

"Please return to your narrative," said Holmes, with a touch of irritability. "You were explaining that the Sumatrans no longer exist? On what basis do you venture this conclusion?"

"Allow me to amend my statement. The Sumatrans on *that* particular island were washed away. After rescuing Walter and his friends, Captain Pickering stopped at the nearest port to reprovision. Whilst there in port, one of the Gregor Valdez sailors came back after a night of drinking and went straight to the cabin the young three friends shared. Remember that lull? That eerie calm weather? It preceded a terrible storm. I believe they called it a typhoon. The winds whipped up waves that engulfed the entire land mass. There were no survivors."

At this point, Holmes got to his feet and paced the room. "No one was left alive?"

"No," she said. "To confirm the story, the boys asked about the island the next time they put into port. The same report was given. More recently, my father hired a fellow from the Royal Geographic Service. This man traveled to my brother's island. He found no living inhabitants. Indeed, he reported no signs of humanity."

Holmes stared at the young woman. Most would have withered under this stern gaze, but Gillian Benson met his eyes with perfect equanimity. Holmes asked, "How long was the journey from Sumatra to Liverpool? I assume that's the port where the ship docked?"

"You are quite correct. Liverpool is the home port of the Gregor Valdez. Let me think about your question, sir. May I see my brother's journal?" Gillian held out a slender hand. Holmes responded by passing her the journal. Flipping through the pages, Gillian peered carefully at the top of one page and then at the headings of subsequent pages. "The Valdez stopped off at no less than ten ports on its way home. I remember Walter talking about the cargo the ship carried. Spices, leather goods, fine blades of all sorts, silks, and exotic wines. They must have been in the water for about a month at the least. More likely a good six weeks."

After answering that simple question, Miss Benson's lower lip trembled. "Please, Mr. Holmes, accept this entreaty of mine and find my brother. Whether or not he marries Ennis Caldwell is of little consequence to me. I say this without any rancor towards her. What matters is my brother's safety. I need to know that he is alive and where he is staying. Once I know that, I will write him and ask him to forgive me for the lapse in his confinement. When I get him back to our estate, I will make new preparations to safeguard Walter during those times when he is indisposed. I know I can keep my brother away from innocent society. Is it not patently clear to you that he does not wish to hurt others? He only accepted the call to change because he had no other viable option. Can you not see past this dreadful outcome and latch firmly to the humanity at his core?"

I was not as easily swayed. The words from the diary had rekindled my memories of warfare. Essentially, the boys had become assassins. Weapons, if you will. In the guise of wolves, I doubted they could be controlled. Furthermore, I doubted that the secret of their transformation could be kept under wraps. Such a change was simply too outré to be kept secret.

"What about Miss Caldwell?" I asked. "What of her need to know whether she was jilted?"

Gillian Benson bowed her head. "When he returns, I will ask my brother what he wants to do next. Her reaction to his altered state was so violent, her fear so distressing, that I doubt either she or he will want to move ahead with the nuptials. However, that is a matter I leave between them. If he wishes me to represent him to Ennis, I shall, of course."

"I cannot imagine a woman alive who is willing to marry a man who changes into a brute," I said stiffly. "Miss Caldwell seemed unwell from her last encounter with your brother and his friends. Perhaps her protestations of love were overblown. Or perhaps she has no desire to toss herself down as a sacrifice the way that the Romans fed slaves to the lions."

"That is not fair," Gillian Benson said, wagging a finger at me like an irritated schoolmarm. "Observe, Doctor, that I sit here whole and without a blemish. That night when Walter and his friends gathered under a full moon, I took food to them."

"Plumeria? The chickens?" supplied Holmes.

"That's right." And she continued in a defiant tone, "We grow the flowers in our glasshouse. I pinned several in my hair. We grow those birds. My brother and his friends gobbled down the chickens. There has never been such a rush to devour the poultry. Once or twice, the boys growled at one another, but—and this is notable!—they never snapped at me. Not even once. If they are to be cast as stone-cold murderers, explain that! You cannot! I am alive to prove they are not heedless killers. Categorizing them as vicious animals logically is proven to be incorrect."

I bit back a smile. This intelligent young woman understood how to talk to Holmes. She wisely had interpreted his mind as one that wrestled with logic and eschewed sentiment.

"If you wish me to pursue finding your brother, you would do well to remember that the road ahead is rough going. I trust you are not faint of heart," Holmes said simply. "It would not do for us to begin a journey and have you doubt your decision. Think hard on this, Miss Benson. Do you want my help or not? I have pledged to the Caldwells to find out what happened to your brother. I can honestly tell them at this exact juncture that he has run off. My advice to the Caldwell family would be to put aside all hopes of matrimony between Miss Caldwell and your brother. Or I can go back and say I am searching for young Walter."

"But he needs to deal honestly with Miss Caldwell!" I fairly shouted it. The idea of the young woman waking up and finding a wolf in her bed was too much for me to bear.

"Yes, Watson," said Holmes. "But as a couple, they can decide how to handle his...disease. He would not be the first spouse to choose to absent himself from his household due to concerns about contagion. Nor, I warrant, will he be the last."

That, of course, was true. Syphilis was rampant in London. Without a reliable treatment, many husbands chose to protect their wives by practicing abstinence. The gentlemen's clubs were full of husbands who slept there rather than visit this plague upon their spouses. But I did not need to share that with Miss Benson. The poor girl had enough to worry her!

Miss Benson's shoulders relaxed and she drew in a quivering sigh. "As you might guess, this has been very trying. My father knows nothing of it. Only that my brother was taken in by a kindly group of Sumatrans. He sent someone to find them so he could tender his thanks. My mother is aware of what happened. She and Walter have always been close. Papa is not what you might consider a tolerant man. In fact, I blame him in large part for what Walter is today. Do you know he didn't even bother to get references for or visit that awful school before he sent Walter away? The word of another gentleman at Papa's club was enough to convince my father that the school was a worthy idea. Papa lacks the milk of human kindness, and I cannot respect him for his choosing to send Walter away. In fact, if there is a villain in all of this, I point my finger at my father!"

She hesitated. "So you see, this is not a decision for my father to make. Mama has her own money. I can share our conversation with her and her alone. Together we will decide what to do next, but...we simply must locate Walter. Goodness only knows what sorts of pain he is suffering. I saw his face as he glanced up at the window where Ennis stood, backlighted by a single candle. Even in his...his form as an animal, his eyes reflected a depth of sadness that touched me deeply. I suspect he is hiding out of shame. Undeserved shame. No, no, no. It will not do to let this go. You must find him, Mr. Holmes. Find him and bring him home. I shall not desert my brother when he needs me."

"All right," said Holmes, rising out of his chair. "Then once I find him, keeping him locked up during a full moon will be your responsibility. Are we agreed?" He offered his hand. His long, slender fingers waited until Miss Benson had risen to her feet and she linked her hand with his.

"Agreed," she said.

12

"Ho!" Sherlock Holmes snapped his fingers as an idea came to mind as we stood in the vast foyer of the Benson home. Turning to Miss Benson, he said, "I nearly forgot. Is it possible that we might have a look at your brother's room? There might be a clue to his present whereabouts. At the very least, I would feel secure in the knowledge that I had examined it thoroughly and did not overlook something crucial to my mandate."

Holmes' voice echoed off the marble floor. Even the carved English walnut panels that surrounded us could not temper the deep tones that resonated from his throat. Of course, he was right. The fact that he hadn't asked earlier amused me, although later he admitted that he'd planned this all along. Catching Miss Benson off guard, appealing to her when she was sure she was done with us, that was all part of his plan.

"Oh," she said. Her ejaculation was more of a tiny grunt than a fully formed word. She repeated, "Walter's room."

Holmes had taught me the virtues of silence. When asked a question, most people hurry to fill the quiet space that follows. By remaining perfectly motionless, we often encourage others to flood the void. My dear friend's quick sideways glance suggested this was exactly what he had planned.

She said slowly, "Truly, is that necessary? It seems so invasive."

Holmes gave her a reassuring chuckle totally out of character with his personality but designed to feign harmlessness. If only Miss Benson could foretell what Holmes might divine from viewing Walter's most recent domicile! I looked away from the young woman, as I was feeling fearful that my expression would expose what I was thinking. For Holmes, a tour of a room was like opening an encyclopedia.

"Yes, it is necessary. Only if you truly want me to locate your brother," Holmes said. There was a warning in his tone. "Any information about his friends would also be of great assistance."

Gillian Benson's eyes brightened with the possibility that her beloved brother might be found. "Of course. I'll have Dennison, Walter's manservant, accompany you. Please wait here. I shall go and write down the information you might need."

Off she went down the long hallway.

**

Moments later we were joined by a man so thin that he looked emaciated. He introduced himself as Dennison.

It was all I could do not to demand that he allow me to examine him on the spot, as I was absolutely certain his pallor and lack of bulk represented an extreme illness of one sort or another. When he turned his rheumy brown eyes on us, I noted the yellow tinge and decided I would write a note to Miss Benson, a missive to suggest this man receive medical treatment. Surely they kept this man out of some sort of familial loyalty because his rotting teeth and the foul odour that emanated from them made a very poor impression indeed. One interaction with Dennison and guests with lesser determination than we had would instantly be rebuffed.

"Right this way," Dennison intoned after handing Holmes an ivory notecard on which, presumably, Miss Benson had written details regarding her brother's friends. Leading us up a sweeping staircase with a curved mahogany bannister, the manservant turned left to take us through carpeted hallways. At the end of our route was a tower room. The space was wholly pleasing, given that the circular shape afforded many west-facing windows with views encompassing a broad expanse of the far-reaching grounds. Availing myself of the landscape, I lingered at one of the windows and enjoyed the view. Below me stretched a colourful panorama. Egg-yolk yellow gorse contrasted with vibrant green meadows, whilst a brown-and-green copse edged a small silvery-blue creek. All in all, it was a soothing vista. Yet when making a mental comparison of it to a tropical island, the viewer would have found this domesticity exceedingly tame.

In size, Walter Benson's singular room was comparable to the flat Holmes and I rented from Mrs. Hudson. The décor was unusual to say the least. Instead of a sturdy four-poster bed, a rope hammock was strung from the ceiling. This swinging bed was tucked into a nook and curtained with draped canvas, possibly from a ship's sail. When Dennison saw where I was looking, he said sadly, "Once young master returned, he found conventional bedding not to his liking. Too constricting, he said. What you see is his attempt to replicate the sleeping area he had on that island." Dennison sniffed. "Mr. Benson was not amused."

"Curious," said Holmes. "What other changes did he make to his accommodations?"

Dennison wore a bleak expression. "Sir, I hardly think it appropriate—"

"That we find this young man before grievous harm comes to him?" asked Holmes while looking down his long aquiline nose. Holmes can be imperious when challenged.

Dennison dipped his head in a semblance of a bow. "Sir." With a sigh, he pointed toward a corner of the room. "There is Mister Walter's teak travel trunk. See the brass fittings? I believe one of the sailors made it during the voyage home and young master purchased it. You do realize, sir, that the young master left the school with naught but the clothes on his back? During his time on the island, well, it doesn't bear thinking about what he did to cover himself."

Turning a tight circle, Dennison considered his surroundings. He stopped when he faced a large vitrine. "That cabinet of curiosities houses most of what young master brought home. He has been very keen to preserve, um, some of the more unusual items."

Sure enough, while beguiled by the pastoral view, I'd ignored a glass-fronted case of imposing size. In my defense, the case was as far away from the windows as possible. The dark wood and lack of illumination conspired to help it blend in with the dark wood paneling. This was a wise precaution to protect the contents.

"Une vitrine," Holmes said under his breath. With hurried strides, he moved to the cabinet only to find that the door was locked. Cupping his hands over his eyes, Holmes tried to peer in, but his own form blocked the small amount of light coming in from the windows. "Do you have a key?" Holmes asked the manservant.

"No. Perhaps young Miss does," said Dennison.

"Please ask her if you can avail yourself of it." Holmes straightened and glared at the man. I could sense Holmes' increasing irritation with how little help Dennison was providing. "And do it quickly. The longer it takes me to track down Walter Benson, the more likely it is he will need a great deal of help. That should weigh heavily on your conscience."

"As you wish," the manservant said. His plodding exit emphasised he was not happy with our visit.

Once Dennison had left us alone, Holmes reached into his jacket pocket and withdrew a small set of lock-picking tools. Whistling under this breath, he poked a slender rod into the keyhole with one hand and pressed another tool into the same hole, a few inches apart. The lock clicked open in a most satisfying manner. Holmes tucked his tool kit away and motioned to me so we could both take a closer look.

Indeed, the case was a veritable treasure trove of primitive items. As I eagerly examined an arrow with a tip that looked to be of oyster shells, Holmes retreated from the case to check out the teak box. Holmes picked the lock on it as well. Meanwhile, I took out my pocket notebook and jotted remarks regarding the contents of the glass-fronted case and the teak box. My notes were designed to refresh my memory later, if need presented itself. In the vitrine was a necklace that mimicked large gray pearls. In actuality it was a strand of smooth grey seeds. My find intrigued me. I was picking up a pressed flower, when Holmes let out a low sound of approval. I turned to face him.

"Look at this!" Holmes held up his prize: a giant rat. The creature took me aback and I nearly tripped over my feet in alarm. Holmes was displaying it by the tail, and the vivacity of the creature was mute testimony to the skills of a talented taxidermist. Once I recovered myself, I noted the animal's body was nearly three feet long. Its tail was curled around the body. I judged it to add another twenty-four inches as well. Nose tip to tail, the beast was an incredible five feet long!

"I believe we have found a preserved example of the giant Sumatran rat." Holmes spoke in an ironic drawl.

"I would say so! That creature is positively astonishing," I marveled.

"More than that," agreed Holmes. "This proves the boy's journal was no hoax. This alone is a powerful indicator that young Benson told the truth in his diary. Why else would he own such a creature? The journal explains its existence in full."

I picked up the thread of the argument. "And of course, since such a creature does exist, then the rest of the story has to be truthful as well."

"Let us just agree it is more likely truthful than not," said Holmes. "While it is possible that Walter Benson lied in his journal, this stuffed creature makes that seem improbable."

I rubbed my chin. "Think about it, Holmes. Why would a boy lie when he was convinced his journal would never see the light of day? Who was he lying to impress?"

"Bravo, Watson. Who indeed? I'll grant you that I find it highly unlikely our Walter would lie about his predicament. Firstly, he was not alone. If Walter was lying, there was a good chance he'd be found out."

"As long as his confederates were alive." I thought that point worth qualifying.

"Just so. And of course, we know they did live through their adventure. So why bother to craft such an outlandish lie in a journal—and keep the book with the lie intact? Secondly, as you put it so eloquently, who was he trying to impress? No one. He had no reason to lie as he created his manuscript, because he didn't know whether his journal would ever see the light of day. Third, according to his diary, this rat is a sacred animal. Why would you bring something like this back with you? The very existence of this stuffed creature suggests it was, or is, important. Notice it was locked away. Sunlight would damage the pelt and over time, the hair would fall off. This was never intended as a display item or a curiosity. Therefore, we can assume it has some other meaning to the boy."

"Hardly a boy," I corrected my friend. "He is now twenty. Or nearly so. His friends are no longer children either."

"And there are three of them," Holmes added. "One man on his own might find hiding his transformation challenging. Three heads put to solving one problem might produce much better results. Taking that into consideration, I now know exactly where we should go to begin our quest."

"And that is?" I asked, raising an eyebrow.

"We know that Walter ran off with his two friends. All three were in their alternative forms as wolves." Holmes held up the notecard Miss Benson had penned for him. She had neatly written the addresses of the country and city homes for Frank Donnelly and George St. Ledger. "Take this, Watson, and tell me, if you will, after reading it where would you go to hide?"

The rough texture of the card suggested an expensive stationer's stock. I scanned two names and their family homes. Of the two, Frank Donnelly's parents' abode, Greene Manor, was outside of Sunningdale, making it by far the closest domicile. As a matter of fact, I reckoned that Greene Manor was no more than twenty miles from where we were now.

"I wonder how far a wolf can travel in one day," I mused aloud.

"A horse can cover thirty miles," said Holmes. "When one thinks of the hunt, and how the horses and foxes are somewhat evenly matched in their efforts to cover ground, I would extrapolate that a wolf could go at least as far as a fox. Therefore, the outer limit of our wolf pack's travel would probably be around thirty miles."

"Then Greene Manor would be the most likely place of shelter for the boys. At the very least, Frank would know the surrounds and whatever outbuildings might serve their needs." Pulling out the railway schedule I'd thought to tuck in my pocket when leaving the flat, I ran a finger under the various routes. "If we hurry, we could catch the local train. While the route takes us out of the way, we would arrive at a station and switch over to a train bound for Berkshire. Given the gravity of the situation at hand, the sooner we get to Greene Manor, the better."

I hesitated handing the card back to Holmes. He's incredibly quick-witted, and he has trained his mind to work through scenarios at such lightning speed he claims he no longer remembers the process. For me, sussing out hidden clues still takes a more methodical effort. In this case, however, I did apply myself to the unanswered questions. The three boys had spent their formative years living in the wilderness. The Sumatrans had taught them skills that would serve them as they hid from civilisation. How best to employ those skills? The city would provide them with a multitude of hidey-holes so that the boys could change without fear of discovery. But staying in London would not make sense. Their particular skills, as wolves, were better suited to the vast out of doors. Furthermore, if spotted, they would arouse hysteria. Outside of the city, one might assume three wolves was a fanciful story told by rubes.

We were coming quickly upon the new full moon. The recent frightful experience with Ennis Caldwell should have been enough to convince the boys that they needed a confederate to lock them up. At the very least, they would need a place where they could transform into their wolf selves, act like the predatory canines they were, and not hurt anybody.

Again, that suggested that the boys needed an untamed place. Uninhabited acreage. A spot where flora and fauna would provide the three young men ample room to live out their primal instincts. A vast expanse of uninhabited forest, or lands with natural cover would suit them.

"Windsor Park," I said, returning the card to Holmes. "If I were going to change into a wolf, I would seek a vast and fertile hunting ground. It borders the Queen's land. There are pubs a-plenty snuggled up to the edges of the park. Furthermore, not just anyone can hunt there. One must register with the park ranger. Great Windsor is a place shut away from casual shooting, else anyone might find himself at the wrong end of a rifle. As for our journey, if we wish to make the local train and switch stations to arrive in Windsor, we had better hurry."

"Well, done," said Holmes, clapping me on the back. "Well done, indeed."

✠ 13 ✠

"I would wager that there's a keen sense of smell involved," Holmes said to me later as we were climbing into a growler on our way to the local train station. We'd given Gillian Benson our promise to do all we could to find her brother. "That particular scent would be important else the wolves would kill other members of their pack. I would hypothesise that Walter Benson's sister smells rather like he does. The plumeria served as an additional deterent, as did the proffered chickens. You have noticed, I am sure, that different households smell differently. That unique odour is most probably a combination of bodily habits, food, smoking habits, and access to items of personal hygiene. Clothing also can harbour or hide various smells."

Our conversation paused while I bought our tickets to London, and Holmes raced off to send a couple of telegrams. Moments later, we found two seats in the back of a quiet car. There, as if to illustrate his earlier thesis about unique odours, Holmes pulled the stuffed rat out from under his coat. Thank goodness, we were facing the back of the car! Until the moment, he withdrew the rat, Holmes had presented a rather comical figure, given that his chest was protruding grossly. He had tucked the animal's head inside his vest and shoved the entire creature down, a scheme that only worked because his knitted vest had enough give to allow the necessary accommodation. Pressing his elegant nose to the dead animal's form, Holmes now examined the dead creature from top to bottom over and over again.

I reflected on how an onlooker might respond to such a scene and decided to hide my amusement rather than share it with the world's greatest detective who was vigorously sniffing the nether regions of a dead rat. Even from my own seat, I could detect a certain robust smell, the combined scents of glue, dead meat, and wet fur.

I interjected, "We know that species have distinctive smells. Otherwise harriers would chase each other instead of chasing down foxes."

"Hence the use of red herrings to put dogs off a trail," Holmes said agreeably. "We know the scent of plumeria was important, and we can guess at the familial smell, too. Otherwise, the wolf people would, in accordance with their wolf natures, destroy their natal packs and therefore put an untimely end to their species."

This made perfect sense to me. I've never studied wolf packs, but Holmes' logic was, as always, unassailable. If the wolves could not govern their urges, the three of them would have turned on each other by now. The fact that had not happened was further proof Holmes' theory seemed sound.

"How do you propose that we find young Walter?" I asked. I was thinking out loud. "Great Windsor is a very, very large tract of land."

Holmes gave me a sly grin. "We will hunt down Walter's pack. Think on it. That royal park was founded by William the Conqueror in the eleventh century. Those who visited came to show obeisance to the King. Or they hoped to pay tribute, and took their chances they might be granted an audience. All and sundry knew to find lodgings nearby and wait for word that the King and his hunting party had enjoyed a good day. Similarly, if the hunt did not go well, the supplicants stayed behind closed doors and prayed for better results the following day. Lodgings that abut the grounds are plentiful. That is my aim: to secure rooms for us overnight. Tomorrow, in the full light of day, we can approach the family of Frank Donnelly. If they turn us away, we can at the very least, speak to the park ranger and warn him that there are creatures loose that might trespass on Her Majesty's property."

"But what if he decides to kill them? Surely, alerting him to their presence puts them at risk!"

"Not if we tell him they are precious denizens of a private zoo that have unfortunately slipped the care of their minder. I would also emphasize there is a generous award for returning them to me unharmed."

I stifled a groan. "Dreadful, but apt. Coinage is cure for many ailments."

"Sadly, that is so. We have three days until next full moon. At that precise time, the three friends might be too strong for us, and yet I feel we have no other choice but to confront them if they are not cooperative. At least if we have the park ranger's assistance, we won't be tackling this problem by ourselves. I don't know about you, but my experience capturing wild animals is sadly lacking."

"As is mine."

After climbing off the train at Paddington Station, Holmes asked me to buy several newspapers while he went to the telegraph office once again. I bought the requested newspapers and a cup of hot chocolate for each of us. With those timely errands accomplished, we hailed a growler to take us through the streets of London to our rooms on Baker Street.

As the carriage bumped along, Holmes took on that dreamy look, an outward sign he had turned inward to contemplate our next moves. With his eyes half-open and his hands totally relaxed in his lap, he could easily pass for an Indian guru rather than the world's greatest detective. Rather than disturb his quietude, I pondered the question of how we would find the boys. Even if we did meet up with them, what would we say to these three castaways? The young men had no reason to trust adults, at least not if the adults were British citizens. After all, it was adults such as us who had sent the boys away to a school that proved so horrible the boys risked life and limb to escape. Their plot had been both daring and dangerous. After all, they might have been thrown overboard by the ship's captain, and no one would have been the wiser.

They could have died when they first landed on the island. They could have angered the rajah and found themselves served up as human sacrifices to the natives' gods. Even if they had passed all of these tests, they might have died at the hands of the Dutch, either in combat or as docile prisoners. In short, when I thought of myself at their tender age, I marveled at their resilience.

How might they react when they discovered we were hunting them? Would we have better luck appealing to them as they kept their human form or should we enlist the help of a skilled gamekeeper and trap the boys as though they were the wild animals they chose to become? I was not sure which course of action would be the most fruitful.

To the best of my reckoning, it had been two nights short of a second fortnight since poor Ennis Caldwell had stared out her window at the horrifying scene that caused Walter Benson to run and hide. How much ground could three wolves cover in one evening? I imagined the answer was quite a lot. After all, first they could run in their animal forms, and once the full moon gave way to the sunrise, the young men could resume their travel in their human form. This, of course, assumed the three friends had the means to pay for any conveyance they wished. That gave me an idea. I waited until we stopped at a cross street and Holmes' eyes snapped open to share my idea.

"I believe we've missed an important opportunity," I ventured. I was unsure of how to couch my reasoning, but I was confident I needed to share my thoughts.

"How so?" asked Holmes, lifting one eyebrow.

"We have been concentrating on these boys in their alternative status, as wolves. They are not animals. Not right now. They are young men, and although Walter Benson embarrassed himself in front of his intended, the other boys, so far as we know, have managed to keep their alternate lives a secret."

Holmes turned his head towards me. "Whatever are you on about, Watson?"

"These boys never expected to have to run and hide. They had repaired to the Bensons' manor house thinking they would be incarcerated by Gillian Benson for one night only, March twenty-sixth, the full moon. Had Ennis Caldwell not seen them in their animal forms, they would have spent a leisurely week or two under the Bensons' roof. It was a cruel twist of fate that Miss Caldwell hurt her ankle so badly she was forced to remain at the Bensons' home. Her presence, the fact she saw them, is what forced them to flee. Therefore, it stands to reason that they lack proper funding. For this was a wholly unexpected adventure. I propose that we track down the banks that keep money for all three boys. Assuredly, one or two or even all three of our young men will have withdrawn funds. They'll need money to keep them fed and sheltered."

Holmes smiled at me. "Watson, I have trained you well."

"Really, Holmes. One might think I was a bumbling idiot before we met."

"No, I do not. But I do believe you were more willing to take people at their word. Now, sadly, you see the world in the same sinister terms as I do. Yes, yes, I know you saw death on the battlefield, but that was straightforward in its expression. One side openly quarreled and took action against another. Sadly, I believe that much carnage that goes on behind the curtains of polite society. Decisions are made, alliances chosen, and people are cast off to live and die as best they can." He sighed. "You have enhanced your natural mental acuity and you have learned how I approach a problem. As a matter of fact, the telegrams I sent from Paddington Station were to a friend who has access to a variety of bank records. We should soon have information regarding any withdrawals made by any member of the families of the three young men. I also believe we shall hear word from your Thomas Henry. In the meantime, I have decided my brother is mistaken."

Holmes tossed me one of the papers I'd just purchased. This particular issue was one I had not yet read, as he was well aware. Scanning the headlines, I noticed a police report on the very heinous crime we'd viewed shortly before leaving the city. The police commissioner had been sorry to announce the death of a fifth prostitute through violent assault. The commissioner went on to assure the public this death was in no way related to the murders now thought of as the

"Jack the Ripper" crimes. As a point of fact, he said there were no similarities in how the murders took place.

I let the paper fall to my lap. "Astonishing!"

"Yes, I know. They are doing their best to enact a cover-up," said Holmes. "Worst of all, I believe Mycroft is going along with this twaddle for reasons that infuriate me!"

"Such as?" I could not untangle the thread Holmes had neatly handed me tied in a bow.

"My brother knows better! He knows that this latest young woman was not a prostitute. He also has at his fingertips reports that prove her death was carried out in a manner very similar to, if not absolutely the same as, the murders of the other women in that area."

I stroked my moustache. Appearing critical of Mycroft would be the wrong strategy, yet admittedly, I wondered why Mycroft Holmes would adopt such a position, knowing it to be *prima facie* untrue. With care, I managed, "What do you suspect is his motivation for such behavior?"

Holmes threw his hands up in the air. "Advancement! He has told me privately that his immediate supervisor is a man incapable of deep thought, much less of strategic planning. For years now, Mycroft has been doing his best to clean up the messes left by Lord Hyslop, the Queen's special appointee, who has been tasked with acting as liason between Scotland Yard and Buckingham Palace."

I made understanding "tut, tut" noises. How queer it is that Mycroft Holmes adores politics and Sherlock Holmes has a deep loathing of them. Perhaps the difference is because as the older brother, Mycroft has used politics to get what he wants, whereas Holmes has succeeded on merit.

"I have told Mycroft repeatedly that if he wants this Jack the Ripper character brought to justice, he need only allow me access to the department's files. With accurate information, I could resolve this matter quickly. But, I suspect Mycroft does not want the matter concluded. Each day this drags on and another woman is killed, more pressure is put on Hyslop. Because he's the type who takes credit when something goes right, he also shucks off blame when something goes wrong. As a consequence, his underlings are afraid to move! They are, quite literally, frozen at their desks, unable to make any sort of progress."

"What is Mycroft's plan?"

"That's the crux of it. His plan is to stay hands off. His goal is to let Hyslop hoist himself by his own petard."

14

We passed a restless night in our own lodgings, as Walter Benson's journal had deeply affected both of us. By prior agreement, we left 221B Baker Street at first light the next morning and took a growler to Paddington Station. There Holmes sent telegrams one more time, whilst I purchased two coffees and a crumpet for each of us, a serviceable breakfast, albeit a light one. By ten a.m., we were in Windsor. We'd been fortunate that the trains had run on time. At this stop, a handful of telegrams awaited us. They had been so recently printed that the sharp tang of ink permeated the pages. At last, Holmes had gotten the information he'd requested from the bankers. All three boys had taken funds amounting roughly to a total of ten pounds or so per person. These withdrawals came from their respective personal accounts.

"Barely enough to pay for food and lodging for a decent length of time," Holmes observed as we stepped out of the dark train station and into the bright spring sunlight. I was still blinking and trying to adjust to the change from dim to full illumination, as Holmes strode to the kerb. There he flagged down our second growler of the day. We climbed in and immediately approved of our new ride. This cab was unusually clean and smelled as though the owner had made liberal use of lemon juice in water to wipe down the seats. It was a real treat!

My stomach rumbled in anticipation of a good luncheon. I believe Holmes might have also have felt hunger pangs because he leaned his head out the window and asked the driver to drop us at a good place to eat. The driver yelled, "The White Hart. It's not far."

"Those small bank withdrawals won't last long," Holmes continued. "Especially for three hearty young men. I'll wager they can eat up that entire amount in one or two good meals."

"Then we can assume they do not anticipate paying for lodging and food," I said. "Such a meager sum proves they won't be independently provisioning themselves. Perforce, they must have decided to seek shelter in one of their family homes until the next full moon. Given that there's a full moon every month, we have two days before they change again."

"Right, and so we'll visit those familiar locations right away, after we stop at Great Windsor."

True to his word, the driver dropped us off at the White Hart, a stucco building crisscrossed with dark wood beams accenting the creamy paint. Holmes ducked to enter the pub, else his head would have struck the ancient oak beam that ran along the front of the building and formed the lintel for the door. The publican greeted us enthusiastically, as one who truly enjoys his work, and pointed to a chalkboard where the day's specials had been painstakingly printed. Holmes chose slices of roast beef and crisply fried potatoes. I was ravenous so I selected blood sausage, an assortment of cheeses, a small loaf of bread, and a bowl of vegetable soup. A much scarred table in a back corner suited us down to the ground, so we took it and exchanged desultory chatter as we waited for our food. At that moment, the only irritant in our world was an exceedingly wobbly table. After putting up with an unsteady surface for a few minutes, Holmes begged a matchbook from the bartender and stuck it under one of the legs.

Since we were already on the premises of the White Hart, we decided the rooms at this establishment would be sufficient for our lodging needs. The fact the publican graciously promised to supply us with breakfast the next day added an irresistible incentive. After we inspected our rooms and found them to be more than adequate, we returned to the pub so we could chat. Holmes said, "I believe we can safely presume that the boys are planning to stay with one or the other of their families. Elsewise they would have withdrawn more money."

I concurred. "Unless they had funds stashed away."

"True." Holmes narrowed his eyes and tapped his index finger against his thin lips. "Hmmm. First we should visit Greene Manor. If we are lucky, all three boys will be there."

A CABMAN DROVE US TO THE VILLAGE OF ASCOT, HOME OF THE famous racetrack. Greene Manor, we quickly learned, was only five miles from the track, so we rode past sturdy trees suggesting that they had seen centuries of history. The conifers tossed down pollen as they bloomed their inconspicuous flowers. Soon the ledge of our carriage door wore a stripe of bright yellow, a colour that showed up cunningly against the black varnish. "Spring is different here," observed Holmes. "Living in the heart of London as we do, we barely note how the world awakens."

"Awakens and heeds the call to reproduce. Notice the white and pink petals on the apple trees, the small and tight blossoms on the mulberry trees, and of course, the peach-coloured bouquets on the quince bushes. There is a fresh sweetness in the air, an innocence. All are prelude to bearing fruit," I said. "I am not sure I could live so far away from London's raw, pulsating energy, but I must admit that each visit I make to the countryside reminds me why people of means keep a country manor in addition to a city house. They are like two sides of a coin, are they not?"

"Certainly if one is so inclined, they offer the best of both worlds," agreed Holmes. "Unless of course, your son becomes a wild animal and roams the planet looking for prey."

"Do you suppose the boys could have rabies?" I wondered out loud. "Perhaps we are looking for a trio of dogs that have contracted the virus. Or three young men who have it."

"Doubtful," said Holmes as he stared out his window. "In fact, I believe this country will be free of the scourge of rabies soon enough. Mycroft mentioned to me that the Home Office has done all it can to eradicate the zoogenic disease. He believes it is only a matter of time before our nation can declare itself free of the problem entirely."

At that point in our conversation, the carriage turned down a lane lined with plane trees, forming a graceful canopy. Their bowed branches parted and opened to an imposing edifice on a relatively narrow graveled driveway. The driver pulled up on the reins, and our ride was concluded.

"Pray, wait here for me," Holmes said to me. "We've given these people no advance warning of our visit. Two strange men might be more overwhelming than one."

Indeed, almost on cue, our carriage was surrounded by yapping dogs. But these were not ferocious animals. No, they were a moving symphony of King Charles Cavalier Spaniels in a variety of coat colours from a coppery red to black and even a tan-and-white. Answering the barks and yips came a harried man with a dark green cap pulled low on his head. His dark trousers were dotted with hay and bits of straw, as if he'd been rolling in a hay mow. His tweed jacket sported leather patches at the elbows, and it wore a fine coat of sawdust. "Oh!" he said when he saw us. Until then, he'd thrown himself into the business of chasing the pups with such single-mindedness that he'd totally ignored our carriage.

Holmes opened his door a slice and stepped out. "Sir? Whom do I have the pleasure of addressing?"

"And who is you?" retorted the man in the cap. "Come back 'ere, you rascal, you." This was a prelude to scooping up one of the dogs. The others danced on two feet, twirling in acrobatic circles around the man in the cap.

"My name is Sherlock Holmes. I'm a consulting detective." Holmes stuck out his hand.

"I'm Barkley. And you're what? A what? A consulting what?" The man in the cap with a dog under one arm echoed.

"A consulting detective," said Holmes. "I am brought in when people need help. Like now. I was wondering if you've seen Frank Donnelly? Or his friends, George St. Ledger, and Walter Benson?"

Barkley sneered at Holmes. "Ain't young master with you?"

Holmes wagged his head no, and tried to explain. "No, but I've been asked to find the three young men. Walter Benson's sister asked me to track him down."

The man in the cap snapped a leash on the collar of the dog he was holding and set the fine looking animal on the ground. The long silky fur undulated as the dog wriggled with joy and promptly wrapped its leash around the man's legs. "Look it here," said the man. "I'm Barkley, and I'm in charge of these dogs. They're show animals, don't you know? I ain't seen the young master or his friends since last night."

Last night! I could hear everything from my bench seat in the cab. Rather than interrupt, I listened intently because if this man had seen the three young men, perhaps our search was over!

"Did they sup with you?" asked Holmes.

"Did they eat with me?" parroted Barkley with a whoop of laughter. "Not very likely. Not at all. I takes me own meal in the kitchen. That's where I was when the three of them came in and started packing up food to take with them. Didn't even ask Moffit, the kitchen girl, to do it for them. No, sir. They used paper and oilcloth and arranged it in a canvas bag, just so."

"Did they say where they were going?" asked Holmes.

"Well, sir, they did and they didn't."

"Please clarify your statement," said Holmes. I recognised that tone. He was two ticks away from losing his temper. Holmes' impatience often tripped him up. I hoped he wouldn't let it get the better of him right now. If so, we wouldn't get the information we needed.

"They did and they didn't," the man repeated. "They said they were going out for the night, and they didn't take a carriage or a horse or nothing like that. So they didn't say exactly, but they must not have been going far."

Holmes softened his voice. "This is important. What were they wearing? Were they carrying anything besides the food?"

"Only that food I told you about. They was wearing jumpers and trousers," said the dog keeper. "Like they was going to watch a cricket game or such."

That was all Holmes was able to get out of the man. The long day had begun to wear on me, and we still had to travel back to the White Hart before we could conclude our efforts. My friend must have realised the time as well, "If they come home this evening, please send someone to contact me. I'm staying overnight at the White Hart."

Holmes reached over and tucked money in the man's pocket as a way of thanking him in advance for his help. In fact, Holmes went one better. "Let me help you, sir, with getting your dogs under control. Do you have a kennel?"

"Aye, but these are house dogs," said the man. "They never spent a night in a kennel."

Really, they were a magnificent spaniels, just lovely, all three of them. The one in the dog keeper's arms was particularly a beauty as it raised liquid brown eyes to his minder.

"Sir, if I might be so bold," started Holmes. "I would not presume to tell you your business. However, we're here in part because we're tracking a wild animal. It might even be a rabid animal, and it has destroyed livestock from nearby estates. You may wish to keep these fine creatures close at hand, lest they be attacked."

"That so?" The man shifted his weight nervously. "The lady of the house would have me for breakfast if anything happened to her little darlings. Can't say that I blame her. A more harmless pack of pups never walked the face of this earth. Can ye help me get them all leashed up?"

"Of course." Holmes' head bobbed up and down as he attempted to corral the two at our feet. I chuckled, imagining him chasing after the small but lively animals. When he had finished snapping leashes on collars, Holmes reminded the dog keeper of the danger. Thanking the man, Holmes hopped back into the carriage. His coat jacket was embroidered with stray hairs. At the level of his knees, there were a collage of small paw prints made from dust.

"My," I said. "You look a sight."

He sighed. "I know. But I have to admit, those animals were credits to their species. The idea of them being eaten turned my stomach."

There were times when Holmes managed to surprise me, to totally catch me off-guard, and this certainly was one of them.

"Again, I am drawn to Windsor Park," I said. We had returned to the White Hart so that Holmes could brush the hairs and dust off of his apparel. Also, it was nearing the supper hour, and I felt peckish.

After Holmes finished his toilette, we repaired to our original table, back in one corner. "Windsor Park is the largest open tract of land nearest to the Donnelly family," I said after we both ordered the shepherd's pie and glasses of stout. "Where else would the boys have sought shelter? No other expanse would offer them such an expansive setting for hunting down food, hiding, seeking shelter, and staying clear of the authorities. Furthermore, if they live in the manor house until they change, they can move back and forth from the house to the park easily.

"There is one other reason that a visit to Windsor might be advantageous, and that's the park ranger. He controls who hunts on the grounds, how many are in the hunting party, what kind of weapons they use, and so on," I continued, finishing a bit of the mashed potatoes from my dish. The cook was to be commended as the meal was excellent. "Such a man might be of help. I have no idea how to capture three wolves, do you?"

Holmes demurred. "No, I do not. I wonder who the current park ranger is. I shall need to send another telegram. Surely one or another of my resources can point me to the appropriate servant of the Crown."

That led me to another question as our server set down the bill. "What do you propose to say to the man? The park ranger? Hallo? Seen any packs of wolves lately?"

Squaring his shoulders, Holmes gave this well-deserved thought. "I don't believe it would be wise to be transparent regarding our purpose. The whole situation is unbelievable, even for us! And we have seen as much evidence as any two people alive except for Miss Benson and Miss Caldwell."

Holmes concluded, "I believe we must prevaricate. The best option is a white lie. Telling the park ranger that we're looking for a trio of wild dogs would work. I could ask that he notify me if he sees any such gang."

"No," I reminded him. "You'll want to say the dogs are rare and expensive purebreds, and their owner wants them back."

With that, Holmes and I paid our cheque. We headed for the staircase leading up to our rooms.

"One moment," Holmes said. He turned on his heel to go and speak to the publican. Minutes later he returned with an empty flour sack. "For the rat," he explained. "Carrying him tucked into my vest has been uncomfortable."

I yawned. "We have a long day ahead of us tomorrow. The new moon will force them to turn—and when they do, they'll be deadly."

Holmes agreed. "Their wolf instinct will drive them to hunt for prey. I hope they have confided in someone trustworthy, who will serve as their gaoler. But failing that, they will undoubtedly go on the prowl. Without someone like the redoubtable Gillian Benson to feed them, they might attack livestock..."

"Or even people," I finished for him.

"I propose we stop by the park ranger's house first thing tomorrow," Holmes said. "At the very least we should warn him."

We walked through narrow hallways to our rooms. "I'm not sure what good that will do. Surely, you won't tell the ranger to watch for a pack of wolves! He will think you are daft, Holmes! Or he'll laugh at you. Either way, he'll dismiss the suggestion that a troupe of wellborn young men could act like dangerous predators. I rather think you'll be dismissed out of hand! Think about it. You need a better plan."

Holmes leaned against a wall covered in a restrained floral wallpaper that must have faded over the years as it gave off a musty smell and one corner had peeled loose. He rubbed the bridge of his nose with one hand, holding his empty flour sack with the other. "All right. First we'll go to Great Windsor Park and speak to the park ranger. I believe it would be best to suggest that a trio of expensive purebred dogs have run away from their owners. That should serve to warn the rangers and safeguard the boys' lives."

"If the park ranger can capture the dogs, er, wolves, think how wondrous that would be!" I said. "Surely we could find a way to incarcerate them once a month, and thus allow them to live normal lives for most of their days on this earth."

"That is very bighearted of you, Watson, although I expect most would not approach this program with your innate generosity. However, you are right. Those boys did not make this choice for malicious or frivolous reasons. They chose it out of all those qualities that anyone would value in an exemplary Englishman. Courage, loyalty, self-sacrifice, and above all, duty. They should not be made to suffer, much less give up all hope of happy lives."

With that, we said goodnight and withdrew to our rooms.

15

The next morning's pleasant drive took us over small hillocks and through verdant meadows. The gentle shade of walnut and apple trees lulled me into a short after-breakfast nap. Our host had been as good as his word, waking us with trays heavily laden. The crisp toast in toast racks, the fragrant marmalade, the robust coffee and silky cream, and the rashers of bacon all went a long way towards convincing us we'd made a good decision by staying at the White Hart. When Holmes opined that he missed having a poached egg, one was promptly delivered. A miracle of culinary good fortune!

Thus we were in high spirits when we stepped into our growler and took off for Windsor Park. Holmes carefully settled the flour bag with its precious cargo on the floor.

One tends to forget how vast the Crown's holdings are until one contemplates entering a Crown Estate. Great Windsor Park sprawls over five-thousand square acres, situated as it is on the border of Surrey and Berkshire Counties. Given the herds of deer that roam the undulating hills, and the nearby lake, Virgina Water, owing to the coverts and woods dotted with ancient oak trees, the park would be ideal for a pack of wolves.

The cabman had laughed at us when we asked him to take us to

Windsor Park. "Aye, and I could spend the better part of the day driving you hither, thither, and yon. Why don't ye tell me what exactly you're after?"

Adhering to the story we'd concocted, Holmes said, "We're searching for three lost dogs. Very valuable ones, you see. Purebred harriers. They got loose from their master, and we've been hired to bring them home again."

Again the cabman laughed. This time his guffaws were even more hearty. "Dressed like you are? Oy, that's a good one, mate. But who am I? Eh, Terry Dodgeman at your service, and if ye don't mind me saying, you'll be wanting the Deputy Ranger. I'll take ye to his lodge."

Holmes and I both suffered a modicum of embarrassment at Mr. Dodgeman's chiding. The cabman was entirely correct. In no manner did we fit the mould of two men looking to retrieve runaway dogs. Blessedly, we needed only to convince the Deputy Ranger that our cause was just. Since the Deputy Ranger served HRH, in a pickle we could rely on Mycroft's name to save us. Or so I reckoned. Mr. Dodgeman's chuckles had given me a chance to reflect on how odd our travails had been. We'd started with a request for help from the family of Miss Ennis Caldwell, moved along to the family home of her fiancé, Walter Benson, and discovered such an outlandish, preposterous occurrence that I still found it unsettling. Benson and two of his friends had willingly allowed themselves to be bitten by a giant rat, and the result of that rat bite was that they transformed into wolves one night a month when the moon was full. Now we hoped to alert the gamekeeper to the possibility that these man-wolves might one day hence roam the sprawling acreage of Windsor. Astonishing!

So much depended on our ability to plead our case convincingly. The Deputy Ranger must believe that these "animals" should be captured alive at all costs. Otherwise, we were sure to see bloodshed and possibly the deaths of three young men whose only crime had been running away from a cruel schoolmaster. My fingers itched with the desire to record my impressions of all that had occurred already and was about to occur. But the cobblestone streets leading to the lodge that had served generation after generation of park rangers were far too rough to accommodate such a specific activity as writing.

We had traveled to the northwest point of the Windsor Park grounds when the cabman turned towards a pastel pink stucco house set among mature trees. A white picket gate was attached to two pink stanchions. Frothing banks of flowering azaleas and rhododendrons in shades of red, pink, and white capped deep green bushes. Graceful magnolia trees, their limbs laden with white flowers, welcomed us.

"Ye should see it in the fall when the trees turn," said our driver. "Makes your heart swell with joy, it does."

Holmes did not answer. The cabman was happy enough to wait for us, as we didn't think our visit would take very long. Wisely, Holmes left the flour bag in the growler.

When the front door opened, we found ourselves in the midst of a frantic gathering. The shy little housemaid bade us wait in the foyer after explaining, "He is awful busy right now. Ye couldn't have come at a worse time, I tell you."

"It is a matter of great importance," Holmes said gravely. "We have come all the way from London."

She scurried off, her stiff black skirt swaying as her feet raced through the house. From our place near the door, we heard urgent muffled words uttered by several masculine voices. One bellowed loud enough for us to hear, "Carnage! When I discover who or what did this—"

His shout was interrupted. Loud footfalls approached and a brute of a man hurried towards us. His face was darkened by hours out of doors, and his hair resembled the quills of a hedgehog with the way it stood on end. His icy blue eyes were cold with the sort of anger that is lethal. Although he wore a tweed jacket with patched elbows, he was attired suitably for walking in the park.

"How can I help you, gents?" he asked in a manner that brooked no nonsense.

Holmes introduced himself and me to Edwin Sullivan, Deputy Park Ranger. "We came on a most urgent mission. I've been hired to retrieve three purebred dogs that have gone missing, animals of enormous value."

Mr. Sullivan's face knotted up like a tangled piece of string. "Excuse me? With all due respect, I'm dealing with a crisis here on the Queen's land and you want me to chase down someone's lost pets?"

"Not exactly," replied Holmes. "As I said, these dogs are extremely valuable, and we have reason to believe they were headed this way. They must be captured alive at all costs."

Sullivan's mouth sagged open. His ruddy face reddened even more and a fleck of spittle flew from his mouth as he said, "Really? See here, I have more important things to do than chase after some rich bloke's dogs. If you're so all fired up about getting them back safe, I suggest you go walk-about our five thousand acres and call for your puppies. I've got five dead deer, shredded to bits, and the Queen is going to have my head on a silver platter—and you want me to waste my time running foolish errands—"

I groaned. "Were they gutted? Eaten from the inside out?"

"How would you know?" Sullivan used his finger to poke me in the chest. "Unless you're the culprit who done it!"

Holmes' look of confusion caught Sullivan's attention. Turning to me, the detective said, "Impossible! Truly impossible! But tonight is a full moon!"

"Ha!" laughed Sullivan. "I don't know what you're on about, but the moon was full last night. Now go on, get out of my sight."

"Come along, Watson," said Holmes. "There's no more we can do here."

"Take us to Windsor Castle," said Holmes, as we hopped back into the growler.

"Yes, sir!" said the cabman. The mournful expressions on our faces must have alerted him to the wisdom of holding his tongue. I couldn't even look at Holmes, due to the immense embarrassment I felt. How could we have gotten the day of the full moon wrong? I shook my head.

A thought came to me: When we had first met and become flatmates, I was doing my best to figure out exactly who Sherlock Holmes was. I made a list of his strong points and his weak ones, as well. I recalled now how he knew nothing of astronomy, and how when I told him that the Earth revolved around the Sun, he had said, "Good. Now I shall do my best to forget it." He'd gone on to say that he wasn't going to clutter up his head with unnecessary information.

Holmes must have remembered the same conversation because he glared at me. "If you dare to point out that I was eager to forget that the Earth revolves around the Sun and other extraneous information, I shall toss you out of this cab straight away."

I burst out laughing. "And you said it was useless information!"

"It was!" he protested. "At the time, it was! The only answer to this miscalculation is that the occurrence of full moons is *not* strictly thirty days apart, and there is a slight variation that hews closely to, but is not exactly, one calendar month."

This failure on our part was all too humiliating! To think that while we were chatting and enjoying our servings of shepherd's pie, we could have found those boys, rounded them up, and made safe their futures was too appalling to consider. With a shake of my head, I tried to clear my mind. Briefly, I entertained the impulse to question Holmes as to why we were heading to Windsor Castle, of all places, but in the end I could not muster the wherewithal to query him.

A little later, we drove through the Henry VIII Gateway and into the Lower Ward. Drawing up to St. George's Chapel with its imposing masonry walls in their Gothic design, the cabman stopped. "Can't go further. Ye have to walk past the chapel and around to the other side. The library's back there."

The pleasant weather, the birdsong, and the memory of the floral display in the park went a long way towards soothing our sour moods. I had no idea what Holmes planned, or why a visit here was in order, but I chose not to ask him to state his purpose. Instead, I strolled along at his side. Once we were directly across from the chapel, I glanced up at the towering edifice. Oh, the history it had seen! I took this opportunity to soak in all of this magnificence.

Whilst Holmes ducked into the library, I waited outside. He came out with a scrap of paper in hand. "To the train station," he yelled at the driver as he threw himself into the cab. "Twenty-nine and a half days," he grumbled. "That's the time between each full moon. Not an exact thirty as we had assumed. So we were led astray. I now have in my possession the entire full moon schedule for the past year up until this coming January."

With a disgusted look on his face, he jammed the paper into his coat pocket.

"What do you propose to do?" I asked.

"Do? Do! Do I look like a man who traipses around searching for lost pets? That is what I am reduced to, Watson. I have never ever taken on a case of a missing person who was simply missing because he roamed the countryside in the guise of a wild animal! What am I? A dogcatcher?"

Our cabman dropped us off at the train station. We arrived in time to catch the next locomotive back to London's Paddington Station. Neither Holmes nor I felt like talking. We did not even discuss visiting the home of Frank Donnelly. There wasn't much use. Our chances of capturing them in their animal form were slim. The boys might have returned to Greene Manor or might not. They could very well have moved on since their wild encounter last night.

I thought Holmes was giving up rather too easily, but short of rounding up a cadre of hunters on horseback at the next full moon, what options did he have? As for tracking down the young men, clearly they had repaired to one or the other of the family homes. Otherwise, they would have withdrawn more funds. Approaching them now seemed foolhardy. They had recently slaked their hunger, and they had no reason to trust us. None.

The sum and total of the situation was that there seemed to be no intelligent way forward. None at all.

I chose to keep my counsel. When Holmes was ready to ask for my opinion, I would give it. We didn't speak of the day's news until late that night after our supper at 221B Baker Street. Holmes had lit his pipe and I was enjoying a glass of sherry. The stuffed rat had been given a place of prominence on top of the bureau in Holmes' room. When I learned of the rat's new home, I suggested that the creature remain shrouded with the flour bag lest the maid see it and fall over in a faint. Holmes paid no attention to my worries. Instead, he said, "I have decided what to do. I shall send a note to Miss Caldwell and suggest that she write to Walter Benson, care of the Donnellys and the St. Ledgers. It occurs to me that I have only two ways of baiting these wild young men. I can use either Ennis Caldwell or Gillian Benson."

My quick intake of breath signaled my horror. "Bait? Holmes, listen to yourself! Have you gone mad?"

"No," he said calmly, packing tobacco into his clay pipe. "I am, as always, in complete control of my faculties. I am also approaching this problem with sterling logic. In their animal forms, the three men could be captured by hunters willing to set traps. Although goodness knows if they have any traps that would catch the wolves humanely. I doubt that. Therefore, the best method would be to encourage the young men to return to their families or to the authorities and ask to be incarcerated. Only those two young women seem to have any sway over Walter Benson. He seems to be the only one of the three young men who still maintains a strong tie to another person. Or persons. Perhaps one or the other of the young women can persuade him that she still cares for him. I doubt that my cajoling him will work nearly so well."

I shrugged. "That's only a partial solution. He'll still need to decide what to do with himself on those nights he turns into a beast."

"And that is not my concern," Holmes said stiffly. I did not respond, and he moderated his words. "Do you think a woman such as Miss Caldwell could love a man under such circumstances? What are the limits of love? Is it even fair for him to ask her to be his wife?"

As a matter of fact, I'd been giving that question a lot of thought and I had a ready answer. "I have known men who are beasts to their wives every day of the month, Holmes. As a young doctor in the first year of my practice, I shadowed an older fellow, Mr. McMurray. He opened my eyes to the ways a man can beat a woman and yet not leave a mark on her. He also informed me of the quiet pain a woman can feel when her husband ignores her most tender emotions. I can say to you with great assurance that one night of shape shifting a month is a small price to pay if both parties acknowledge what is happening and how to cope with it."

16

The next morning, the papers were full of another attack by Jack the Ripper. Although the body had only just been found, the coroner thought she might have been killed one or two days ago. Otherwise, the sad details of her demise matched those of the other victims. That is, the poor young miss had suffered numerous indignities to her body. She'd been found by a rag man, setting out for a day of digging through trash bins hoping for a scrap of cloth. The poor fellow suspected he would have nightmares for the rest of his life, or so he said when *The Times* reporter interviewed him. Lestrade had been on the scene long enough to give a statement to the reporter. "We don't have any leads yet. We'd be most grateful to anyone who can shed any light."

Angered by what he read, Holmes got up from his breakfast and stomped around the room. "Why won't Mycroft allow me to pursue this case? It is, without a doubt, the most vicious and singular set of crimes that will go down in history. For decades to come, criminologists will talk about Jack the Ripper, and yet here I am, the foremost consulting detective in the world—and my own brother won't let me work on this debauchery!" he growled, as he paced like a caged animal. "What must I do to convince Mycroft to let me help?"

"The answer is simple," I said, as I spread nectarine jam on my toast.

"Tell me! If you are so fortunate and so shrewd as to have an answer to my conundrum, what evil impulse encourages you to keep such information to yourself?" Holmes said.

"The answer is," and I paused for dramatic effect, "you can do nothing. Nothing! Not one thing, Holmes. Unless you are invited to the party, you cannot take a turn on the dance floor. You know as well as I do that I am right. Anything less than a fine friend would fill your head with lies and promises and schemes. But I am telling you the truth and you know it. Now find some other puzzle to occupy that prodigious brain of yours." I finished my last bite of toast and washed it down with tea. "Following up on our conversation of the night before, what do you plan to tell Caldwell and his daughter?"

We formulated a plan. Holmes would write to Colonel Caldwell and his daughter to say we were still investigating the matter, but that we were sure Walter Benson was alive. Holmes would add that as soon as we had permission from the Benson family, we would share more. Next, he would write to Gillian Benson and tell her what we suspected had happened at Windsor Park. Although we could not say with absolute positivity that her brother had been involved, there surely were more than enough reasons to convince us that Walter and his friends were behind the savage attack on the Queen's deer.

"I shall also ask Miss Benson how she wants me to proceed, especially in regard to the inquiries from Miss Caldwell. I cannot honestly say I found Walter, of course, but Barkley saw him and therefore, I am fairly certain he is safe. I know that all three of the young men withdrew meager funds from the Bank of London. On the basis of that, I can with some degree of accuracy assume that they have decided to stay together as a group and probably sought lodging at one or the other of their own homes. After I tend to whatever is happening here in London, I could go back to Brookhaven Manor and try to speak to young Walter, providing he is there. If they have moved on, surely they would have gone up to Birmingham where St. Ledger's family lives."

He sighed. "All in all, this is turning out to be a boring missing person case."

"How can you say that?" I shot back at him. "Have you ever heard the like? A man is missing because he turns into a wolf once a month? Really, Holmes. Don't you plan to immediately go back to Brookhaven Manor and track the young man down?" To me, it sounded as if Holmes had given up very early on.

"I see no sense in it. If I had a letter from Miss Benson, I could pass it along to her brother. His sister's tender love might bring him home, but short of capturing him and caging him, I can't imagine a way I can persuade him, do you?"

No, as a matter of fact, I didn't, and I was rather tired of arguing with myself. I could only see one way out, and that was for the three men to entrust themselves to Gillian Benson. The trio had been through so much, and they'd done it without the guidance of fatherly love. In point of fact, one could argue that so-called fatherly love was what had dragged Walter Benson away from the bosom of his family in the first place.

I nodded. "I have turned this over and over in my head and I believe you are right, Holmes. It might be best for Gillian Benson to do that instead of sending you on a wild goose chase as a hapless, empty-handed courier. Gillian would take good care of her brother and his friends. She's seen all three of them at their worst, and still feels great love for her brother. I believe she's the best person to persuade Walter and his friends to consider what lies ahead. Perhaps if she sits down with the young men, they can work out what to do next."

Our conversation ended there because a messenger arrived with a note for me. It was from Thomas Henry Knopf. He wondered if I were back in town, and whether I had made any progress regarding his strange patient at Bethlehem Hospital. Also, he wanted me to know that Mr. Wren had been found, wandering the streets of London in a terribly disheveled and unhygienic state.

"Dash it all," I said, putting the note aside. "I'd completely put the matter of Mr. Wren out of my mind. He's back at Bethlehem. Isn't that curious? Thomas Henry says he was found wandering the streets yet again. He thinks I should come and see Mr. Wren."

"I wonder," said Holmes, acting as if he hadn't heard me, "what Mr. Flower would think of the giant Sumatran rat? Do you think we could share a cab and make a short diversion? We can go from the British Museum to the Bethlehem Hospital. From there we could go to the Diogenes Club and I could pen letters to both Miss Caldwell and Miss Benson."

17

Of course, I indulged Holmes and allowed him his detour. In actuality, I was not terribly keen on going back to the Bethlehem Hospital even though I was curious about Mr. Wren. The sense of obligation I owed Thomas Henry Knopf, as one army medic to another, was wearing rather thin. I shivered and tried to put my nasty errand out of my mind when we were deposited in front of the British Museum.

Holmes and I hurried up the broad expanse of stairs and into the building. My friend was bringing along his flour bag. The bulging shape suggested the sack was once again home to that strange rat we'd found in Walter Benson's room. All in all, it was nearly four feet long, if you counted from the tip of its tail. The greyish-brown fur was decidedly more plush than that of any rodent I had seen before, and since one daily sees a dead rat or mouse on the streets of London, I knew the difference in the pelts.

"Really, Holmes," I said with a touch of impatience. The shape of the flour bag gave away what he was carrying. "How long must you drag that grotesque souvenir around?"

"At least until I get a few answers," he replied. Now that we were moving towards a goal, Holmes was congenial once again. "Specifically, I want Flower to tell me if he has ever seen the like."

"Do you plan to tell him about the castaway boys and their adventure?" We were midway down a hall. My innocent question caused Holmes to freeze in place.

"Watson, you are brilliant. If ever a man might know more about this strange tale, Flower would be the one, for sure. If nothing else, he might even be able to propose a cure for the malady."

I scoffed at that. "You put too much faith in the man, Holmes. He may be a genius but he is not a miracle worker, and that is precisely what a problem like this would take. Also, there are ethical issues to consider. Is it remiss of you to share the secrets we've learned?"

"I was tasked with bringing Walter Benson home," said Holmes. "Mr. Flower is a man of high reputation. If I do not turn to him for help, then I shall have missed an opportunity to complete my job."

"I thought you were giving up!" I said in frustration.

He gave me that sly smile of his. "Only for that moment. Thinking of Flower has given me a new purpose."

We asked a docent to point the way to Flower's office. He did and escorted us to our destination. In the small reception area outside the glass-paned door, we heard raised voices. "Never! That is not what an institution such as the British Museum is for! No, no, no! You will not turn this place into a weapon! I forbid you! Now if you have no more threats to lob my way, good day to you!"

Holmes and I stepped to one side to let Lord Reginald Hyslop, the Secretary of Defense and the Queen's chosen liaison between Scotland Yard and the military, hurry past us. Hyslop was obviously stinging from the refusal he'd been dealt by Flower, because the Secretary did not even take notice of our presence. His eyes were narrowly focused straight ahead.

"Well, well, well," said Holmes. "Didn't we just see him at Mycroft's office? Not that long ago?"

"Yes, indeed. For a man charged with protecting the Realm, Hyslop seems to be quite the gadfly, doesn't he?" I stared at the man's retreating back. Not for all the gold in the Queen's Jewels would I want his job. The memories of my fallen brothers-in-arms haunted me nearly every night. To think of sending young men off to die sent a chill through me.

"Holmes! Watson!" Flower's cheerful voice expressed his pleasure at finding us waiting outside of his office. "Richards, thank you for bringing me these welcome guests."

"My pleasure, sir," said Richards. His voice surprised me because he was obviously a lot younger than I had first thought. I chided myself for not paying more attention to the man when we'd first encountered him. I was sure that Holmes knew every secret of Richards' life, down to his shoe size.

"Come in, come in, and make yourselves comfortable," said Flower. But that proved nigh unto impossible given the accumulation of papers, pamphlets, books, and general clutter. After surveying the messy landscape, Holmes and I simultaneously decided to remain standing.

"This won't take but a minute," said Holmes. "I brought something with me. I was hoping you could identify it."

I opened my mouth to protest, as we already knew what the dead creature was, but I quickly reconsidered as Holmes went on to spin a yarn. "A friend asked us if we had any idea what it is. I believe his grandfather is a sea captain, and this is a family treasure he picked up on his voyages." With that, Holmes drew the rat out of the bag.

"I say!" Flower crowed with delight. "I've never seen the like! Oh, bravo, Holmes! I shall be very busy indeed trying to identify this wee fellow. May I keep him?"

"Only for a fortnight or so," said Holmes. "Sad to say, I have to return him to his owner. He is rather cunning, is he not?"

"Indeed, he is," said Flower, as he picked up the dead rat and cradled it as lovingly as any father ever held a newborn baby. "Indeed, he is."

"Then you know nothing about this...creature?" Holmes raised his eyebrows.

"Not a thing," said Flower with great gusto. "However, I am keen to make its acquaintance."

Outside the British Museum, Holmes hailed a cab for the Diogenes Club and proposed that we have our lunch there. I couldn't argue with his choice. When we climbed in, he shouted the club name to the driver in a loud voice.

We'd only gone a few blocks when he turned and stared out the window. "Still with us," he said with satisfaction.

"What do you mean?" I asked.

"We've been followed since London. A man is tailing us even now."

"That's absurd!"

"Not really. Remember when we last exited from the Diogenes Club? He came with us."

"And you never said anything?'

Holmes shrugged. "What was there to say?"

"You might have warned me!"

"Come now, Watson. He's only following us. He's not doing any harm."

I fumed, but Holmes ignored my anger. He said, "This visit was yet another dead end. I could see no reason to burden Flower with details of my assignment because he knew nothing about the rat."

I nodded absentmindedly. I was disappointed in Flower's response as well. I understood the man's respect for scientific method, but I regretted the fact he would not engage in speculation of any kind. In fact, I'd found his obstinance rather irritating. All in all, this day was not turning out as I had hoped. Holmes seemed to have given up on finding Walter Benson. He was turning the problem over to Benson's sister. Flower had nothing to tell us about the giant rat. We were being followed. Thomas Henry was still having problems with Mr. Wren.

Suddenly, I decided I would much rather be back in Windsor Park enjoying the floral displays. Then again, a nice meal at the Diogenes Club would provide a small bright spot in what would be an otherwise depressing day. We arrived at the kerb, and I noted with interest how the growler following us came to an abrupt stop as well, even though no one got out of it.

"Hmmm," Holmes muttered to himself as we climbed out. "The man assigned to follow us isn't sure what to do. Good."

Once inside the club, Holmes beckoned one of the clerks. "Euston? You keep back copies of *The Times*, do you not?"

"Indeed, sir. Up to one year, we have them," said Euston with a bored expression. Then again, the members of the Diogenes Club favor anonymity and silence over any external show of enthusiasm.

Holmes shoved a scrap of paper into Euston's hands. "I want that back. Please bring me the issues for these dates, as well as the day before and after. Dr. Watson and I shall be in the dining room." With that, Holmes stalked off for the dining room with me following on his heels. Briefly, I considered asking Holmes what that errand was all about, but in the end I decided the smell of roasting chicken was more intriguing than a stack of mouldy old newspapers. Holmes took his time selecting tomatoes in aspic, haricot vert, crispy potatoes, and the roast chicken. I had never eaten anything in aspic, so I said, "I'll have the same, please."

We were sipping glasses of wine when Euston appeared. Or more precisely, a stack of newspapers with a pair of legs in perfectly creased trousers appeared. I say this because the papers towered even with Euston's eyebrows. Using his foot, the man pulled out an unoccupied chair and unceremoniously dumped the papers into it.

"Watson, I need your help," Holmes said. "We shall divide the stack of papers. I want both of us to go through our own half and peruse them."

I signaled the waiter for a refill of my glass of wine. "What are we looking for, Holmes?"

"Any anomalies. Odd deaths. Reports of people dying. Crime reports from Scotland Yard. Even announcements by outstanding politicians. For the days in front of you only, all right?" Holmes' eyes fairly glistened as he grew excited with the possibilities. He pushed his well-worn scrap of paper my way. I yawned. "Very well."

The decision was made to use my notebook as a repository of our findings. We committed to writing down the date, persons involved, type of behavior, and so on. Also, Holmes asked that I record where all of the interesting circumstances occurred.

This chore kept us busy until our meals were ready. The aspic came, wobbly and shiny. It was savoury beef stock with a few sad tomatoes enshrined inside it. The taste was regrettable. I wouldn't recommend it, but Holmes liked his so I gave him mine. The rest of the meal was superb. Both Holmes and I tucked in, savouring every morsel.

Once our hunger was diminished, we scanned newspapers whilst sipping cups of tea. Indeed, we were hard at it for quite some time. Our waiter came back several times, and he wore a grimace suggesting he heartily wished we would finish our messy business and move on. But we did not hurry. Systematically, we ploughed this fertile field. When we were finished, Holmes grabbed up the paper from my notebook. Using his index finger as a marker, he quickly read down the list of remarks. "Perfection," he said, as he tucked it into his pocket.

As Holmes signed for our expenses, we stood and started for the door. Our exit was blocked as a contingent of important-acting men came down the hallway. Their heads were tilted towards each other so they could share confidences. So involved in their conversation were they that they paid no heed to the fact Holmes and I were blocked by their progress, which was exceedingly slow as they talked in low tones, going back and forth with great solemnity.

One of the men glanced away from the other to get his bearings. It was Hyslop, and the man he was with was some sort of naval captain, judging by his uniform. The blue double-breasted tailcoat with eight gold buttons was worn with blue trousers with gold lace down the side. Medals were pinned to the man's chest.

Holmes mused to himself, "I wonder what Hyslop is up to and who he is with? Surely, he's recently come from seeing Mycroft. Elsewise, he wouldn't be here."

"Do you want to go and visit your brother?" I asked. At last we were out in the hall and that option presented itself.

Holmes seemed to marshal his thoughts. At last, he said, "No. But I still need to write some correspondence. In fact, it's more important than ever. I'll summon one of the staff members and request writing materials."

So he did. We were admitted into a quiet room, one with a desk, a sitting chair, and a selection of books. From time to time, members needed to work out particularly troublesome assignments, and thus a few rooms were so appointed for men needing quiet spots where they could pen a report or a response. Holmes rested his fists on his hips. "Look around, Watson. These walls have witnessed the creation of laws, treaties, and the like. Is it not marvelous?"

"Yes, I suppose so," I said. Picking a book of Shakespeare off the shelves, I made myself comfortable in one of the armchairs. In fact, I was so entirely comfortable that I dozed off. When I awakened, Holmes was sealing three individual envelopes. "There now. All done. I shall leave these with the club manager at the front desk with strict instructions to put them into the post. Come, Watson. Let us see what secrets Bethlehem Hospital will reveal to us."

ONCE WE WERE IN THE CAB AND HEADING TOWARDS BETHLEHEM Hospital, I asked, "What did you learn from the newspapers?"

Holmes' smile was thin. "I prefer to keep my thoughts to myself for the time being. A theory is in its infancy, and if I tap on that thin protective eggshell too soon, the chick won't hatch."

I found this totally unsatisfactory and said as much. Holmes replied, "Be that as it may, it will have to do for now." Waving his hands in front of his face as if arranging imaginary puzzle pieces in the air, Holmes added, "A picture is forming. Pray allow it the time it needs to become clearer. Tell me, what does your friend Thomas Henry say about his time in Her Majesty's service? Does he look back on it and feel a sense of valour?"

My brow creased. I couldn't hide my confusion. "What on earth leads you to ask that, Holmes? Thomas Henry is, like all of us who served, eager to put that period behind him."

"Yes, yes," Holmes said with irritation. Waving away my response with one hand, he continued, "But, as an example, you came back from Afghanistan wounded, yet filled with a sense of Crown and Country. One never hears you complain about your treatment by your commanding officers."

"There is a reason for that," I said. My voice thickened with emotion. "So many young soldiers died in my care. Some were hopeless cases. Others could have gone either way, but in the end, they lacked the strength or the will to pull through. A few were more dead than alive after they were patched up and sent home. How could I see all that and not count myself as a lucky man?"

The cab pulled to a stop at the front of Bethlehem Hospital. As we stepped out, our driver sped away as quickly as possible, not waiting for the cab doors to be shut. Holmes shook his head in dismay at this rude behavior, but I understood the driver's reluctance. "I don't blame him, Holmes. If I had a choice, I would still be in the cab with him, heading back to Baker Street. This building was intended to provide solace and it projects an air of menace."

Holmes ignored my remark. Slowly he raised his eyes to the height of the towering walls. As the guard waved us through the gates, I shuddered involuntarily. We could hear water running off the walls of a tunnel in front of us. It rushed into the iron grate on the ground. The way forward involved passing through these thick walls with their cloying dampness. When once we again stepped into the open, we stared up at the decaying stone structure that housed the insane and cast us into darkness. Iron bars gleamed against the windows like long grinning metal teeth in ghastly mouths. The effect was disturbing.

Holmes stared at the building with his mouth set firmly, as though reaching a conclusion and committing to it. His eyes narrowed. His entire body tensed with coiled energy. I followed my friend down the long curving drive that meandered the length of the towering building. A bleak cupola stared down on us, like a bird of prey ready to snatch us up. We passed the six enormous Ionic columns, and I felt the weight of our venture bear down on us. Holmes moved swiftly up the stone stairs, hesitating only when he stood before the main entrance of the hospital. The heavy wooden doors dwarfed my friend. Then he raised his fist and, unless I am mistaken, he paused before banging on the heavy doors repeatedly. Surely, he was thinking of the misery that waited on the other side of that barrier!

An orderly opened the door to us. He was a rough sort of fellow, as most of them seemed to be. His jacket had once been white, I assume. The stains of dried blood, food, and dirt along with the gray sheen of general grime rendered the garment a distinct mushroom-coloured hue that was both distasteful and unsanitary. In addition, his general demeanor was that of irritation at our arrival.

The orderly brusquely asked our names. His was Philpot. When I introduced myself and Sherlock Holmes, Philpot's eyes flickered with recognition and his mouth turned even more sullen. My credentials have long been established, and I am listed on the roster of visiting physicians. For that I was thankful, because I fear that any pause for reflection would have been injurious to our plans. I explained we'd arrived to talk to Dr. Knopf, and Philpot's face closed up. Rather than wave us through, the man physically blocked our path to Thomas Henry's office.

"He's busy," the Philpot said, exposing shards of teeth. "Dr. Knopf told me specific, not to let folks in. He said to tell everyone and anyone that he's got his hands full and come back some other time."

Holmes stepped forward. His hand slipped into his pocket and when he withdrew it, I caught sight of a gold coin. So did Philpot. "That is all right," said Holmes with an air of congeniality. "But in truth, we didn't really come to see Dr. Knopf. We heard an old friend is here. We promised his wife that we'd check on him."

Holmes held the coin between his thumb and fingers in order to flash the gold at the man standing between us and admission to the hospital. "In fact, Dr. Watson knows exactly where his patient is being held. We don't need to bother Dr. Knopf. No one needs to know we are here. We won't bother you one whit, Philpot."

The orderly's eyes were riveted to the coin. The pink tip of his tongue slithered out to lick his lips. Going from the coin to Holmes' expectant face and then back to the coin again, Philpot took all of this in.

"Seeing as how you won't be bothering Dr. Knopf none," he began. "I don't rightly see the harm."

Holmes rotated his hand so that the coin was resting flat on his palm. Philpot snatched it in the wink of an eye. "Go on with you."

Before the man could change his mind, I led us through corridors glistening with moisture and mould on the crumbling walls. Although my knowledge of the building was not extensive, after my first visit I had sketched the floorplan as a map for my own use. Since then, I have done my best to fill it in as I learn my way around. In truth, vast areas of my sketch were unlabeled, but others I had marked with, "Tile flooring changes here," and "Cell marked #67 at the corner." As we climbed down slippery steps, the air became foul and musty with the smell of unwashed bodies, rotting food, and full slop buckets. Even without the map to hand, the memory of my sketch served my purpose.

As always, I tried not to show distaste. Eventually, my senses would adjust and the odour would be less objectionable. That was the only way one could stomach this place: adjusting to the foul conditions and blocking them out. I admonished myself to ignore the howls of pain, the pleading, and the general moaning that swelled to a crescendo the deeper we went into the asylum. Harking back to my military training, I kept my eyes straight ahead, focused and alert. My shoulders wanted to curl inwards, to protect me from my surroundings, but I forced myself to pin them back and hold my head high. I did not dare to glance over at Holmes to see how the ambience of this dismal place affected him. I simply kept moving forward towards our goal.

Holmes whispered to me, "Watson, I have been thinking about that strange patient, Mr. Wren. And about Thomas Henry. As you know, I don't trust your old friend. I believe he is covering something up, and it's clearly something going on here at the hospital. I have a plan. Once we're inside Thomas Henry's office, I will have a seizure. Not a real one. Just enough of one to make Thomas Henry a believer. Play your part by making sure that Thomas Henry knows that I have suffered from seizures in the past. I'll see to the rest."

I turned to stare at him. "Toward what purpose?"

"To stay overnight," he answered.

"Heavens no!" I grabbed my friend by the arm and managed a stage whisper: "On what basis did you construct this folly? Did you bump your head in the carriage? Whatever it is that you have against poor Thomas Henry, let it drop. The adventure of the past few days has fired your imagination and somehow Thomas Henry has gotten under your skin, but now you've gone too far. Come along. Let's turn around. Let me see you home. Once we are back at Baker Street—"

But he tore his arm out of my hand. "Not a chance, Watson. There is mischief happening here. Of that I am sure."

"Yes, of course there is! You could scarcely have a building filled chock-a-block with the insane and not have mischief. That's the nature of that particular beast. But if you think this is worth endangering your life, you are in dire need of a sedative, Holmes. Trust me. I only came here today because I owe it to a fellow soldier to answer his cry for help. Thomas Henry wanted me to check on Mr. Wren and so I shall."

"That is exactly what I am doing!" said Holmes in a tone of exasperation. "Can't you see? This poor Mr. Wren has run away twice. We know nothing of his past, except he must have had a seafaring life at one point, and yet he is being held here against his wishes. Many a vagrant in the same situation would welcome a solitary cell, a warm blanket, a hot meal, and a roof over his head. But not this one. Tell me, what is that man's story? And how can I trust a liar like Thomas Henry Knopf to care for an indigent like that?"

"That's hardly enough to warrant a night among London's most disturbed citizens!"

"I have a hunch!" Holmes said.

Holmes' protest left me with an open mouth and a look of shock on my face, I am sure. "Less than two hours ago, you talked about sending important letters out to Miss Caldwell and to Miss Benson. Then you wanted to get Flower to examine that poor dead rat. Next, you demanded to go to the Diogenes Club and peruse old newspapers. There you wrote letters to three people, not two. Now you say we must visit Thomas Henry, a man you've decided is a liar! Oh, and you are determined to spend the night in an insane asylum! And for what earthly purpose? Holmes, what are you playing at? A hunch? Since when did you traffic in supposition?"

This brought a change to my friend's face. He had gone from impassioned to angry in a flash. "What is a hunch, Watson? Use your head! A hunch happens when the mind takes in unformed, uncategorized information and attempts to give it meaning before this protean matter can be properly recognised for its true nature! All my faculties, so well-trained and keen, are telling me there is a problem here, it concerns Mr. Wren, and that I must see this problem with my own eyes to tackle it. Now, if you are through chattering like a chipmunk, I suggest we go on in."

Each step weighed terribly on my heart. It was broad daylight outside, but dark and damp in here, giving the building a foul scent made more pungent by a variety of sour body odours. I tried not to engage the hollowed out eyes set in the pitiful faces we passed as they stared out at us from behind locked cells. The more comfortable rooms for civilized patients were on the floors above us. These at the lower levels were those poor souls who had abandoned all hope. I did not want to know their stories. Jesus said that the poor would always be with us, but was it necessary for them to suffer so? Could we not find a way to help them?

Twice I opened my mouth to speak to Holmes, but I shook my head because I could not find the right words. I could guess at Holmes' intention and it chilled me to my marrow.

I paused when we arrived at Mr. Wren's cell. As before, the man was huddled in the farthest corner, as distant from the door as he possibly could get. A first glance might suggest the cell was empty. The straw and hay were fresh, a dirty blanket was heaped and crumpled in one corner. Holmes made quick work of the lock with his set of picks. A test of the hinges proved they would protest with a loud squeal, so Holmes spat on them, starting at the top and working his way down. Once his saliva had lubricated the mechanisms, he confidently swung the door open.

We both squatted next to that pile of blankets, and for the briefest of seconds, I feared we'd been tricked and Mr. Wren had been moved. But he was there, as we learned when a bony foot stuck out from the folds of the disgusting woven wool. Holmes reached out and gently tapped a bony protrusion at the top of the pile. I assumed it was the jut of a shoulder.

Nothing happened. As a matter of fact, the stillness was eerie. Was Mr. Wren dead? That was a frequent occurrence here in Bethlehem: the denizens, having no more reason to live, simply slipped the mortal grasp of this forlorn hell on earth. But Holmes is nothing if not persistent. He reached out and took Mr. Wren by the shoulder. He shook the man lightly, and Mr. Wren's head poked up from the mess of fabric. His eyes tried to pry themselves open. On closer examination, I could see the crust that had dried, forming a sickly yellow-green shiny matter that glued the eyes shut.

"Wait here," I said. Sprinting down the hall, I ran to one of the faucets built into a nook in the stucco wall. Turning it on, I soaked my clean cotton handkerchief in the flow of water. Wringing it out lightly, I took it back to Mr. Wren's cell. Very gently, I pressed the wet cloth to his eyes. The cool water had a reviving effect on the man. The moisture loosened the matter that had gummed his eyelids shut, and I gently wiped it away. Slowly he unpeeled the lids and opened his eyes to stare at us. I folded the handkerchief over and used the clean portion to wipe off Mr. Wren's skin. In the sallow light of the cell, I got a good look at him for the first time. "My word!" I said. "He's not jaundiced. He's Asian!"

"Exactly," Holmes said.

"Help me," Mr. Wren said, as he grabbed me by the hand. The man's fetid stench nearly overpowered me. My nose began to twitch in revolt brought on by the smell. Mr. Wren's grip was more intense than I would have suspected. He wouldn't let go of me. "I beg you, sirs. Help me."

"We are here to do exactly that," said Holmes. "You have my word." He'd been watching my ministrations with the sort of attention a doting father gives his newborn baby.

But Holmes didn't get to keep that promise because we heard voices at the end of the hallway.

18

Holmes whispered to Mr. Wren, "Stay strong. Say nothing. I shall come back for you. You have my word."

Mr. Wren nodded.

Holmes and I hurried out of the cell. He pulled the barred door shut behind us. By taking off his coat, he was able to wrap the lock mechanism and deafen the sound of it as it clicked behind us. Holmes' eyes flashed angrily, as he gazed around at the daunting edifice. "I never knew," he lamented, as we took off down the hall, running the way we'd come, away from the advancing voices, moving as fast as we could go. With my map in my head, I retraced our path and rather than climbing the stairs to and pausing at the ground floor, we ascended the floors to the level of Thomas Henry's office.

Holmes grabbed me by the shoulders and stared into my eyes. "I must spend the night here," he said. "Please come for me at nine, but if that fails, I'll be on the rooftop at eleven. All is arranged."

"What!" I spat out. "Details! I need details."

"No," said Holmes. "Any more information and my plan will not work."

Under my breath, I whispered such curses as I had learned in Afghanistan.

Holmes understood the gist of what I was saying.

We were now close enough to hear voices coming from Thomas Henry's office. They seemed to suggest we would be interrupting some sort of meeting. No less than three voices spoke, other than Thomas Henry's.

"Countless lives..."

"Her Majesty will be pleased..."

"Small sacrifices. Superior fighting forces..."

"Rewarded for your service and your contribution..."

Holmes grabbed me by the shoulders and whispered, "Remember, everything depends on you."

"You cannot be serious, Holmes!" I whispered.

"If all else fails," he said, retaining a grip on my sleeve, "I'll be on the roof."

I pushed him away. "What a load of rubbish! You'll do no such thing. You'll walk out the way you came in."

"The roof," he repeated.

Without warning, Holmes hurried through the outer room and threw open the door to Thomas Henry's office. If I had not followed him, my friend would have walked in without me! I hurried along behind the great Sherlock Holmes.

⁂ 19 ⁂

Thomas Henry was seated behind his desk and handing over a sheaf of papers. In his left hand, there rested an onyx fountain pen. The man across from Thomas Henry was none other than Lord Hyslop, and next to him was the naval captain we'd seen at the Diogenes Club. Thomas Henry and his guests looked astonished to see Holmes and me. Lord Hyslop did a double-take and then practically bounced to his feet. "Sherlock! I saw your brother earlier today. How are you, my lad?" But his *joie de vivre* was forced, and I wondered if his exuberance was a cover-up. If so, for what?

"Very well, sir."

"Keeping busy?" Lord Hyslop crossed his arms over his chest and spread his legs wide, assuming a posture that would have looked more appropriate on the deck of a naval vessel. All he lacked was a spyglass.

"Yes, sir."

"Still running all over and doing...what? Sniffing around for other people?"

Holmes bristled. Before he could respond, Lord Hyslop said, "But then, you are a second son. Mycroft is making your father proud, I daresay."

It was a remark calculated to wound deeply.

Turning to me, Hyslop said, "As for you, John Watson, your reputation precedes you as well. A failed soldier. Damaged on the battlefield, and now on the dole."

I swallowed hard as his words found their mark.

Rarely has one man done so much damage to others without aid of a lethal weapon. Bile rose in my throat. I hated taking a pension. It diminished and demoralized me. Of the two pains, my wound and my pride, taking the money was more acute. To deal with my own discomfort, I turned my attention to Holmes.

Whilst it is true that Sherlock Holmes has taken an untraditional path, I feel it my duty to point out that if not for the untraditional amongst us, man would never move forward in any arena. True, the untried path presents a singular challenge, as it is always fresh and each hurdle is a surprise. Then should we not celebrate those who part ways with the expected and who forge new pathways so that all of us can benefit? I think so.

This whole time, the naval captain observed everything, staring first at Holmes and then at me. My body tensed, waiting for the officer to do something. But what?

"I'm off," he said suddenly, as he leapt out of the wooden seat. Pushing past me without benefit of introduction, the naval captain left the room. Hyslop, for a split-second, looked bewildered. Then he recovered.

"Good day," said Hyslop, tucking his tricorn against his chest and making a courtly bow. Then Hyslop was gone, too.

Holmes' brow furrowed as it does when he is deep in thought.

As a trained observer and a medical man, I forced myself to take a mental step back and review the situation. Hyslop had been doing all that he could to make us tuck tail and run. Why? What was his game? There was something sinister happening here, something even more evil than I had previously suspected. Holmes had sensed it, too. And I could not wait to be shed of this place.

At that very moment, a piercing scream tore through the walls. The ghastly sound penetrated our very bones. Holmes leapt backwards, falling against the door in terror. He banged his head against the solid surface with a resounding thud as he slid to the floor.

"Holmes!" I cried, as I managed to latch onto Holmes' lapels and hoist him to his feet. But keeping my own balance was a struggle because Holmes is taller than I, and we weigh about the same.

Thomas Henry bolted from his desk and aided me by wrapping an arm around Holmes' waist. I changed my grip to support Holmes under his shoulders. With effort, Thomas Henry and I led the detective to the small horsehair sofa and had him lie down. Holmes' eyes fluttered up into his head and his breathing became rapid and shallow. Spittle formed at the corners of his mouth, as his body thrashed about violently!

"It is a seizure!" I shouted, in alarm.

"No more! No more!" Holmes bellowed, clawing at some unseen monsters.

"Hold him down!" Thomas Henry ordered. "I'll get my kit and a sedative!"

I struggled to subdue my friend, trying to keep him still and quiet. Immediately after Thomas Henry left the room, Holmes went perfectly still. His eyes returned to their normal position as he offered me a broad wink. "Excellent, Watson," he whispered. "I'm fine; just follow my lead and recommend my staying here for the night. Mention that this isn't my first attack." His words were hurried, as he endeavored to give me instructions before Thomas Henry's return.

I whispered, "Holmes, stop this! Let's end this charade! I've had enough of these people!" My own heart was pounding, and my nerves were rattled.

"Not now, Watson," Holmes said in a tone so low that I had to strain to hear him. "Listen closely. Do not let Thomas Henry give me a sedative. Make any excuse you have to. Do you understand? I must stay the night! Come 'round tomorrow morning for me at nine—and if I'm not available, you must come again at eleven. I'll meet you on the rooftop. Now, play along. Tell Thomas Henry that I have had these bouts before. Everything hinges on your acting ability, old friend! Do not forget me, Watson. Eleven o'clock on the roof, precisely!"

I nodded, wondering what scheme was running through his mind. Footsteps rang out in the hallway.

"He's coming!" Holmes whispered. Again, he took on the symptoms of a delirium-induced seizure.

Thomas Henry hurried into the room. In one hand, he held a syringe. When he leaned close to inject Holmes with the sedative, I used my arm as a barrier. Keeping Thomas Henry away from Holmes, I explained, "There will be no need for that, Thomas Henry. I'm acquainted with these spells Holmes has. All he needs is a little peace and quiet."

At the sound of my voice, Holmes started to calm and closed his eyes. With a low sigh, he pretended to drift away.

"What happened?" Thomas Henry asked. He still held the needle in one hand.

"I'm not sure," I replied, shaking my head. "But he's experienced these before. Ever since our last case together... I'm afraid propriety forbids my furthering any of the facts of the crime, but I can assure you, it was most violent. As you can plainly see, the nature of the inquiry made a powerful impression on Holmes."

Thomas Henry nodded. Though he looked eager for me to continue, I felt it necessary to put an end to the conversation before our ruse was found out. "Thomas Henry, I would not wish this place on any man, let alone my friend, Sherlock Holmes, but I'm without options. I dare not risk another seizure in the cab back to Baker Street. Do you think it possible that he stay the night? Not in the ward, of course, but perhaps here in your office?"

"Of course, John, but I do wish that you would let me examine him." Thomas Henry still held the syringe. His expression said he believed me, but his posture suggested he needed convincing.

Holmes' body tensed at Thomas Henry's suggestion. I hurriedly intervened. "That will not be necessary," I protested, as evenly as possible. "As I've told you, I am well acquainted with these attacks and all he needs is rest. An exam would be a waste of your valuable time. Furthermore, Holmes would be angry with me for allowing you to examine him without his prior consent. He is a very private man."

"Very well," Thomas Henry replied, stiffly, "I shall do as you ask, but I do not have to like it. What happens should he awaken and not find anyone here?"

This I had not considered. To be fair, I'd not had the chance to concern myself with such trivialities. I hesitated and Thomas Henry looked at me curiously as he waited for an answer.

Any further protestations on my part might cause the good doctor to grow suspicious. I quickly formulated a plan—one which would rely heavily on my ability to master the art of deception and sleight of hand. "Hmm, you do have a point," I responded to Thomas Henry. "To play it safe, perhaps a sedative will be necessary. Give me the needle and a cotton swab, please."

Ever so slightly, Holmes' body tensed. I hoped that my gentleness and matter-of-fact manner would disarm both the detective and my old colleague. Thomas Henry handed me the syringe.

I stared down at it. "Where's the cotton? I must sterilize the area. Holmes is susceptible to many maladies. I do not want an infection from this place to be one of them."

Thomas Henry walked to a small table and removed a cotton ball from the alcohol jar. The sharp fumes from the jar hit me hard. This was real. Holmes was pretending, but this was real. Handing the soaked cotton to me, Thomas Henry leaned over me until he practically set his weight against my back.

"Roll up his sleeve, will you?" I asked. I had to distract Thomas Henry.

The doctor did as instructed and thus gave me room to move. I snapped my fingers against the cylinder to release any air bubbles. I swabbed Holmes' exposed skin with the alcohol and held the cotton in place, pressing it against the detective's vein. I could feel Holmes' pulse rising, as I brought the needle down so that the pointed tip indented the flesh, but he lay perfectly still. His trust in me was implicit. "This is for your own good, Holmes," I said quietly. Changing my position, I blocked Thomas Henry's view as I pressed the cotton swab against the fabric of my trousers and squeezed out as much of the alcohol as I could. Then I pretended to wipe Holmes' skin with the cotton. I pressed the sharp tip of the needle against his flesh and felt the small give, as the point penetrated the flesh. But immediately—I covered the tip with the cotton and withdrew the needle from the skin. Only then did I depress the plunger. Liquid squirted out and was immediately absorbed by the cotton. When the syringe was empty, I dabbed at the small droplet of blood on Holmes' arm and tossed the cotton away. I glanced up at Thomas Henry and smiled. He gave me a nod of approval. As far as the doctor was concerned, he had witnessed my administering a potent sedative to Sherlock Holmes.

Holmes, now aware of my subterfuge, reacted properly to the injection. He did not stir. The ruse had worked just as I had planned.

Proud of the trick I'd pulled, I folded Holmes' arms across his chest. Thomas Henry retrieved a woolen blanket from a supply cabinet outside of the antechamber and covered my dear friend. I didn't like playing Thomas Henry for a fool, but I was sure that Holmes had his reasons.

"I don't think he'll be any trouble, Thomas Henry. We'd best let Holmes rest undisturbed." I rose from the sofa and ushered Thomas Henry out of the room. Mechanically, the doctor locked the door and placed the key in his vest pocket. At first, I was alarmed; then I found myself chuckling. The very idea of locking Holmes in a room! Why, to Holmes, a lock was child's play!

"What amuses you so, John?"

Caught off guard, I stumbled for an answer. "Oh, it's nothing. I was just imagining Holmes' reaction when he learns that he spent the night in Bedlam."

Thomas Henry spun me 'round, angrily. "I fail to see the humour, John! And we do not appreciate the name Bedlam. Many strange things have happened here as of late, and I wouldn't want something untoward to happen to either of you."

I reeled back. *Was that a threat?*

The doctor's face flushed, and then Thomas Henry said something that troubled me further. "Make no mistake. What we do here has value! What we are learning from the soldiers we treat will help us protect our Nation! No more sending helpless young men into battle!"

His hand flew up and covered his mouth. His eyes were wide. "I am sorry. I've been under a lot of stress."

I realised that I had seen a side of Thomas Henry that I was not meant to see. This incident with Holmes and my apparent amusement had caused Thomas Henry to drop all pretense. His zealotry unnerved me. A chill swept through me. I was leaving behind my good friend! As cunning as Holmes was, would he be up to the task of survival in this horrible place? I worried about the detective's safety. Warring impulses battled inside me. Blast Holmes and his dangerous ideas! How could I leave him behind in this hell hole?

Suddenly, I was about to call off the whole affair and was prepared to tear the door from its hinges, if necessary, to free my friend! But before I could enact my new wishes, Thomas Henry slowly shook off his outburst, the way a dog flings off water after a bath.

"Forgive me," he said.

Feeling chastised and embarrassed at my own feeble attempt to recover from my mental lapse, I was still troubled. Something was horribly wrong with my old colleague. Thomas Henry had another agenda. An agenda that mattered to him personally. Before I could probe his thinking, he smiled sheepishly and repeated himself. "Forgive my foolishness. It's this place. It gets to everyone. You know it does. You've felt its oppression, too."

Yes, of that he was certain, and I was, too.

Thomas Henry led me to a consultation room down the hall. This place was empty except for a desk and two straight-backed chairs. Taking one of them and dragging it behind the desk, I waited while Thomas Henry grabbed his own chair and turned it around to face me. For what seemed like a long time, he searched my face as if looking for any signs of betrayal. I prayed there was none.

My supplication must have been heard because Thomas Henry seemed mollified. With that unpleasantness behind us, we spoke for some time on the matter of Mr. Wren. According to my friend, Mr. Wren was nearly dead when they found him. Thomas Henry's voice changed in pitch, growing higher and more nasal. He had trouble keeping his hands still as he talked. He said, "I can't imagine why Mr. Wren keeps running away. As far as we know, he has no family. I believe he has lost blood, which is exceedingly odd, because how or why is beyond me. But enough of that, tell me about your friend Holmes. Has he overextended himself?"

The abrupt change of topic made me leery.

"No more than usual," I said. "Holmes is Holmes."

But Thomas Henry continued to ask probing questions. "Has he worked on any taxing cases lately? I know you have been out of town. Where exactly did you go? What were you doing? How is this brother of his, Mycroft? I've heard he is a government employee. What does he do? Where did you travel to and when did you get back?"

He kept firing questions at me. My instinct told me that Thomas Henry's queries were no longer innocent. I did my best to fob them off, but he had become an aggressive inquisitor. I resorted to short answers: "No, yes, the country, looking at flowers, visiting old friends, Mycroft is fine, he's a bureaucrat, we came home yesterday."

At first, I hoped that it was my imagination and I was being overly sensitive, but as he continued to probe with evermore pointed questions, I came to distrust his interest. Soon I would not be able to fend off his prying inquiries. Desperate for a way to retreat, I feigned drowsiness. At length I made my excuses for ending our conversation by yawning rudely—in Thomas Henry's face!

"I say," I began, "you must excuse me, Thomas Henry. Holmes and I were up until the wee hours. I was getting caught up on my correspondence. He was reading newspapers. We both lost track of the time. Please forgive me, but I believe I need to go home and crawl into bed."

Thomas Henry's glare told me that he was discomforted by my attempt to end our talk. However, he must have recognised that he was rousing my suspicions by continuing to press me about Holmes.

After my apology, Thomas Henry quickly recovered and resumed the polite and professional manner he'd cultivated. "Let me find a hansom for you, old friend," he said. Rising from his chair, he opened the office door. I heard him tell an orderly to flag down a carriage. Thank goodness, Philpot was nowhere to be seen. I didn't know how I'd explain being here with Thomas Henry when Holmes and I had promised not to disturb the doctor.

I told Thomas Henry I'd call to see how Holmes was on the morrow.

At that, Thomas Henry grew guarded. "Do you not trust me? Are you concerned about your friend's well-being under my care? Really, Watson—"

"See here. Holmes and I are flatmates. Of course, I will ask about him on the morrow. I would do the same if it were you in his place," and with that, I managed to calm Thomas Henry down.

As the orderly walked me to the front entrance of the asylum, I realized I had not been pretending my fatigue. Despite the nap I'd had at the Diogenes Club, I was bone-tired and grateful, whilst at the same time apprehensive about leaving Bethlehem. As I stepped into the cab, I stared back at the monstrous edifice where my dear friend, the world's greatest detective, would be spending the night. My journey back to Baker Street seemed to take forever as I worried over my friend's safety. Arriving home, I changed into my nightshirt and on a whim, grabbed my revolver. I dragged an armchair from the parlor over to my bedroom window and gratefully plopped down into it. I rested my arms on the sill and peered into the night. Of course, I could not see the asylum from my post. However, being there and staring out at the general direction somehow gave me comfort. Oddly, I felt closer to Holmes than if he'd been in his own room.

The dark, brooding facades of the buildings before me could hide a thousand villains, but on this night, as I scoured the lifeless street below, nothing moved. The mantel clock chimed at the quarter hour, and my eyes grew heavier. Feeling the comfortable weight of my revolver in my lap, I dozed into a fitful sleep.

I awoke with a start when my pistol fell to the floor. My breath had condensed moisture on the window and the pane it had fogged over. Glancing at my watch, I saw the time to be half past seven. I groaned at my own discomfort. My bones were stiff and creaking from the unaccustomed position. There is a good reason one does not usually sleep all night in a chair. Nonetheless, I groggily rose and returned the chair to its usual place in the parlour.

There was a persistent, gnawing sensation of impending doom, as I waited for Mrs. Hudson to bring up breakfast and the morning papers. I tried to dispel these unwanted and unwarranted emotions, but to no avail. Impatiently, I paced the floor and worried about Holmes. My aimless wanderings through the rooms of our apartment created enough of a stir for Mrs. Hudson to know that I was awake, and it wasn't long before her gentle knock brought the invigorating aromas of steaming coffee and rolls into the apartment. I thanked her for her promptness and poured myself a cup of coffee. I set *The Times* off to one side.

Knowing that my disheveled appearance worried her, I escorted the landlady to the door. My abrupt manner offered her no explanation or comfort, and I was left to munch on a roll and browse the paper in peace. Thankfully, that good woman is accustomed to her tenants acting oddly!

20

Lestrade rapped upon the door a few minutes later. It was nearly eight. I suspected he'd timed his visit to concur with when Mrs. Hudson served our first meal of the day. "Where's Holmes?" he asked, before sliding into the chair my flatmate normally used.

"Why do you ask?" I said guardedly.

"He sent me this," Lestrade tossed an envelope on the table. It nearly missed the marmalade. I took that as a hint. Sliding the toast rack within his reach, I said, "Help yourself. I'll ring for tea. Or would you prefer coffee?"

"Good old English tea will do me fine," said Lestrade, as he grabbed a piece of toast and slathered it with Mrs. Hudson's excellent nectarine marmalade. I rang for Mrs. Hudson and asked for more tea, toast, and marmalade. Then I settled back down and opened the envelope. In Holmes' scrawl it said:

Dear Lestrade,

I know who Jack the Ripper is. Come to 221B Baker tomorrow morning around eight. Watson will instruct you further.

S. Holmes

"Is this some sort of joke?" Lestrade's rodent-like face reminded me of the Giant Sumatran Rat. I wondered what Flower was making of that trophy. Jerking myself back to the matter at hand, I answered, "I have no earthly idea."

"Then I'll ask you again. Where is Mr. Holmes? I don't have time for his games," said Lestrade. But his attempt to sound menacing was seriously eroded by the smear of marmalade gleaming from his moustache.

"He is at the Bethlehem Hospital, or at least, that is where I left him late yesterday afternoon, and where I plan to meet him at nine this morning. Care to join me?" I genteelly dabbed at my own whiskers to make sure I wasn't wearing marmalade as well.

"Ha! I always said he was mad!" Lestrade chortled with glee. "Let me finish my tea. You going to eat the other half of that toast? What do you suppose he's on about, regarding those women as was savaged by the Ripper?"

In all candour, I could maintain my ignorance.

"How'd he wind up in Bedlam?" Lestrade asked after we'd climbed into a hansom. His tone was almost idle, as if he didn't much care one way or the other, and he really did not think the admission to such a place to be out of character for Holmes.

"He had a hunch," I said. The closer our carriage came to the hospital, the more I worried. Holmes had been there overnight. I had seen the torturous cures enacted on patients in the name of science. None of them had the slightest bit of merit. Would Thomas Henry stoop so low so as to subject Holmes to such barbarity? I shivered.

"You all right?" Lestrade asked. His tiny eyes studied me. "Holmes is there at the asylum as a consultant, isn't he? You don't mean to tell me—"

"Yes and no," I admitted. It seemed best that Lestrade be aware that drastic measures might be needed.

"Yes and no?!" Lestrade fairly shouted. "What are you on about, Dr. Watson? Holmes is a strange one, that's for sure, but I wouldn't send my worst enemy to that place. No way! It's horrifying. Do you mean to tell me that Mr. Holmes isn't walking freely about the place?"

I nodded. "To be honest, I cannot vouch for whether he's free to do as he wishes or—"

"Upon my word! And I thought you were his friend! Whatever possessed you to allow him to be—" and fortunately, Lestrade's tirade was abruptly ended because our cab had pulled up outside of Bethlehem Hospital. Lestrade ordered the driver to wait for us.

I would be remiss if I didn't admit that during our short ride, with Lestrade babbling on and on, my mood had darkened considerably. As we hurried to the front entrance, Lestrade kept peppering me with questions I could not answer. An attendant led us to the administrative area, where a woman behind a desk inquired as to the purpose of our visit. Typically, the orderlies greet me and let me do as I am wont. However, this woman considered herself some sort of gatekeeper. As I struggled to explain our mission, she stared at me coldly. In her severe dress and haughty manner, the woman provoked my immediate dislike. I was none too gallant with my reply to her demand for our credentials. "My good woman, I am Dr. John H. Watson, and this is Inspector Lestrade of Scotland Yard. We are here to retrieve Mr. Sherlock Holmes, who was an overnight visitor of Dr. Thomas Henry Knopf. Now, if you would be so kind as to inform Mr. Holmes and the doctor that we are here, we shall let you get on with your business."

The mentioning of Sherlock Holmes' name caused the woman to have a curious reaction. The colour drained from her face. Her dark hair contrasted to her newly acquired pallor, and the dull grey of her gown did nothing to compliment her complexion. I stared at her hawklike nose and thin lips. Her hands trembled. Her mouth hung open most unattractively as she proceeded to examine her papers. (I assumed she was in search of Holmes' name on a list.)

"I'm sorry, sir," she said at length, "but I have no record of a Sherlock Holmes as a patient here."

"A patient? What?" Lestrade shouted.

I interceded. "I said nothing at all referring to Sherlock Holmes as a patient! He was a guest of Dr. Thomas Henry Knopf!" My voice rose with frustration as my words echoed off the walls.

Lestrade stepped in front of me. Flashing his badge, he confronted the woman. "Now listen here. I'm Inspector Lestrade of Scotland Yard!

Either you produce Mr. Holmes or contact someone who will. It makes no never mind to me. We'll set the matter straight, with or without your cooperation. Which will it be?"

"Inspector," she replied coldly, "you may threaten me all you like, but I can assure you that Mr. Holmes is not on the grounds. It's against the policy of the hospital to allow visitors overnight. And, as far as Dr. Knopf is concerned, he's been called away on urgent business. In fact, I was informed that he left sometime late yesterday after making his rounds. Therefore, it is impossible that he spoke with Mr. Holmes last evening! Now, unless you have a warrant to search these premises, I will bid you both a good day."

She tapped her papers to order them and turned her back on us. With purposeful efficiency, she opened a ledger and copied down numbers. Her slender fingers moved at an astonishing pace.

"B-b-but..." I stammered.

"You better come along with me, Dr. Watson," said Lestrade, grabbing my sleeve and ushering me out the door. "If this is another wild goose chase cooked up by you and Mr. Holmes to make me look a fool, I can assure you that it will not sit so well with my superiors."

He hustled me back out the front entrance of the hospital.

"To the Yard!" Lestrade shouted at the driver sitting in the carriage, as we climbed in.

The door had only just closed when I whirled on the policeman. "Lestrade, I tell you, Holmes is in there. I left him there in Dr. Knopf's office last night. He's probably in grave danger!"

"Tut, tut, doctor. Holmes is probably back at your flat, laughing—laughing, I might add, at my great expense."

"Lestrade, you are a fool!" I spat out the words. My fears for Holmes were compounded by my bitter regret for the disposition of Mr. Wren. If Holmes had been found out, if Thomas Henry had sussed out Holmes' curiosity about Mr. Wren, who could say what might have happened to that poor Asian wretch?

Lestrade demanded that we travel to Scotland Yard so we hailed yet another cab and made the trip without any further conversation. Lestrade can be a spiteful buffoon—for no sooner had we arrived at the entrance of the Yard when he flung open the door and pushed me out of the carriage. He followed me, practically leaping to the ground. With a rap, he signaled the cabman to drive on. "I'm sure you can find your own way home, doctor," said Lestrade. "If there's nothing else..."

"Wait!" I yelled, as I grabbed Lestrade by the arm. "You cannot walk away from this situation. This is no joking matter. I'm telling you that Holmes saw this coming. Lestrade, give me the courtesy of explaining our case."

"This better be good," said the angry inspector. "Let's go inside so we can talk."

IN SHORT ORDER WE WERE IN THAT CLOSET THAT LESTRADE CALLS his office. I told the inspector about Mr. Wren. "Thomas Henry keeps saying the man has disappeared, and then Mr. Wren is rediscovered. Each time I see the poor wretch, he's in worse shape. Why, I don't even believe he's a citizen! I wonder if he's being held here against his will."

"What do you mean?" asked Lestrade. He sat behind the most extraordinarily messy desk I have ever seen in my life. As a matter of fact, his teacup rested on a stack of papers with headers blaring: "Official! Eyes Only!" But Lestrade used those reports as doilies. I could not believe his cavalier attitude towards his documents, which I suspected might mean justice or incarceration, life or death, poverty or inheritance, to goodness knew how many citizens. But that was a matter for another day.

"Mr. Wren is Asian. He's spent time on a ship out on the ocean. He certainly does not present himself like a citizen of the realm." I paused to organize a coherent argument and found my logic sadly lacking. "You see, none of this makes any sense. Thomas Henry specifically asked me to come and consult with him regarding this man, Mr. Wren. Holmes spotted the fallacy that Thomas Henry told us. When Holmes pressed Thomas Henry, he—Thomas Henry, not Holmes—all but ran off like a frightened bunny rabbit. Yet, Thomas Henry turned around and asked me to come back and examine Mr. Wren after the man was returned to Bedlam. And yesterday, Holmes did as he often does. He ingested great heaps of information, racing through newspapers, and thinking in that faraway manner of his, and then he said that he wanted to test a theory."

Lestrade was trying to follow my meandering thoughts, but I was not making it easy. In truth, I was also confused.

"Lestrade, Holmes suspected he would not be released. Now, why would that be? Unless there is some sort of nefarious plot in action, why didn't Thomas Henry simply send Holmes back to his flat, like any other doctor might after a patient had been successfully treated for a seizure?"

"Maybe Holmes is sicker than you think," said Lestrade.

"Even so, wouldn't Thomas Henry let me know? Wouldn't he call on Sherlock Holmes' brother, Mycroft?" I sat straight up in my chair. "That's it, Lestrade. We must go to Mycroft. He'll know what's happened."

Seeing that Lestrade wasn't completely convinced that I'd landed on a productive course of action, I supplemented my plea by explaining, "There are two men who keep showing up, over and over, on the outskirts of our lives. Almost as if they are following us or we are following them. Of course, we aren't following them. At least, not by design, but these coincidences merit inquiries as to whether they're pursuing the same line of thinking that Holmes is."

Lestrade's hands flew up in the air. "I have no idea what you're on about, Dr. Watson. You aren't making sense."

I knew that I wasn't. Just as Holmes had explained earlier, I was putting together pieces of a puzzle. Right now, I had little to go on, but a few of the pieces had snapped into place.

"Come with me to speak to Mycroft Holmes. Do that, and I shan't bother you again, Inspector."

When Lestrade hesitated, I added, "If Holmes really did find out who Jack the Ripper is, don't you want to be there to claim credit for his discovery?"

Lestrade turned an unappealing shade of crimson. "That wouldn't be right."

"Oh, ho, but it is. Remember, Holmes sent you a note. He wants you to have the credit. Think what this will do for your standing in Scotland Yard."

That was enough to pry a reluctant Lestrade away from the comforts of his messy desk and out into the streets where we hailed another growler.

At the Diogenes Club, I explained to the manager my mission to see Mycroft Holmes. "And this is Inspector Lestrade from Scotland Yard. He wants to see Mycroft Holmes, too."

"Ha," said the club manager. "Too bad you didn't show up ten minutes ago."

"Did we miss Mycroft?" I asked.

"No, sir. But Mr. Holmes personally sent a note to you, saying not to bother him. Could have saved yourself a trip." With a wave of his hand, the manager indicated the roster, the book all members and visitors must sign and state their purpose upon entering. I'd already scribbled my name, but Lestrade was too in awe of our surroundings. He stood there in the foyer like a dumbstruck young lad seeing his first girl. "Glory be," he murmured. "I never."

With the tip of my finger, I pushed the roster book his way. "You need to sign in. Everyone must."

As Lestrade was taking his time, and writing very precisely on the right-hand page, I noticed on the left that Hyslop and Percival had come and gone, beating us here by a half an hour or so. That confirmed...what? That their efforts somehow overlapped the circles that Sherlock Holmes and I were twisted in?

Despite the alleged message for me to go away, I led Lestrade to Mycroft's office. The elder Holmes brother glared at me as I rapped once and entered. One of his minions tried to hold me back, but Mycroft could see from the look on my face that I was not to be trifled with. As a matter of fact, my trusty revolver was tucked into my pocket. One way or the other I was going to get Sherlock Holmes out of that asylum.

"Yes?" Mycroft rocked back in his chair and steepled his fingers together.

"Your brother is being held captive in the Bethlehem Hospital. As his nearest kin, it is up to you to sign him out," I said. "And by the way, this is Inspector Lestrade of Scotland Yard."

I suspected Mycroft knew Lestrade, but I wasn't taking any chances.

Lestrade was doing his utmost to appear unimpressed by his surroundings, but the dozens of men typing, filing, and working at desks down here could not help but be overwhelming. This was our shadow government. And this place was as much of a function of the running of our Nation as Parliament or the Queen's Red Boxes. Instinctively, Lestrade knew that. I didn't need to insult the man's intelligence by saying as much.

"No." Mycroft stared at me.

"Excuse me?"

"No. I shall not petition for Sherlock's release. Not at this moment." Mycroft's smile was sly and I saw a hint of his brother in it, but unlike Sherlock's sly smile, which is born out of his quick wit, in Mycroft's expression there was a hint of dissembling.

I nearly flew across the desk, and I would have done, if Lestrade had not grabbed me by the arm and held me back.

"You would leave your brother there? In that madhouse? Among those poor demented souls?"

"For the time being, yes." Mycroft seemed exceedingly pleased with himself.

I shook with rage. "You cannot be serious, Mycroft Holmes. What sort of brother are you?"

"Right now, the greater good is served by leaving my brother where he is." Mycroft tilted his head as if studying me. "Surely, as a military man who was willing to sacrifice his life for his Country, you share the same love for our Nation."

"How dare you compare my life as a soldier with what's happening to your brother! He sent you a message. He must have asked for your help!"

Mycroft picked up a crumpled ball from the top of his trash. "Indeed, he did. And I sent a message to you saying you should not bother me. I told you that I shall help him. But not right now."

Lestrade pulled on my arm, trying to remove me from Mycroft's presence. My rage was so severe that all I saw was a blinding flash of red. Even in the heat of battle, I've rarely felt such loathing, and certainly not such anger. If I could have, I would have ripped Mycroft Holmes' head right off of his body.

❦

Out on the street, Lestrade sighed. "I never. Do you have brothers?"

Without waiting for me to answer, he went on. "I do. There's six of us. Three boys and three girls. There's nothing I wouldn't do for my kin. Nothing. Even though I've taken an oath to serve the Queen, I say that family comes first. What a queer doing this is. To think that Sherlock Holmes can't depend on his own brother. Who would have guessed it?"

"Well, Sherlock Holmes can depend on me." I stepped out into the street and waved down a hansom. "He predicted this might happen. His final words to me were that if I couldn't see him at nine, I was to come back and he'd be on the roof at eleven."

"The roof?" Lestrade opened the door of the carriage for me. "What on earth? That makes no sense."

We were both inside the carriage when I said, "The roof makes no sense to you. Not to me either, but Holmes must have a plan. It's not like him to be whimsical, especially in matters this important. I was there when he told Mr. Wren to stay strong and that he would get the man out of Bethlehem. I watched as he sent three letters. One to you, one to Mycroft, and I do not know who received the third, but I'd wager that his missives set a plan in motion."

Lestrade stuck out his lower lip. "All right. I can always tell my guv I was chasing down a lead regarding the Ripper. I'm with you, Dr. Watson. What do you propose we do?"

"I guess we stand outside of Bethlehem Hospital and wait for a sign," I said. "Holmes did not ask me to storm the gates, and he knows I would have, if he'd asked. He did not ask me to force Mycroft's hand, and he could have. Nor did he ask me to sneak into the building and get him out. All of those were possibilities. He didn't ask you to do any of that either, right?"

"Right." Lestrade nodded thoughtfully. "What sort of sign do you suppose he'll send?"

"I do not know. All I know is that I shall be on the outside of the hospital, watchful and hopeful. When the sign comes, I shall do whatever is required of me to help my friend. As for you, I should think you'll do the same because the chance exists that Holmes can help you capture the Ripper."

"Indeed," said Lestrade. "Count me in."

21

So we found ourselves standing awkwardly on the kerb, directly across from the Bethlehem Hospital. The cabman asked if we wanted him to wait. I pulled my timepiece out of the watch-pocket of my vest. It was nearly eleven o'clock.

"Please do," I said. If Holmes was as good as his word, and I expected no less from him, then when he escaped, he would be bringing Mr. Wren with him. Even if Holmes was able to stand around and wait for a carriage, I had no idea what sort of shape Mr. Wren would be in. Better to be prepared.

Lestrade leaned against the trunk of a plane tree. "Funny, I never thought about someone going inside that place voluntarily."

With a shiver, I said, "Believe me, no one would. Holmes felt it was all-important. I cannot help but think he was onto some dastardly plot or he would have never proposed such a perilous—"

But I didn't get to finish my thought because a crescent of blue was rising behind the hospital. At first, I didn't understand what I was seeing. I blinked and squinted. I stared.

"Look it! One of those hot air balloons!" said Lestrade. His index finger was pointing straight ahead of us like the nose on a fine hunting dog. As I followed the digit's direction, the crescent grew. Such a marvelous sight! The silk balloon itself had been dyed a brilliant blue, like the bluebells that bloom in an English woodland. As it rose slowly, majestically, I could make out lines of rope that ran from the top down the side and then...

The balloon rose a little more and the woven rattan gondola came into view. The gold of the basket contrasted with the brilliant blue and the milder, gentler blue of the clear skies behind the contraption. Dots of white clouds formed a perfect backdrop. A whooshing sound accompanied a flame, and a spike of blue fire roared upwards and towards the mouth of the balloon, heating the air in such a way to send the whole airship higher.

By now a small crowd had gathered. Children who had been playing hopscotch had run back to their houses to call to their mothers. Women in their aprons came out to stare at the blue globe as it grew and grew and drifted closer and closer to the hospital. That's when I saw them, Holmes and a slight figure, who was bent over and shuffling. My friend was on the roof of the hospital, and I could tell by the way he moved that he was shepherding Mr. Wren along, but to what purpose? Shading my eyes with one hand, I squinted up at them. The sun was at their backs, making it terribly difficult to see. But Lestrade spotted what I had missed.

"Look! There's a ladder! It's trailing!" He pointed to a rope ladder hanging down off the gondola. The pliable sides bent and swayed as the balloon continued its ascent. I remembered what S.A. André had explained during his lecture at the Diogenes Club.

"There are different currents at differing altitudes," I said, repeating what I'd heard from the Swedish explorer. "By adjusting the blasts of hot air, and leveraging the height of the balloon, the pilot can move north or south, east or west, once he finds the right air current."

"That balloon can't go very far," observed Lestrade.

"Why not?"

"It's tethered. See? There's a rope connecting it to something behind the hospital building. It's keeping the balloon from sailing off and away. And look it! See up there? You suppose that's Holmes?" He pointed at the two huddled figures. One of the two looked like he was leaping towards that dangling rope ladder.

"Yes, yes, I'm sure it is!" But to myself, I thought, *Holmes, I don't know whether you are a genius or an idiot.* How was he going to hoist Mr. Wren and carry him along on their escape? Holmes was strong, to be sure, and athletic. But carrying the weight of another man, knowing that dropping him would cost that man his life, was far too risky. Mr. Wren was weak. I doubted seriously that he could cling to the ladder, even for a few minutes. If the balloon needed longer than that to be reeled in, Mr. Wren might fall to his death!

"What is Holmes planning to do?" asked Lestrade. It was as if the words came out of my own mouth. I couldn't answer. Instead, I watched the spectacle unfolding and asked myself: *What would I do if I were Holmes?*

The rope ladder was being dragged the length of the rooftop. Holmes and Mr. Wren were standing in the center of the space. As I watched, Holmes' arms reached skyward in anticipation of grabbing the ladder as it made a pass. Curiously, Mr. Wren stood upright, next to Holmes. Was it possible that the sickly man was stronger than I had thought? Thomas Henry had said that he was amazed at his patient's muscles despite the fact he was emaciated. Even so, trusting that Mr. Wren could hang on was taking a chance. A life or death gamble. Equally, trusting Holmes to hold onto Mr. Wren was a risk on my friend's part. What other options did Holmes have? A sense of despair had temporarily overwhelmed me until I saw this daring plan.

I held my breath. With one outstretched hand, Holmes managed to snag the ladder. The chatter of voices swelled as the number of onlookers grew. What had started as a dozen was now thirty or forty people joining us on the kerb, staring up at the spectacle in the sky. One little boy asked, "Is this the circus?" I wished I could have laughed, but I was too worried for the safety of the two men. Before our eyes, the scene was unfolding—dreamlike, exhilarating, and frightening. The colours alone were breathtaking: the pale blue hydrogen flame, the golden wicker gondola, the brown leather straps on the gondola, the soft blue sky and drifting white clouds, and the vivid bluebell blue of the silk balloon envelope. As one of those clouds glided in front of the sun, and the glare from the sun's rays was diluted, I could see Holmes had one leg hooked over the ladder, and then his foot wedged under a lower rung. This had the effect of locking his lower body in place. He was clinging with both hands to the ladder, and Mr. Wren was somehow attached to Holmes, or so it seemed. By what mechanism, I could not tell.

How long could the pilot keep the balloon in one place? Long enough for Holmes to make whatever arrangements he needed to safeguard the sickly patient? My heart crowded my throat, even as the throng that milled around Lestrade and me oohed and ahhhed with excitement.

With a roar, a blast of flame leapt up and the resultant hot air gently lifted the balloon. A thin sheen of perspiration broke out on my forehead. I still couldn't see what bound Holmes and Mr. Wren together, but as the balloon drifted incrementally higher, the crowd called out their encouragement. One woman shrieked. A child began to cry. Slowly the balloon lifted higher.

Just as slowly, it began its descent. At first, I doubted my eyes. Was the silk envelope moving or not? I locked my eyes onto the balloon, counting the crisscrossed diamond shapes formed by the ropes that linked the envelope to the gondola. Yes, the number of diamonds decreased, an indication the balloon was being hauled back on its tether.

"Come on," I said to Lestrade. "We must reposition ourselves."

"Let me tell our cabman to meet us around back," Lestrade wisely said. Because the crowd had grown, the carriage could not get through the throng. To meet us, the driver would have to circle several blocks. I could barely see the roof of the cab over the tops of all the gathered heads. Then the conveyance took off, moving away from the growing mass of people.

Lestrade rejoined me. "He'll meet us there. We can get there first, though." With a nod, he pushed a pathway through the bystanders. When we'd cleared the crowd, Lestrade and I both broke into a trot. The Bethlehem Hospital's main building is a forbidding edifice, a large and sprawling place covering what would be multiple city blocks. Added to that, on each end are wings, equally as large. So Lestrade and I found ourselves running for what seemed like an eternity, only to turn the corner and lope along the side of the wing before we could turn a corner again. That's when we spotted a ground crew of six people studying the envelope floating overhead, whilst reeling in the balloon, hand-over-hand. Their activity demanded caution and attention to detail. If at any point the balloon listed to one side or drifted in such a way that it might run into the nearby trees, the crew foreman shouted for a complete stop. A length of the tether was extended, in the hopes of stabilizing the balloon. This descent would be a time-consuming matter, especially because the balloon was so close to the building. If the silk fabric of the envelope snagged, it could rupture or tear. The emission of hot air would send the balloon plummeting to the ground, and the impact could be disastrous. The balloon would go from a controlled landing to an out-of-control fall.

Without asking, Lestrade and I both pitched in to help. We added our body weight to the tethers. "Heave!" shouted one of the crew members. The rope tensed and did its best to work against us by pulling in the direction of the sky.

The process reminded me of reeling in a large trout. You gave the line enough play to accord the fish its battle, and as it wearied, you reeled it in. Unfortunately, positioned as I was, almost directly under the gondola, I had no way of seeing what sort of state Holmes was in. That meant I had no opportunity of making sure that he and Mr. Wren were still aboard and safe in the gondola. All I could do was help with the tether.

"Coming down! Grab it!" one of the crew members shouted. Two continued to pull on the tether whilst guiding that thick rope to the side, keeping it from tangling up in the envelope. With practiced movements, four other crew members grasped the bottom of the gondola and pulled it toward the earth. They eased the basket to the ground. Because the sides of the gondola come up about four feet high, once on terra firma the passengers needed help climbing out. The pilot worked to turn off the hydrogen jets while a doddering man was gently lifted up over the side of the wicker basket and moved out of the way. Mr. Wren was too wobbly to stand on his own, so Lestrade and I rushed to his side. The odour of unwashed flesh, of fetid soil, and of sickness was so strong I thought I might get sick.

"Who is this?" Lestrade asked as he slipped an arm under Mr.

Wren's shoulders. Lestrade's lack of concern about the man's hygiene was most welcome under these trying circumstances.

"This is Mr. Wren," I explained. "I've got him, if you want to see to Holmes."

Lestrade did as I asked, offering Holmes a hand. Two crew members had lifted Holmes under the armpits, and Lestrade steadied my friend as he stepped over the side of the basket. A quick glance told me that Holmes was disheveled, but fine. Under his eyes, dark circles had appeared, and his narrow face seemed even more gaunt than usual. He and Lestrade exchanged a greeting before stumbling my way. I was ever so glad to see my old friend.

"Holmes!" I shouted. "Thank goodness you are all right!"

But at that exact moment, he stumbled and nearly fell. I grabbed his arm and quickly realised his time in Bedlam and his responsibility for Mr. Wren's safety had seriously depleted all of Holmes' strength.

22

Holmes and Mr. Wren were filthy, tired, hungry, and extremely dehydrated. We hurriedly got them back to 221B Baker Street. Lestrade helped Holmes and I helped Mr. Wren up the stairs. After working in an army field hospital, it wasn't difficult for me to care for them, once they were situated on the sofa and in a bed.

"Better be getting back to the police station," Lestrade said. "When this fellow and Holmes are on the mend, let me know. I'll come 'round and interview them. Seems to me like there's a bad lot at the hospital. Elsewise, why not let Holmes go home? Doesn't make a bit of sense. They had to guess you'd be harping after his release."

I agreed. "I don't know what to make of Mycroft Holmes' strange behavior."

As soon as Mrs. Hudson realized we had two men in the flat who were doing poorly, she fluttered around like Florence Nightingale herself. She's particularly devoted to Holmes, but her good nature quickly expanded to include our new visitor, Mr. Wren. The dear landlady carried up copious jugs of hot water, as well as a selection of flannels and a fresh bar of soap. Holmes was not as dirty as Mr. Wren, so once he'd had a couple of glasses of water, he was able to clean himself in his room. After he had freshened up, he rested in his favorite armchair and sipped copious cups of tea while picking his way through an assortment of tiny sandwiches originally destined for a church luncheon. "I'm sure the church ladies will understand," said Mrs. Hudson.

The job of bathing Mr. Wren was unpleasant, and one I could not delegate. Not in good conscience. As an army doctor, I had seen worse patients. Peeling off the older man's filthy rags afforded me the opportunity to inspect his numerous wounds. His garments had stiffened with dried blood, but it did not appear to have come from his person. Small puncture marks suggested he'd been using drugs or had his blood drawn. Given his level of dehydration, I would bet on the latter.

There was little more to learn about him. As I'd come to realise, Mr. Wren was, indeed, Asian. His hair must have turned from black to white, given the rest of his natural colouring. I tried to speak with him, and in his eyes was a flicker of understanding, but the poor man was too exhausted to communicate.

After several abortive attempts at asking questions, I chose to repeat soothing words, over and over again. Once the washing up was finished, I dressed the man in an old pair of my pajamas and led him to the divan. Mrs. Hudson had thoughtfully covered it with clean sheets. She assisted me in getting Mr. Wren tucked in.

The good woman spooned bone broth into the man's mouth. What a curious image that was! Her being the very soul of rectitude, and the man on her sofa having been treated like a piece of human flotsam. What a curious dichotomy! No mother could have been gentler than our kind landlady.

After Mr. Wren fell asleep, Mrs. Hudson hesitated at our door. In one hand was an empty bowl that had held the last drops of soup. In the other was a towel she'd used under our guest's mouth to catch any spillage. "What on earth happened to that poor man?" she asked, whilst staring down at him. "It's as if someone tried to drain him dry."

"Honestly, I do not know. That is rather what Holmes and I were struggling to work out when all of this happened. As soon as Holmes rests up, I know he will join me in expressing his gratitude. You are indeed a marvel, Mrs. Hudson."

She coloured and coughed. "I'm only doing what the Good Book says I should."

If the idea of having a man from China under her roof bothered her, she never turned a hair. This was beyond the normal foolish business that Holmes and I regularly presented her with, and I was heartily glad that her kindness and Christianity extended to a suffering man of another race.

Holmes slept for eighteen hours straight after his balloon flight. He woke up to eat and promised me that he'd reveal the details of his adventure in the fullness of time. I found this highly unsatisfactory. When he asked me to send 'round a note to Mycroft, indicating that he was back at 221B Baker Street, I flatly refused. "Your brother's churlish conduct cannot be condoned. If he has any interest in your well-being, it is incumbent on him to prove it. I won't be a party to easing his troubled mind. If you do write him, you are welcome to say he'll have many amends to make if he cares about getting back into my good books."

Despite my refusal, Holmes managed a few lines and sent them out in the post. The message did not seem to move Mycroft one way or the other. Certainly, he did not answer back. But Mycroft Holmes was the only person in London who did not record his admiration for his brother! Those who saw the rescue told reporters that Sherlock Holmes must be the bravest man in all of London! The onlookers fairly gushed with sentiment regarding Holmes' daring rescue.

In addition to praise for Sherlock Holmes, S. A. André received accolades from the newspapers. There was a general acknowledgement that his efforts and those of his crew were "heroic, death-defying, and spectacular."

I had thanked the balloonist and his crew in person as we loaded Holmes and Mr. Wren into the carriage, but my gratitude seemed to fall short of the mark, so I also wrote Mr. André a letter praising his timely and skillful intervention. I promised that if he found himself in need of funding for his explorations, I would do everything I could to aid and abet him in raising money.

Over the successive few days, as Mr. Wren grew stronger, Mrs. Hudson continued to see that our guest was fed properly. Indeed, she cared for him the way one might an invalid. On the third day of Mr. Wren's stay at our flat, he mentioned to Mrs. Hudson a recipe his mother had made as a tonic for restoring good health. "I'd be pleased for you to teach me to make such a broth," said Mrs. Hudson with genuine enthusiasm. "That would be a welcome addition to my meager repertoire of dishes. If you'll give me the ingredients you need, I'll fetch them from the market."

"Holmes? Are you ever going to tell me what's going on?" I asked, as I handed him *The Times* one morning, four days from his escape. "Even some inkling of how long Mr. Wren will be our houseguest might prove useful."

I asked this as Mr. Wren was downstairs in the kitchen directing Mrs. Hudson in the making of a healing soup.

Removing his pipe from his mouth, Holmes said, "Are you eager to be shed of him? Does he offend you?"

I scoffed. "Not at all, but you do. You ask too much of me, Holmes, and give too little in return. You have answers to the questions that bedeviled us both, but you refuse to share what you learned or your solution to this puzzle. To this day, I still do not know why you insisted on spending the night in Bedlam, particularly since you knew you, too, would be held prisoner. Blast it all! I was worried sick!"

"Poor, misused, Watson." He chuckled. "I have every intention of sharing all of the tiny details. However, you must admit that this is also Mr. Wren's tale to tell. Before you grow too angry with me, he and I have discussed your need to know. He begged me for a few days to muster his strength, but you'll be included in our discussion forthwith."

In the event, explanations came sooner rather than later. The next day Mrs. Hudson again invited Mr. Wren into her kitchen to oversee making a healthful dish. They were chopping herbs, when upstairs in our flat, we were visited by Lord Hyslop and Captain Pickering.

"Where is he?" Hyslop demanded, pushing rudely past me and into our sitting room.

Holmes rose to his feet with great dignity. "What is the meaning of this? When did our city fall victim to marshal law? Who gave you permission to force your way into our private residence?"

Hyslop now advanced upon Holmes. The Secretary of Defence stood inches from Holmes' face, standing in a menacing pose with his fists knotted and a pulsating artery in his neck. "I come in the name of National Security and in service of the Crown!"

"Then you certainly must be carrying paperwork," said Holmes, rocking back on his heels. His eyes never flickered away from Hyslop's steely gaze. Holmes added, "I doubt you could make a decision like this by yourself. What sort of legal demand are you making?"

"None!" yelled Hyslop. "Only that I am the Queen's good servant. You, sir, are harboring a fugitive. Hand him over!"

This whole time, Pickering stood with one hand on the hilt of his sword, blocking our doorway, imitating a pose of many statues of Lord Nelson. But his posturing was ineffective. In fact, he looked dashedly silly as I stared at him. Both Pickering and Hyslop were crushing the civil liberties that have so long been established in our great nation. As a matter of fact, I had the sudden urge to whistle for a carriage and propose that we all ride out to Runnymede and pay our respects to the island where the Magna Carta had been signed.

"As you can see," said Sherlock Holmes, "Dr. Watson and I are quite alone. We are flatmates. There is no third person here. If you do not believe me, you are welcome to search. I suggest you look first under the divan. May I offer you a cleaning towel? There is a bit of dusting that needs doing."

Lord Hyslop's face grew more florid by the second. In my pocket was my small revolver. After the events at the hospital, I found the weight of it to be a source of great comfort. Naturally, I had no desire to use the little gun, but just as naturally, I wanted this strange visit to come to an end.

"So you are telling us that you do not know where Chen Wen is? An escaped Chinese national who might, as we speak, be spreading a loathsome and dangerous virus?" Captain Pickering asked. The furrow between his brows was deep, and he too, had adopted a posture of command. Whereas Hyslop was attempting to intimidate Sherlock Holmes, Pickering had chosen me as his target.

Frankly, I had had enough. "See, here. If you have a bill of charges, produce it. Otherwise, vacate yourselves from our premises or we will have to toss you out on your ear.There's no one here but Holmes and me. You are welcome to look for yourselves, but I warn you, the ice you tread on gets thinner by the heartbeat. My friend here is being celebrated as a national hero for his bravery. One day, when you have recovered your senses and look back on this, I am confident you will recognise you picked the wrong side of this situation. There is no one braver or more patriotic than Sherlock Holmes. If you doubt that, ask his brother, Mycroft."

"And who do you think sent us here?" asked Hyslop.

As soon as the words were out of his mouth, he regretted them. You could see his brain catching up with his tongue, and his instant chagrin. Sherlock Holmes, however, thought this hilarious. "Mycroft sent you here? My, my. That brother of mine has high-priced guard dogs, doesn't he, Watson? How does it feel to be let off the leash?"

With that, Hyslop turned on his heel. "Pickering? Come along. We're done here."

23

As soon as the two men left, I turned on Holmes. "You have not played fairly with me. You have dodged my questions. Now we have been backed up against the wall, and I am ignorant of the reason for this intolerable treatment. Have I not shown you that I support you whenever ask? I believe I have, but you can't ask me to defend what I don't know in detail!"

Holmes sighed deeply as he slumped down into one of the straight-back chairs positioned around our dining table. His eyes stared off into the distance. "You are right. I had thought we'd bought a little time. It was a miscalculation on my part. Mr. Wren needed the chance to recover his strength—"

"Balderdash. You were procrastinating," I said, angrily.

"True," Holmes said.

"Why? What could you possibly have gained by—" but my complaint was interrupted by yet another knock at our door. This new intrusion further irritated me. "Blast it. When did our flat become a train station?"

"When I decided I could not speculate any longer," said Holmes, in a sad and tired voice. Indeed, I have never before and rarely since, seen him so defeated. His slouching shoulders, his abject depression, and even the downwards turn of his mouth suggested he was miserable.

"You had best better answer it," I said. I still retained a hold on my anger, and I was reluctant to let it go. Whatever Holmes was hiding, he'd played me wrong. I deserved more consideration. "Let us see what your shenanigans have introduced into our home."

If one can truly be said to "drag his feet," that is exactly what Holmes did. His walk to the door was laboured. When his hand touched the knob, he hesitated long enough to square his shoulders and lift his chin. With a click, the latch unlocked, with a squeak, the door creaked open, and with a start I realized I was staring at three young men, presumably Benson, Donnelly, and St. Ledger.

"Do come in," said Holmes. "I have been expecting you."

I choked back a gasp. Whilst we'd never seen photos of the missing boys, the descriptions had been more than adequate. St. Ledger was the tallest and clearly the most adult, while Donnelly looked distinctly younger. Benson wore the most tragic expression, a response identifying him as a bereft lover, and I knew in an instant that he really did love Ennis Caldwell with all his heart. His resemblance to his sister, Gillian, was remarkable.

Side-by-side, the young men showed the lasting signs of a rugged lifestyle, given their ruddy complexions, their lean physiques, and the tiny crinkles around their eyes and mouths that are unusual in society dandies of the same general age. To a man, their handshakes were firm and decisive. But their eyes reflected a deep pain, an agony almost searing. Also of note was the way they huddled next to each other, with George St. Ledger taking point, but the two younger men at his flanks in the sort of formation that suggested time on the battlefield.

Holmes gestured to our armchairs and the sofa, encouraging the young men to sit. Before taking a seat, George glanced around, wide-eyed, and asked, "Where is he?"

Holmes wore the sort of blank face he often chose when attempting neutrality in order to provoke a result. "He?"

George turned on Holmes with anger flashing in his eyes. "You know exactly whom I am referring to."

Holmes waited in the silence that followed, a common tactic of his for provoking someone to expand upon a topic. Sure enough, George St. Ledger took the initiative: "Do not attempt to play games with us, Mr. Holmes. We have been through too much together. The only reason we're here is to fetch Chen. Where is he?" As George spoke, he rubbed his palms over the fabric of his trousers. This he did repeatedly, in the manner of a nervous habit.

"If you mean Mr. Wen Chen, he is in the kitchen below us."

This was confirmation that Mr. Wren was actually "Wen Chen" or "Chen" from Walter Benson's journal.

"Your old friend is currently teaching our landlady how to make one of his favorite dishes, I believe," Holmes spoke quietly but with authority. "Do you wish to discuss the matter at hand with or without him? I leave the decision up to you, gentlemen."

In response, George, who was clearly the group's spokesperson, said, "Of course we want Chen to be involved. We wouldn't be alive today if Chen hadn't stepped in and taken us—" His voice broke with emotion, and my heart ached for the young man. I said, "Holmes? I'll run downstairs and fetch Chen. Perhaps you could offer these young men some refreshment whilst I'm gone."

With that, I took my leave of the party. At this point it would be disingenuous to neglect to mention how profoundly the presence of the young castaways moved me. My hand grasped the bannister on the stairway with an intensity that even frightened me! "Stop it!" I whispered to myself. I'd seen active combat, men running from guns, and of course, men dying in droves, but to witness these three young men, knowing how they had participated in a ritual that turned them into wild animals, plucked at my heartstrings. What choices we make as human beings! How precious survival is to us! And even more significantly, the nobility of mankind stunned me. These three had put their lives on the line for each other and for a small tribe with whom they had had very little in common. It was one thing to go to war knowing your efforts were sanctioned and applauded by an entire nation. But this choice took so much courage, because it involved an allegiance to those other than one's natal family and one's country of birth. The castaways' decision proved to me that the bonds of friendship can be every bit as strong as those forged by blood.

I had long suspected as much, and now I had witnessed proof.

A DELIGHTFUL FRAGRANCE WAFTING UP FROM THE KITCHEN promised that our next meal would be a real treat. Mrs. Hudson was bent over a large pot, stirring a golden liquid with an exotic scent. Cumin, cinnamon, and coriander filled the air. Mr. Wen stood at her elbow, carefully adding chopped vegetables into the mixture. The two cooks were clearly enjoying themselves. I couldn't help but smile because I'd never seen Mrs. Hudson performing domestic duties such as this, and her happiness delighted me. So much so that I hated to interrupt, but I did.

"Mr. Wen? Please join us upstairs. Your young friends are here: Messers Benson, Donnelly, and St. Ledger. I believe Miss Benson explained our involvement in their dilemma." I did my best to reflect my compassion in the timbre of my voice. My instincts told me this meeting would be bittersweet. The way Mr. Wen received my invitation confirmed that I was right. With great deliberation, he set down the cutting board he had been using. That's when I noticed the knife in his right hand. My heart skipped a beat. The former fugitive was close enough to Mrs. Hudson that he could end her life if he wanted. Inwardly, I cursed myself for not noticing the weapon before speaking.

My concern was unfounded. Mr. Wen set down the knife. He pressed his hands together in the universal pose for prayer. He bowed from the waist to Mrs. Hudson, a gesture steeped in admiration. "Thank you very much, Mrs. Hudson," he said in a clear and almost unaccented manner. "I found our time together most enjoyable. I hope you have the information you need to duplicate this recipe."

The sweet woman's face puckered up with worry. "Indeed, I do. Are you suggesting, sir, that I shall never see you again?"

"I believe that is highly probable," he said, again bowing from the waist. "Therefore, I wish you Godspeed, kind lady. I hope you'll enjoy this meal and think of the poor man you treated with such charity."

Pivoting like a military man, Mr. Wen turned to me. "Dr. Watson? Please lead the way."

WHEN WE MOUNTED THE STAIRS, I WONDERED IF I SHOULD HAVE asked Mrs. Hudson for refreshments, but my idea was immediately banished when I opened the door to the flat. Holmes had served all three young men generous tumblers of his best brandy. They had chosen to sit in a straight line on the divan and sip their drinks. Since he rarely offered this prized liquor to guests, my sense of anxiety was heightened. Of course, Mr. Wen greeted our new friends with undisguised affection. Holmes handed both of us glasses of the golden liquor and bade us to sit down.

"I should very much like to see if my deductions are accurate or if there's been a serious error in my thinking," started Holmes. "Because solving puzzles is my livelihood, I beg your indulgence while I narrate what I believe to be your story. Is that satisfactory?"

George St. Ledger nodded, and the others took their cue from him. Walter Benson was holding his tumbler with such ferocity that I worried it might break in his hand. Frank Donnelly seemed relieved. Mr. Wen held up one finger as a signal that he wished to speak. "First, I have this to say: Thank you for saving my life, Mr. Holmes. I will not give you cause to regret it. You risked your life, and I am grateful. Secondly, my proper name is Wen Chen. In my culture, the family name precedes the first name. Those brutes at the Bethlehem Hospital thought I was saying, 'Wren.'"

"The Bethlehem Hospital?" George St. Ledger said with a start. "Chen, whatever happened? Are you quite all right?"

Chen stared down into the depths of his amber drink. The aroma of the wood casket where the beverage had cured added a smoky tang to the air. "George, I believe Mr. Holmes is poised to enlighten you with the details."

George nodded, mollified.

"So as I understand it," said Holmes. "The three of you young men hoped to run away from the harsh conditions of your boarding school. You became stowaways on the Matilda Briggs, the same ship where Mr. Wen was the cook."

Their silence sent a message of agreement, so Holmes continued,

"The Captain put you off at the nearest island. There you were introduced to a tribe of Sumatrans, natives of that place. They treated you kindly and accepted you as members of their tribe. All was well and good until the first full moon. At that time, they herded you into cages and hoisted the cages high by tossing a rope over the limb of a banyan tree. You were held captive for one purpose, and that was to assure your safety. The entire tribe with the exception of a handful of young mothers and their babes, turned into wolves for the duration of the full moon."

I felt a tightening in my chest. This story was so fantastical, and Holmes told it in a manner so cool, that the disparity was emphasised. Who in his right mind would believe such an account?

"This came to be an accepted practice. With the exception of those few hours once a month when the moon was full, you not only lived a harmonious life with the natives, you also flourished. They treated you with great acceptance, almost as if you'd been born into their own families."

Frank Donnelly had been rubbing his open palms against the fabric of his trousers, and now he worked this gesture harder and harder. Walter looked downcast, almost ashamed, whilst George's expression of worry had deepened. The young man's eyes had darkened from a light hazel to a nut brown.

"You probably would have lived the rest of your natural lives there among the natives, being treated like one of the tribe, except that a Dutch ship found its way to the island. Initially they planned to exploit the peppercorn trees. However, the spice traders quickly determined they could capture the natives to sell them as slaves and that act would give the Dutchmen a windfall of wealth as well as unlimited and exclusive access to the various spices that grew on that island. When the islanders spotted the Dutch flag, they quickly realised what was happening. They had had enough experience with the Dutch on other islands in the archipelago that they could predict what was coming. The chief tribesman, Kiawonka, presented you with options. You could all three stay as you were. You could live, fight, and die as the men you are today. Or you could submit yourselves to the bite of a native rat, the precursor to becoming a wolf one night a month."

Here I could not help myself. I studied the three young men intently. Was it possible Holmes had gotten everything all wrong? Would they erupt in laughter? Or anger? Or storm out of the flat?

In the event, they did none of the above. George glanced at his friends. A nod of agreement passed among them. He said, "Yes. We had that option. At the time, it did not seem like a choice. Even when we were at school, we'd heard tales about the blood-thirsty Dutchmen. We knew that England was fighting the Dutch when we left the UK. If we'd stayed as we were, the Dutch would have no problem slaughtering us. We were not skilled warriors. We had no special weapons. We had been taught to use rudimentary spears for fishing and catching wild boar, but none of that would prepare us for fighting battle-hardened men. And we owed allegiance to the Sumatrans! They had taken us in, shared what little they had, and they were more than willing to lay down their lives for us!"

"Our skin colour did not matter to them," piped up Frank. He had a high, girlish voice. "Once they realised we had no parents to guide us, they took us in. I would rather have lived with Kiawonka than with my own father! Kiawonka was so much kinder to me. How could I refuse to help him defend his family? I couldn't! I figured I would die, but I wanted my death to mean something. I wanted to die for a purpose."

Frank had curled in upon himself, letting his shoulders and his head droop. He'd taken the middle seat on the divan and now he reminded me of some burrowing animal. His eyes stayed on the floor.

Walter was more spirited. He said, "My own father had rejected me, yet Kiawonka, my Sumatran father, was more than willing to lay down his life for me! How could I not join him in battle? I was proud to fight by his side!"

"Yes," said Holmes. "I imagine you were. Chen Wen, too. Am I right?"

Chen Wen raised wet eyes and looked from one boy to another. "I am proud of all of you. You lived with courage. You showed respect for people who opened their homes to you. As an Asian, I have been called many names. Chinaman is the least of them. I have been kicked and hit and chained up like a dog. But the Sumatrans treated me as a man. I would rather die than go back to being treated like a Chinaman in a white person's world."

"The four of you did not expect to survive the battle, did you?" Holmes asked. "And you never expected to come back to England."

"Why would we? The first ship in six years comes to the island and it is Dutch? Our parents did not send anyone to look for us. We shouldn't have been that hard to find. A few questions at the boat dock would have been sufficient," said Frank, bitterly. "But our parents didn't want us back! Oh, they might say they did, but their actions told a different tale."

Holmes continued, "But you did survive the battle with the Dutch, and when an English ship finally weighed anchor off the shore, you decided to come home after all."

"The Sumatran chief made the decision for us. Kiawonka knew the Dutch would learn of the battle. He knew they would come back to the island and try to get revenge. And they did. The Dutch annihilated many of our friends during the initial battle. Then the Dutch came back and massacred most of the natives. The rest scattered and hid in the jungle. Later a typhoon swamped the island. We found out about the devastation when Captain Pickering put into one of the ports," said George.

"Pickering," Chen spat out the name. "He is a snake. He is despicable."

Holmes nodded. "Pickering saw your transformation. After all, you were on his ship for six weeks."

"We locked ourselves up in our room. It was our intention to never hurt anyone. Ever," said Frank. His eyes swam in a flood of unspilled tears. Clearly, of the three young men, he was the most sensitive. That was why his friends had put him in the middle, a naturally protected position on the divan.

George picked up the train of thought, "But Pickering heard us change. He broke down our door. He's ambitious, hungry for advancement, and he has friends in high places. He wants to use us!"

"To infect the entire British army!" said Frank. "To turn innocent men into animals so they can better fight this country's enemies! And he didn't even ask us if we agreed! He kept us on his ship for as long as he could, draining our blood, trying to test it. We finally escaped by offering a sailor a bribe, telling him our parents would pay to get us back!"

"I encouraged them to leave whilst I stayed behind," said Chen, in a sad voice. "I had nowhere to go. The sailor knew that no one would pay to release me. I told the boys that maybe if Pickering had me, he would leave them alone. I did not expect that..."

"That he would use you so immorally," Holmes finished the sentence. "He locked you up in Bedlam Hospital. There he could observe you, with Thomas Henry Knopf's assistance. When you changed, Pickering brought you young women. He thought maybe you would breed more wolves. When that didn't work, he took samples of your blood."

"Holmes," I interjected. "Are you saying that Chen here is Jack the Ripper?"

Chen buried his face in his hands. "I never meant to hurt them. I did not know what I was doing. They locked those women up with me, and I woke up to find they were dead. I am so ashamed."

"You had no choice in the matter," said Holmes. "You were nothing more than an experiment. Thomas Henry did not know what he was involved in. Not at first. That's why he called you in, Watson. He was genuinely confused. But then Pickering and Hyslop offered him money and a partnership, and suddenly, he was onboard with their scheme."

I did not ask about Mycroft. I did not want to know if he was involved.

24

A pounding on the door surprised all of us. Holmes was closest to the window, so he looked out. "It's Pickering, Hyslop, and Thomas Henry Knopf," he said.

The young men scrambled to their feet, looking around the sitting room for a place to hide. I was appalled but that quickly changed to anger. How dare those men come and hunt the boys down! And to come to our residence?

"Crawl under our beds," said Holmes, directing his suggestion to Chen and the boys. "I shall delay them and do my best to turn the scoundrels away."

I helped the four to do as Holmes suggested. When my friend opened the door, I was seated on the sofa, reading a book. At the last possible second, I noticed the six glasses of Scotch and hurriedly piled books around them. It was a rather pathetic display, but it did the job.

"Where are they?" demanded Pickering.

"They who?" asked Holmes, strolling over to the fireplace so he could lean against it.

"Chen and the boys," said Hyslop.

"Chen?" I asked, looking up from the volume of poems I was reading. "Who is Chen?"

Thomas Henry's face reddened with anger. "You cannot cheat me out of this, Watson. I have earned this reward! You meddling—" and he threw himself at me.

But Holmes stuck out his foot, tripping Thomas Henry so that he came down hard against the side table. His lip was broken open and a streak of blood ran down his chin as he landed awkwardly on the carpet. I used that distraction to draw my pistol. "By what right do any of you have to barge into our flat? Get out!"

"I am here on the Crown's behalf," said Hyslop with a sneer. "You are hiding something valuable, something vital to our national interest."

"Really?" Holmes sounded amused. "That sounds intriguing. I wonder what you are talking about."

Thomas Henry used his sleeve to wipe away the blood. Rolling to his knees, he pushed up off of the floor. He stood pointing his index finger at me like a bayonet. "Dash it all, Watson. You know what war is like! Think of the lives we could save! Soldiers who turn into wolves? The terror of it all would strike in the hearts of our enemies. The fear inspired by the change would be a vast tactical advantage!"

Standing near the doorway, Pickering had been simmering with anger. His eyes had darted from my pistol to Holmes and back again. His hands twitched as if he wished to throttle me and the tips of his ears had gone red with rage, but he struggled to keep his voice level. "Let us discuss this as civilised men. There's a great deal of money to be made if we capture these four...monsters. I've seen firsthand the sort of damage they can do to a human body. The Commander in Chief is willing to pay us a great deal for bringing them to the War Office. Alive or dead, it does not matter."

But Thomas Henry interrupted, "Alive. Until we are sure of the process for replicating the transformation, I need them alive."

Pickering waved his hand in a dismissive gesture. "Yes, yes. Point being there's so much at stake here. A great deal of money has been set aside for acquisition of these...beasts. If we cannot appeal to your patriotism, perhaps there's a payment that might help you see your way clear. Holmes? Your brother has been ordered to stand down. He is fully aware how important these creatures are. You are not a stupid man. Tell us where we can find them and we'll see that the money is deposited in your bank account."

Holmes' smile was tight and it did not reach his eyes. "I have no idea what you're talking about. As Dr. Watson said, you have no right to be here. I join him in asking that you leave. Now."

Hyslop's upper lip curled in a churlish manner. "Believe me, I have no desire to waste another moment in these shabby surroundings. However, I am here on behalf of Her Royal Majesty, Queen Victoria, and I shall not leave until I get what we've come for."

I'd had enough. Staying seated, I pointed my pistol at the ceiling and fired off a shot. The resultant impact sent bits of plaster showering down on all of us.

Then I got to my feet. "Leave or I'll use this on each of you. Don't you think a jury will agree with a man defending his own domicile? I do."

Hyslop had backed towards the door and now bumped into Pickering. Thomas Henry shook his head at me. "But John, we served—"

"We served together to defend the English way of life. Or have you forgotten what William Pitt, the Younger, said? 'The poorest man may in his cottage bid defiance to all the forces of the Crown,' and thus I say to you, get out now or I'll turn my pistol on each one of you!" I shouted. To punctuate my demand, I fired off another shot.

This time our unwelcome guests left.

Fortunately Mrs. Hudson was out for the evening at a church service or we would have been hard put to explain my gunshots.

We gave the intruders ten minutes before we helped our guests out from under our beds. "We cannot stay here," said Holmes, as he assisted Chen in getting to his feet. "None of us can."

"But surely they're waiting and watching," said Frank. His pallor made his freckles more prominent.

"Yes," I agreed, "but there's another way to leave this building." From a dresser drawer, I withdrew a rope ladder. Tying the ends of it to my bedposts, I explained, "In the middle of the night, no one will be out and about. We'll toss this out of my bedroom window. We can climb down and run through the alley to the other side of the block. From there we can hail a growler to take us to Paddington Station."

"Where do you propose we go?" George was the tactical one of the bunch.

"I suggest we repair to Brookhaven Manor," said Holmes. "There is much to discuss, and the older Bensons are away."

❧

We arrived at the front door of Brookhaven Manor around four in the morning. We'd taken the first train we could get out of Paddington, and sadly, it had made a multitude of stops, extending the duration of our trip. Fortunately, Gillian Benson is a light sleeper, and she came as soon as we knocked. Throwing her arms around her brother, she sobbed a little, but the young lady was too sensible to lose all control of her emotions. We'd slept a bit on the train, exhausted by the strain of the day and by the exertion of climbing out my window, down the ladder, and skulking our way through the back alley. Gillian saw the fatigue on our faces. Quickly, she installed us in rooms and made us comfortable.

The next morning, all of us rose early. I suspect the weighty matters ahead had stolen any chance of a good night's sleep. Gillian had sent the servants away. She herself had brewed strong pots of tea and set out cold slices of ham, hot bacon, cheeses, and bread. The three young men came downstairs together and asked if they might spend time in the library without the rest of us.

Holmes asked, "You aren't planning to run off, are you? If so, let us know so we can plan for our own safety accordingly."

"Of course not," said George.

"We simply need time to talk," said Frank.

"To discuss our options," added Walter. "Sister? Will you send a message to Ennis and ask that she join us? I should very much like to see her and explain myself."

"I will," said Gillian. Dark circles ringed her puffy eyes.

Chen looked from one boy to the next. "Do I need to be involved in this talk?"

"Not yet," said George. The young man was a natural-born leader. They closed themselves up in the library, there at Brookhaven Manor, and on occasion, their voices rose in disagreement and echoed throughout the edifice, but in the end, they formulated a plan. Only a few doubts lingered, and those would be quickly dispatched.

They came back about an hour later. We were still sipping tea at the dining room table. The boys wore solemn expressions and their eyes looked distinctly sad. George said, "We've talked. There are a few questions I wish to pose to Mr. Holmes. Sir?"

"Yes?" Holmes got to his feet and paced, as is his custom. Then he leaned against the trim of one of the large windows in the dining room. His noble face was alert with curiosity.

"Do you think, under any circumstances, that the British government will ever let us go?" George's voice trembled a little bit.

Holmes reply came quickly. "No. Even if Hyslop, Pickering, and Knopf all gave up, now that word of your condition has penetrated the various levels of government, I think it impossible for them to forget what they know. I would liken it to unringing a bell."

"Dr. Watson?" Frank addressed me. "Is there any chance we could be cured of this?"

I'd been wondering the same thing. Reluctantly, I said, "I don't see how. At least not in your lifetime. Remember, it took decades for us to find a cure for smallpox, and that was rather common. Your situation is unique. There are only four of you. We do not have a concerted national effort to eradicate this...disease."

Walter asked, "Do you think we are contagious, Dr. Watson?"

"I don't know." I hated my answer, but I was being truthful.

A silence followed. Gillian Benson spoke up, "I promise you that I shall do everything in my power to lock you up once a month. I shall spare no expense figuring out the best way to keep you isolated."

Her brother went over to her chair. He knelt beside her and wrapped his arms around her shoulders. "Gillian? It wasn't your fault. And there's nothing you can do, Sister. Even if you lock us away, the government will find us. If not this month, the next or the one after that."

"But Walter, what if we took a ship and went to Bermuda? Or Australia? Anywhere else!" Gillian's eyes brimmed with tears. "Please, please, please. I missed you so much while you were gone. Now you're home. I don't want to lose you again."

He kissed her cheek. "They will come for us, Gillian. We shall never be safe. And if they find us, they will use us. They will turn us into weapons. Even if they cannot figure out how to copy this curse, they'll hold us captive and turn us loose on the enemies of the Crown. Don't you see? They will never think of us as human. Ever. We'll be pawns. Worse than slaves, because slaves can have a multitude of purposes. We shall have but one, to kill."

"What about the plumeria?" I asked. "Could you not be surrounded by that?"

Holmes gave me a sad smile. "To what end? Once word gets out that these four exist, the government will hunt them like animals. To everyone else, these are not four persons. They are four weapons. Weapons are aimed and discharged. That's all."

"Would you want to fight for our government?" It was a last ditch effort, but I felt it only fair to explore it.

The young men traded glances. Chen said, "Doctor? You saw what I did to those young women."

But Holmes was the one who answered. His face had darkened. "The government has given you short shrift, Mr. Wen. They worry that someone intimately connected to the throne is behind the mutilation of the women. In that respect, you are free. Men such as my brother will not purse you. They have decided to turn a blind eye to the murders of the ladies. They see their tragic deaths as just retribution for their sinful lives."

Chen shook his head sadly. "I hate myself for what I did."

"It was not your fault," Holmes said firmly.

Chen's eyes were full of misery. "That is true. Nothing I did was done on purpose. And yet it haunts me. They delivered the women to me in my cell as I was in the midst of changing. In the cold light of day, they removed the corpses. It disgusts me. If I am captured by the War

Office, I will commit suicide. They cannot keep me alive. I won't allow it. The powers there would use me indiscriminately, and I cannot be a party to that."

George chose to change the subject. "I am looking forward to meeting Ennis Caldwell, as Walter has spoken glowingly of her. The weather is brilliant. How shall we spend this beautiful day and evening?"

Walter gave us a brave smile. "Yes, there is much here to explore. The grounds at Brookhaven are full of natural beauty. I suggest we take a long ramble. Sister? When will Ennis arrive?"

"Not for several hours." Gillian lifted her chin and tried to smile back at her brother.

"Well, then, let's take a walk outside until she comes." Walter offered his sister his hand.

25

A little past dawn the next day at Brookhaven Manor, we walked out to the meadow, which was still cool from the damp night air. Dew clung to our boots and the hems of our trousers as we made our solemn procession. Ennis was with us, after having arrived the afternoon before. She and Walter had talked for hours behind closed doors. They had emerged holding hands. They faced us with reddened eyes, and demeanors that suggested the resolution of a weighty matter.

As that young man had suggested earlier, all of us had enjoyed some time out of doors, admiring the grounds of Brookhaven Manor. All of us, that is, except Holmes. He preferred to peruse the Bensons' extensive library. Later in the day, I joined him there. We both found comfort in the wisdom of the ages as captured in those books.

All that we had done, all that we had said, had served to strengthen our sense of purpose. Now we stepped forward in a tightly knit group, unified by our grim decision. Each step crushed pine needles, and to my delight, they released their pungent fragrance. The birds watched us and called warnings to one another, even as a few occupied the highest boughs and acted as sentries. A grey squirrel, startled while burying an acorn, ran in front of our group, hurrying past Walter as he led the way with a quiet sense of resolution. His mind was long past being made up, and he described himself to me when we met very early at the breakfast table as, "Eager for my next adventure."

I prayed that was just around the corner. My gun never felt so heavy in my pocket. With each footfall, it bumped my hip and reminded me of its cold efficiency. I have often thought of my pistol as a protector, but today I saw it as an enemy because of the deadly task ahead. Holmes' right hand dangled as he carried a revolver. The muzzle was too long to fit comfortably in his pants pocket, so he held it rather loosely down at his side. Landover and Ducky, the elderly gamekeepers, had answered our call for assistance. The two old friends wore somber expressions and carried their rifles as if they were off to hunt pheasant. But an onlooker would find it curious how they'd strapped four stretchers to their backs. These would perform the solemn duty of transporting the dead back to the cart.

Ennis Caldwell carried a small linen bag. Inside were four blindfolds, sewn by hand. Ennis and Gillian had sat up all night working on them. A last act of love, I tagged it in my mind, for that was exactly what those blindfolds represented.

The young men walked ahead with Chen, their faces solemn but resolute. To keep their best clothes for their final viewing, the four had chosen to wear old garments, and they had picked these with an eye to sentiment. George had chosen his cricket gear, owing to his love of the sport. Frank had worn tails, because he wanted to remember his first ball, and a girl he'd danced with but would never see again. Chen wore native garb from his country, a sort of cotton wrapper, but he'd added trousers in a nod to our English sensibilities. Walter wore his hiking gear, and I must admit, he looked quite dashing. Once in a while, I would wonder how Ennis would carry on, but each time I glanced her way, I saw her mouth was firm and her eyes dry. I believe this was her final gift to Walter, her attempt at acting as if she was fine with his decision. How could she be? I wasn't, but I also had accepted there was no other logical course of action.

Every so many steps, the four men would glance one another to see how their friends were bearing up under this terrible weight. I feared the women would collapse under the strain, but as Holmes had said,

"They have a right to be there, and they understand what is required of them, Watson. If it were your brother or your lover, would you have him meet his end alone? I would not. I would have to put aside all my sentiment and be strong, at least for a short while, and then I would grieve."

Of course, Holmes was right. The young men and their wise friend had discussed every aspect of their decision and come to this sad conclusion. At least they did not need to carry it out all alone.

They had made decisions no man takes lightly, and for three men so young, they had shown remarkable maturity and steady purpose. Chen, for his part, had lived a good life, and he had thrown his lot in with his three young protégés. Of all of them, he knew most clearly what their future might hold, if the government caught up with them. Throughout the day before and late into the evening, Holmes and I had discussed with each other a multitude of other solutions, from wrought iron cages to drug-induced comas, but in the end, we had to allow that there was but one way, and one way only, to eradicate their closely held secret, that murderous impulse inherent in all men but given free rein to this quartet once a month.

The sun was coming up. At the top of a small rise, Walter hesitated. As he cast his eyes towards his friends, they nodded in silent agreement. Gillian had carried a trug over one arm, and now she peeled back the napkin to reveal two bottles of a fine Champagne. With a smile that broke my heart, she handed them to her brother. Walter took them and passed them to his friends, whilst he looked down on his sister with great tenderness. A strand of her hair had worked its way free, so he gently tucked it behind one of her tiny pink ears. "It'll be all right, old thing. This is the right decision. You know that. I love you."

She nodded and a tear spilled down her face, but she did not allow herself the luxury of sobbing.

Frank popped the first cork and George popped the second. They handed the bottles to Walter and Chen. After hoisting the bottles to their lips and drinking long thirsty gulps, they passed the bottles to Frank and George. But before Walter partook of the bubbling wine, he paused long enough to raise his green bottle and say, "There is so much beauty in this world. I trust there will be equal measures of enjoyment in the next."

After a few more gulps, the men handed the half-empty bottles back to Ennis and Gillian. They hugged both women. They shook hands with all of us men, somehow managing not to look down at our weapons.

"Are we all ready?" asked Walter. The four shook hands and clapped one another on the back. After they stepped away, Walter noted their nods of approval. "All right," he said as he led the way to the top of that small rise. The sun was behind them and cast their silhouettes in stark relief. A songbird overhead sang out the most delicate melody. A light breeze picked up the leaves of a nearby oak tree and ruffled them lightly. The bright light of the sun, coming as it was from behind the four men, made it impossible to see their features. Ennis stepped towards them and handed over the individual blindfolds. When she fumbled while tying them on, Gillian and I offered our help and got the job done quickly.

Then the blindfolded men needed assistance in arranging themselves. Very gently, Gillian and I placed them here and here and here and here. We'd judged it best for them to stand two feet apart. This had been the gamekeeper's suggestion when Landover had been presented with the idea. Of all of us, he was the only person who'd seen anything remotely like what we were doing, and that sad legacy was his souvenir from the war in the Crimea. Now Landover found spots for the rest of us, moving Holmes to one end, me to the side of Holmes, Ducky next, and leaving a spot for himself. By agreement, we'd decided against a verbal command. Instead Ennis would drop a handkerchief as a signal.

I felt queasy as I raised my gun and sighted it. George was the tallest of the three, so I adjusted my aim and squared my muzzle with his heart. Ennis stood off to one side, holding her white handkerchief by two trembling fingers and looking for all the world like the most miserable person I've ever seen, but she still choked back her sobs. When all of our guns were trained, Holmes gave her a nod.

That white scrap of linen fluttered to the ground like a falling angel.

The *boom-boom-boom-boom* of the guns was deafening, especially coming as it did almost simultaneously. The four silhouettes jerked and went limp, hitting the grass with thumps. Immediately, I switched from executioner to doctor, and I examined the bodies. All four had been shot cleanly through the heart. Walter's fingers twitched, but he had no pulse. When I double-checked his fingers, I saw that he was holding a ribboned lock of Ennis' hair.

Our grim task was done.

—THE END—

ACKNOWLEDGMENTS

This book would not have been possible without the assistance of many people. I am grateful to Roberta Lutton that she trusted me with the work of her late husband, CJ Lutton. I hope that I've "done CJ proud."

Elaine Viets and Don Crinklaw were instrumental as editors and cheerleaders. Truly, they were indispensable on so many levels.

Craig Stephen Copland offered wonderful advice as a seasoned Sherlockian.

My production team of Stacey Ducker and Silvia Mihalcea are the best of the best. I don't know what I did to deserve such terrific ladies in my life. And their patience with me? And their encouragement? Unbelievable. Thank you both!

—JCS

ABOUT THE AUTHORS

CJ (Carl John) Lutton was a Renaissance man, "a person who has wide interests and is an expert in several areas." In addition to serving in the US Army for four years in Germany, CJ worked many jobs throughout his life: digging graves at cemeteries, running a print shop, owning an advertising agency, teaching at a correctional institution, and working at a high school. He even tried out for a position as quarterback for the New York Jets! Throughout his life, he wrote. Among other works, he completed four books and had notes for others that featured Sher-lockHolmes and his sidekick, Dr. John Watson.

Joanna Campbell Slan is the author of more than 40 books,both fiction and nonfiction. She's a USA Today Bestselling Author, an Amazon Top 100 Mystery Author, and a National BestsellingAuthor. Slan's historical fiction, Death of a Schoolgirl, won theDaphne du Maurier Award of Excellence. For more information, go to www.thesh-erlockstories.com

www.ingramcontent.com/pod-product-compliance
Lightning Source LLC
Chambersburg PA
CBHW060806310726
48980CB00002B/257

* 9 7 8 0 9 6 6 4 7 0 7 9 6 *